WHERE ARE THEY

A LUCA MYSTERY
BOOK 12

DAN PETROSINI

Print ISBN: 978-1-960286-12-3
Naples, FL
Library of Congress Control Number: 2023903983

ACKNOWLEDGMENTS

Special thanks to Julie, Stephanie and Jennifer for their love and support, and thanks to Squad Sergeant Craig Perrilli for his counsel on the real world of law enforcement. He helps me keep it real.

OTHER BOOKS BY DAN

Complicit Witness

Push Back

Ambition Cliff

1

———

I opened the front door and was hit with two blasts of heat. Living in Southwest Florida, one type was predictable. The other seeped out of my client. This woman was so alluring, she could make a bishop pray like St. Augustine: *"Lord, make me chaste—but not yet."*

"Mr. Luca?"

She was three levels past stunning. "Yes, Mrs. Talbot?"

"Please call me Ann." She offered a manicured hand. It was smooth as a baby's cheek.

"I'm Frank. Uh, come on in."

I stepped aside, uncomfortable letting such a knockout into my house. Mary Ann and Jessie were out shopping, and there was no shortage of nosy neighbors to ignite rumors. Plus, with my history . . .

This was my first case as a private investigator, and already I'd learned a lesson; if I were to do this for more than the one-year leave I'd taken, I'd need to rent an office.

As she looked at the flimsy license on the wall, I studied the way her dress clung to her curves.

"You worked as a detective for the Collier County sheriff, am I correct?"

"Yes, ma'am. Homicide."

She stiffened.

"But I've got fifteen years of other experience, including missing persons."

"I hope you can find my husband."

"I'll do my best."

I looked at my notes. "You said his name is John Talbot and he's fifty-three. Did you bring the pictures I asked for?"

"Yes. Here are some photos."

John Talbot was good looking. His salt-and-pepper hair looked like mine. But by the way his shirt hugged his chest, he was in much better shape.

"Was it a business trip?"

"Yes, to Atlanta. He went there often."

"What day was this?"

"A week ago, March first. He went to see one of his customers. He usually goes up there once a month."

Her husband had an engineering consultancy company, Talbot and Associates. The client he'd gone to visit was Southeastern Construction Corp. She provided a contact and I asked, "You said he went to Atlanta regularly. Was there anything unusual the day he left? Did he have extra baggage or anything like that?"

"No, everything was normal. John called me from the airport, said he was on a flight leaving at seven and would get to Fort Myers around nine. John said he'd be home before ten."

"And that was the last you heard from him?"

"Yes. I was worried and called him continually, but he never answered. I called the police, and they said it was too early and I had to wait." She exhaled heavily. "I feel they're just not taking it seriously, so I checked around and was given your name."

Mrs. Talbot knew a Lee County detective I'd worked a handful of cases with.

"What airline was he flying?"

"Delta."

"Is there any reason your husband would have taken off?"

She crossed her shapely legs. "Believe me, I've racked my brain trying to think of something. Why would he have called if he was running away? He simply could have said he was staying an extra day."

I tended to agree, but he could have been looking for a head start. I didn't want to tell her it was a good way to buy time to melt into another state or country. Her husband may never have even gone to Atlanta.

When someone went missing, especially an adult, days passed before any real search occurred, and even that tended to be limited.

"Have you noticed any money missing or transferred out of an account?"

"John handled our finances, but it doesn't appear as if anything is missing."

"Have you contacted the credit cards for any activity?"

"Yes, there's been nothing since he bought a drink at the Hartsfield Airport."

"What about cell phone usage?"

"I asked Verizon, but they required a good deal of paperwork to complete. I'm hoping to get it soon."

Privacy was important, and I was leery of all the intrusions technology had created. But in a case like this, it was one of the easiest ways to determine where someone had been.

"Let me know as soon as you get it. Now, I'm interested

to know, when he called you, if you could tell he was actually at the airport."

"Oh, definitely."

"How can you be sure?"

"I heard the loudspeaker, in the background, say something about boarding a flight."

"You have no doubt?"

"None, John was at the airport."

I didn't want to tell her it could have been any airport. "How did he get to the Fort Myers airport?"

"He took his car, a white Genesis. I don't know the model, but it's the smaller one."

"You have the plate number?"

"I'll get it for you."

"Good. I'm going to need your husband's closest friends and business associates."

I wrote down the names and contact details and said, "All right, I'll get right to work on this."

"Do you think John's all right?"

There were two answers. Unless she wanted to get away from her husband, neither of them were good. "I can't say at this point. Let me investigate—"

Her lip seemed to quiver. "You can tell me; I want to know."

The question running through my mind since her call was whether she was involved in the disappearance. "As soon as I have something to report, I'll let you know."

She nodded.

I slid a document across the desk. "I'll need you to sign this agreement. It proves I'm working on your behalf. My fee is fifty an hour plus expenses."

She picked up a pen. "No problem."

I stood. "Okay. Let me get started."

She smiled. "It just occurred to me that you look like George Clooney."

"People do say that."

"You're actually better looking than him."

Did she bat her eyes?

"Uh, let me show you out."

We shook, and she held my hand a second too long. I was hoping she was feeling that I was her best chance at locating her husband.

2

————

Initially, I was wary of the attention thrown on me when I took my leave, but the publicity had generated a dozen calls looking to hire me. All the cases were mundane affairs.

After watching Mrs. Talbot sashay down the driveway, I called Derrick.

"Hey, buddy, how'd it go at physical therapy?"

"It's getting old."

"You have to do the work. It's the only way to get back on your feet."

"I know, just bitching a little. How'd it go with that woman, Talbot?"

I wanted to tell him she was one of the prettiest women on the planet, but said, "Good. Her name is Ann. She didn't give me much. I don't know if he's in trouble or was looking to start a new life."

"What'd she say?"

"Her husband, John, calls her before seven. The guy says he's at the Atlanta airport and is catching a flight at seven.

Said he'd get into Fort Myers at nine and be home before ten. But he was a no-show. Never called again, just disappeared. She reported it but was getting frustrated, felt they were blowing her off and was recommended to me."

"Assume they checked the hospitals."

"Yep, no John Does in Collier or Lee."

"Hmm. Any marriage issues?"

"None that she mentioned, but we'll need to dig in there."

"No doubt, but first we should start with the airport. They have tons of video. Maybe he got a call or something and left the airport."

"Yeah, fortunately, he was supposed to fly Delta, and Frankie can help."

"He's a good guy."

"Yeah. I want you to find out as much as you can on Talbot and his wife. She gave me a bunch of contacts; I'll text you some. We need to see if there was anything in the background that could have led him to run or get whacked."

"Can't wait to get started. I'm bored out of my mind sitting home."

"It's coming your way."

I sent a text with the information to Derrick. He still hadn't recovered from the shooting, and I still hadn't gotten over the guilt I felt over it. Nor had I forgiven the sheriff for his lack of support. It was another reminder of how poisonous politics were. The truth didn't matter; it was all about looking good.

Dialing the phone, I heard the garage door open. The girls were home. I shut the door to my office, waiting for my contact at Delta to answer.

MARY ANN WAS in the kitchen. Jessie was out back, practicing gymnastic moves on what little grass we had.

"You're home early."

"She found a dress she liked right away."

"You mean I got another girl who shops like a man?"

I loved that Mary Ann shopped and rarely browsed. If she was looking for jeans, she'd go straight to that section of the store and find a pair she liked. There was no flipping through racks of blouses or looking at shoes like most women did.

"She has our DNA. How did your meeting go? I understand she's quite the looker."

"What? Who told you that?"

"Miriam. You know how nosy she is."

Neighbors. Why couldn't they be as attentive when a crime happened?

"Geez, get the woman a job or something."

"What is the case about?"

"Her husband said he was on a seven p.m. flight out of Atlanta and called her from the airport. But I found out he was never booked on it and had actually taken an earlier flight that landed in Fort Myers at six p.m."

"Why would he mislead her?"

"There's a possibility she was mistaken. It looks like he was looking to buy time before going home."

"A girlfriend?"

I didn't want to tell Mary Ann the guy would have been nuts to cheat on his wife. "Could very well be that, or something else he didn't want his wife to know about."

THERE WAS a chance someone had picked up Talbot from the airport. Sweeping a parking lot the size of the airport's for

Talbot's car was not something I'd expected to be doing as a PI.

Talbot was only supposed to be gone for a day. I was betting he'd parked in a short-term lot.

Circling the lot made me dizzy. If I were working for the sheriff, I'd have had a couple of rookies doing the looking. I exited the covered parking garage without seeing his car.

Pulling into the long-term lot, my cell rang. It was my client.

"Hello, Mrs. Talbot."

"Hello, Frank. Please call me Ann."

Her voice was breathy.

"Sure. What's going on?"

"Two things. I received the phone records from Verizon, but there's no call from Atlanta. It shows Fort Myers."

"Yeah, I confirmed your husband took an earlier flight out of Atlanta."

"But why? And where is he?"

"You said you had two things."

"Oh, I went online to check AMEX for activity, and there was a charge from Regional Southwest Airport for twenty-eight dollars. It wasn't there before, but it's backdated to March second."

I headed for the parking lot's exit. Talbot had paid for more than a day's worth of short-term parking.

"All right. Your husband arrived earlier than expected and left in his own car. Send me over the phone records."

"I can bring them over, or we could meet tonight."

"Uhm, I-I'm busy tonight. If you don't mind, can you put them in my mailbox?"

"Oh, okay."

I hung up quickly. Pushing her out of my mind, I focused on her husband. *Where were you, John?*

He'd come in early, buying a block of time before his wife expected him home. Why? What did he have to do? I needed to find his car. It had to be fast because it didn't sound like he'd run. At least not voluntarily.

3

———————

THE BELL CHIMED, AND I HUSTLED TO THE DOOR. IT WAS Derrick and Lynn.

"Your first day and you're late?"

I kissed his wife. "I'll take it from here."

"What time should I get him?"

"Give us two hours."

She pecked Derrick's cheek, and I wheeled him into the den.

"You want anything?"

"No, I'm just happy to be out of the house."

"What did you find out on the Talbots?"

"They came down from Connecticut right after they married, over twenty years ago. John and Ann Talbot are low-keyed, but the family up north has money and connections. His grandfather even served as chief of staff for the governor up there."

"Wonder why they left?"

"One of John's friends said he hated the winters and taxes."

"He landed in the right place."

"They live in Park Shore, in a house valued at a million five. His business, Talbot Consulting, has four employees. Brian Blade is his right-hand man. He said Talbot cherry-picked his clients and that their services were expensive. He gave me the contact at the customer Talbot went to see, and they said it was a normal visit to go over structural issues on a new job they were about to break ground on."

"That was good thinking, saves me time knowing why he went to Atlanta. You know, even though you've been sitting on your ass, you still got it, kid."

"And you're still a wise guy."

"What did you expect? You know what else they were working on?"

"He said they'd been hired for two big projects in town, the Gulfshore Playhouse and the renovation of Artis."

"What's that?"

"The Philharmonic."

"Oh yeah, I don't know why they changed the name."

Derrick shrugged. "There's no doubt he's well-connected to get those jobs."

"Probably, but he could be donating his services."

"I asked about that, and Blade said no."

"Like I said, there's no rust on you, kid. What about their marriage?"

"By all accounts they're happy. Never had kids though."

"Don't know what they're missing."

"Couldn't tell if it was a conscious decision or a medical issue."

"It'll come out. Right now, we need to find the car."

"Is the sheriff looking for it?"

"Supposed to be. I let Lee County know about it too, and they put it on their sheet."

"Good. What's next?"

"I have a printout of the calls Talbot made the last fifteen days. You want to run it down?"

"Absolutely."

"Start going through it. I'm going to see the wife. I want to take a look around the house and grab any electronics he used."

I SNAKED ALONG BELAIR LANE, turning onto Willowhead Drive. Talbot's one-story house sat on a narrow lot but backed up to a lake. Its beige color dated the home, but they'd redone the landscaping. Derrick said it was worth a million and a half. Unless they'd remodeled the interior, it was accurate.

"Nice to see you, Frank."

Ann was in another red dress. She was no wallflower. "Same here. As I mentioned, I'd like to look around his office, if you don't mind. And I'll need to check any laptops or computers he used."

"John took his iPad with him. I asked Apple for help locating it, but they denied me because of privacy laws. I'm his wife, for God's sake, and he's missing."

"Between the tech and phone companies, I can tell you they don't make it easy. I've got my partner going over your husband's phone records. By any chance did he have Find My Device on the tablet?"

"What's that?"

"An app to trace a misplaced device."

"Oh. Not that I know of. Here's his office."

I watched her buns sway as she led me into a room right off the foyer. It had dark wood floors and a glass-and-stainless-steel desk. Architectural drawings and pictures of groundbreaking ceremonies hung on the walls.

"No desktop in here?"

"John uses his tablet most of the time."

"No other computers?"

"There's one in our bedroom. You want to see it?"

Bedroom? Could it get any more uncomfortable? "Uh, yeah. Let me look around here first."

Three narrow drawers ran across the top of the desk. Fishing through them, I didn't find anything interesting. I combed through the drawers of a credenza that was covered with pictures of the couple playing tennis and on the water.

"You own a boat?"

"Yes, we keep it at Naples Bay Resort."

"That's the place with all the covered buildings, right?"

"Yes, it reminds me of Portofino."

There wasn't anything out of the ordinary in the unit, and I went to the closet. A gray firebox sat on the floor. "May I?"

"Of course."

I rifled through the files. Most of the paperwork was estate related: trust documents, wills, and insurance policies. The home's deed and auto titles made up the rest.

"You want to see his computer in the bedroom?"

I did but was uncomfortable. "Sure. He has his own closet?"

"Yes, come this way."

We skirted a remodeled kitchen, with modern lacquered cabinets and white countertops, into the family room. I followed her into the master bedroom. She had a great walk.

"Where's the computer?"

"In my closet."

Ugh. This was getting too personal. She walked into a large room. It was a closet like a Ferrari was a car. It looked like the women's department at Nordstrom. I averted my eyes from the lingerie section and headed to a desktop sitting on a vanity spanning an entire wall. I was lucky it was an HP, as I was inept at navigating Macs.

Opening the browser, I went straight for the history tab. Sticking in a thumb drive, I copied the list of sites visited from the PC. "How often does your husband use this?"

"Not often, but at times he does. Some websites just don't work the same on an iPad."

Didn't *not often* and *at times* have the same meaning? "I'd like to have a look in his closet."

She pointed across the hallway. Her husband had a quarter of the clothing she did, but it was still double what I owned. I checked his sports jackets for anything in the pockets but only came up with a ticket to a charity event. I went through a bank of drawers. The bottom drawer was filled with sweaters.

Digging to the bottom, I came up with a magazine. I did a double take when I saw the name.

4

———

The publication was *Swinger Magazine*. I peeked out the closet. Ann was sitting on the bed, checking her nails. I thumbed through the magazine. There were articles with pictures of everyday people and pages of personal ads from swingers looking to meet other swingers.

Were the Talbots engaging in sex with other couples? A snake writhed in my stomach. The thought of someone allowing his wife to have sex with another man, possibly even watching, was enough to throw a splash of bile against the back of my throat.

I put the magazine back. It was their choice how they led their lives, and it wasn't illegal. I tucked the information into the back of my mind, but it crept back. If this turned out to be a homicide, it might be relevant.

Some man might have had buyer's remorse allowing Talbot to screw his wife, or maybe it was Talbot pursuing someone's spouse outside of the couple's swapping activities that drove the husband to kill Talbot.

Ann smiled as I left the closet. "You find anything?"

Did she know the magazine was there? For a second, I

wondered whether it was an elaborate way of feeling me out. "Do the two of you socialize much?"

"About as much as anyone else. We have tennis friends and one or two couples at the marina that we get together with occasionally."

I was dying to ask her if they exchanged partners when they did. "It might be useful to talk to them."

As she gave me the contact info, it was tough not to envision her romping around. Finishing up, I headed back to my office with one more question than I came with.

———

I PULLED INTO OUR DRIVEWAY. A woman was sitting in a Honda across from our house.

"Who is that lady out there?"

The doorbell rang as Mary Ann said, "She wants to see you, been waiting for over an hour."

"About what?"

"Her daughter."

I swung the door open. "Can I help you?"

"Frank Luca?"

"Yes, ma'am."

"Oh, thank God."

Though I couldn't see Mary Ann, I knew she was rolling her eyes. The woman introduced herself and said she needed my help locating her daughter. If it weren't a kid, I'd have questioned the wisdom of pursuing two missing persons at the same time.

I stepped aside. "Come in."

Sherrie Coyle had close-cropped hair and was about forty. She sat at the edge of the chair.

"It's my daughter, Carla. She's been gone for three days."

"How old is she?"

I cringed when she said, "Eighteen."

"Do you have any idea where she might have gone?"

"No, but I know she's probably with Teddy."

"And he is?"

"Her boyfriend."

"She ran away with him?"

"Not exactly. You see, she had a big fight with my husband over Teddy. Jeremy hates the kid and told her to stop seeing him."

"Did you report her as missing?"

"Yeah, I went to the police, but when I told them she was probably with her boyfriend, they said she was an adult."

"How old is Teddy?"

"I think he's twenty-one."

"What's his last name?"

"I, uh, don't know."

"Do you know if he has a job?"

She shook her head. I wanted to shake some sense into her.

"And you're sure she's with him?"

"She better be. I mean, Teddy's not the boyfriend I'd have liked Carla to have, but deep down, he's a good kid."

"Have you tried contacting Teddy?"

"Yes, he won't tell me where she is."

"But you believe he knows?"

"She has to be with him."

"What did he say when you asked about her?"

"That he doesn't know where she is. But I can tell he's lying."

"Where does Teddy live?"

"I don't know. He doesn't live with his parents. His father is in jail, and his mother is on drugs."

At least she had a valid reason not to be enamored about who her kid was dating. "You have his phone number, right?"

"Yeah, I took it off her phone one day."

I wrote down the number. "Do you have any reason to believe she may be in danger?"

"Not really. I'm worried sick about where she is, where's she sleeping . . ."

"Who is her best friend?"

"Carla has really been keeping to herself and Teddy since she graduated from Golden Gate High."

"Is she working?"

Another shake of the head.

"When she was in school, who was her best friend?"

"Nancy Cardinale. She lives a couple of blocks away from us and works at Bed Bath and Beyond on Airport-Pulling Road."

"Is she close with any family?"

"Just my husband's sister, Lara. She lives in Winter Park."

I slid my engagement agreement across the desk. "You'll need to sign this, and I'll get going."

She started reading. "Fifty an hour? I can't afford that. I mean, how long is this going to take?"

"I don't know. I'm hoping it will be quick." I reached for the document and crossed out the fee. "I've got a daughter, so I'll reduce it to forty."

Mary Ann was doing her laps as I showed Mrs. Coyle to the door. "She's a good swimmer."

"It helps keep her MS at bay."

"I'm sorry."

"No need to be, she's a fighter and is doing great. Anyway, I'll be in touch."

I went back to my office and sent a text:

Teddy, my name is Frank Luca. I'm a private investigator. The Coyles hired me to locate their daughter. I realize she's an adult, but all I'm interested in knowing she is safe. Please tell me where I can see her, and I promise not to tell the parents. We can meet in a public place if you wish.

After an hour without a reply, I sent another text telling Teddy I wasn't going away. Fifteen minutes of silence passed, and I headed out to see Carla's girlfriend.

The traffic on Airport-Pulling was lighter than usual. I pulled into the parking lot when my phone rang. It was Sergeant Trillo, a contact of mine in the Lee County Sheriff's Office.

"What's up, Ray?"

"We found the car you were looking for."

"John Talbot's Genesis?"

5

"YEP, IT WAS UP IN LEHIGH ACRES, OFF MILWAUKEE Boulevard, stripped to the bone."

"Any signs of blood in the vehicle."

"Nothing."

"You going to bring it in?"

"Yeah. A tow truck is on the way."

"Will you have forensics go over it?"

"No. There's no reason to. At this point, it's just an abandoned vehicle. I know the owner is missing, but we have nothing more to go on."

"I'll have his wife report it stolen."

"It won't change much."

This was bad news. It meant Talbot, unless he was an elaborate schemer, was likely dead. I wasn't looking forward to letting his wife know.

Cranking up the AC, I sat in my car, considering the possibilities. The slimmest of chances was Talbot taking off, leaving his car behind, and it was stolen. It was more likely that Talbot was killed or kidnapped and the car dumped in a place the perpetrators knew would make it appear stolen.

The other possibility was a carjacking. We'd only had one in Naples since I'd moved here. I couldn't completely discount it, but unless Talbot had gone north after landing early into Fort Myers, it was a long shot.

It all started with a lie. Talbot made up a story to tell his wife, and now it was almost certain he was dead. In addition to finding out what had happened and who did it, Talbot's body had to be recovered.

I needed to inform Ann Talbot, but my desire for efficiency had me stepping into the heat to talk to Carla Coyle's friend at Bed Bath & Beyond.

THE MIDDAY SUN beat on my back as I walked to my Ford Escape with a lead on Teddy. I dialed up the air and went to see Mrs. Talbot. I usually avoided Pine Ridge Road because of the traffic, but it was the direct route to Park Shore.

An automatic in these types of cases is considering the spouse a primary suspect. Ann Talbot seemed like the picture-perfect woman to be married to. But the truth was you never really knew anyone.

Just when you thought you did, they'd surprise you. The problem was the unexpected revelations were overwhelmingly disappointing.

She'd need closer examination. I regretted not taking a long look at the will and trust documents. As a homicide detective, I'd learned jealousy and passion were a distant second to greed.

Ann Talbot was in baby-blue pants and a sleeveless blouse. She was a doll, and I couldn't believe she'd participate in any kind of swapping. She opened the door, and her smile was half the normal wattage.

"Uh, hi. Come in."

The cool air felt good, but I had no interest in hanging around. My MO was to get the bad news out as quickly as possible. There was no benefit in delay. In fact, holding it screwed me up.

I didn't follow her down the hall. "There's been a development."

She whipped around, concern dripping from her face. "About John?"

People said the strangest things when they were scared. "Yes. His car was found."

"That's positive, right?"

"It's good that it's been located. It may give us something to work with, but it means he's either taken off or there has been foul play."

"He, he, wouldn't leave . . . it makes no sense." She leaned against a side table.

"There's a chance he could be incapacitated, in a hospital somewhere."

"My girlfriends and I called every facility from here to Sarasota."

"At this point, we know he came in on an earlier flight, paid the parking, and left the airport."

"And you have the car."

I nodded. "You have my word, I'll find out what happened."

She swallowed. "You believe he's dead, don't you?"

"I didn't say that. However, it's a possibility you have to prepare yourself for."

Her lip quivered.

"Did your husband have any enemies? Anyone he had a running feud or argument with?"

"John was the nicest person, to everyone. When I first

met him, he'd get riled up at times and argue with people, you know, about politics, but he changed when he hit forty and wouldn't get upset or go back at anyone, no matter what they said."

I wished I'd had a metamorphosis at forty. "What about anyone work-related?"

"He never said there were problems."

"Are you sure? He worked on some big projects where a lot of money is involved. Any misunderstandings or differences of opinion that he shared with you?"

"No, I wish I could help."

"Was your husband in or ever had an affair?"

"I certainly hope not."

"I'm sorry, but I have to ask. It could be a jilted lover."

She had a weird smirk on her face. "I understand."

"What about you?"

"What about me?"

"Are you having an affair or had one in the last two years or so?"

She frowned. "Really? And if I did or didn't, what relevancy does it have?"

It was clear she didn't want to answer. "It could be that someone wasn't satisfied with a fling and, uh, wanted more out a relationship with you. He could have decided the way to do it was to remove your husband from the picture."

"Sounds like a movie to me."

"After fifteen years as a homicide detective, I can assure you it happens more often than you'd think."

"Never boring, was it?"

With her deflection, I knew the answer. Unless she was involved in a conspiracy to kill her husband, why share it? If there was extramarital activity, maybe she felt confident the partner or partners weren't threats.

"It certainly wasn't. Have you had an affair or not?"

"I did."

"Is it ongoing?"

"No. It's over."

"How recent?"

"A few months ago."

"I understand how delicate this is, but I'm going to need their names."

"They had nothing to do with John."

There was more than one. "Maybe, but we need to eliminate—"

"You'd be wasting your time."

"Trust me on this. I'll be discreet and check their backgrounds."

She gave me two names. I wanted to ask whether they were swingers but didn't want to push her any further. There was a good chance I'd uncover it if they were.

Leaving her house, my mind drifted back to the magazine I'd found. I knew zilch about swingers, and what I did know came from an untrustworthy source: TV. It led me to believe these people popped in and out of sexual relationships with no attachments.

It was an assumption that defied the human condition.

6

———————

IT WAS ONE AUTOMOBILE-RELATED BUSINESS AFTER ANOTHER on this stretch of Taylor Road. They were all independent shops. Pulling into the lot for Quarry Auto Parts, I wondered if the strategy to cluster the stores would help them fend off the growing heft of national chains.

Signs shouted Quarry's expertise in servicing BMWs, making for plenty of potential customers in Naples. The interior could've passed for a dealership with its cleanliness and artfully lighted displays.

Standing behind podiums, two men in ties tapped their computers. The skinny guy to the left raised his head. "It's a great day at Quarry Motors. How may I assist you?"

"I can't remember the guy who works here. I think it was Teddy or something."

"Teddy Delrio?"

"He's about twenty?"

"Yes, that's him.

"Can I talk to him, please?"

"Did he service your vehicle?"

"No, this is a personal matter."

I was ready for pushback, but he disappeared into the back of the building.

A skinny kid in blue overalls came out with the customer rep. Earrings in both ears, he eyed me suspiciously as he wiped his hands with a cloth.

"Teddy, why don't we step outside a second?" I took a step toward the door, but Teddy stayed put, cracking his knuckles.

"Come on, I want to talk about the text I sent you."

We stepped into the humidity and he said, "What do you want?"

"Just to know that Carla Coyle is safe."

"How would I know?"

"Oh, come on, Teddy. Tell me where the kid is."

"I told you, I don't know."

"When was the last time you saw her?"

"I don't know, like a month ago."

"You expect me to believe that?"

"Believe whatever you want, man."

"All the parents want to know is that their daughter is safe. She's an adult, and if she doesn't want to see them, she's free to make that decision."

Teddy stared at his boots.

"Look, Teddy, one day you may have a kid of your own, and trust me, you'll need to know that she's safe for the rest of your life. That's all I'm asking."

He shrugged. "Look, I gotta get back to work."

Mary Ann stuck her head out the slider. "Is it almost ready?"

I opened the grill and checked the turkey burgers. "Yup.

Get Jessie."

Plating the food, my girls came onto the deck with a bowl of vegetables. Since Mary Ann's MS diagnosis, she was on a healthy diet craze, and I was pulled along. It wasn't easy, but I was getting used to it and had lost five pounds.

"No buns?"

"Dad, you haven't had bread in, like, a month."

"I know, but we're eating burgers."

"Your father just likes to remind me he's sacrificing."

"Aw, come on, I need my carbs."

Jessie picked up a serving spoon. "Here, Dad, have some cauliflower rice instead."

Mary Ann said, "How's your first case going?"

"They found his car today, up in Lee County."

"That's not good, right, Dad?"

"No, it's not."

"Are the forensics people going to check it over?"

"No. But if I was working up there, I'd make sure they'd tear that vehicle apart."

Mary Ann said, "You don't know that, Frank."

"Oh yes, I do." I turned to Jessie. "And here's a lesson for you. Never underestimate the impact of your willpower. You can get things done, even if others say it's not possible. You just have to stick to your beliefs and push ahead. It's the only way to accomplish something."

"Don't worry, Dad, I won't give up. I'm a Luca."

I grinned. "You certainly are."

ABOUT TO CALL DERRICK, I realized I had never looked at the browsing history from the computer in Ann Talbot's closet. I popped the thumb drive in and scrolled. Man, did this lady like to shop.

I didn't recognize a couple of names and had to look up the websites. Did we really need so many places for women to buy clothes? I knew the answer; if they weren't selling, they'd vanish.

Paging down, I stared at the next entry: Swinglifestyle.com. Was it her, him, or both of them? Popping the link into the search bar, the site came up. The title of the lead article rocked me: "You Want Me to Do What? A Guide to BDSM Swingers Boundaries."

I couldn't make out what the photo accompanying the article was trying to portray. Scrolling down, I hit a section called Hot Topics. Its lead was "How to Politely Turn Down a Couple in the Lifestyle." I guess you really never knew what pressing questions others faced.

Next up was, "A Look at Why Couples May Divorce After Swinging." No need for an explanation; I was certain most people knew why.

Then there was, "A Look at Slave Dom Couples in the BDSM Lifestyle." You know what? I'd rather not invade their privacy.

I thought about what I had found. Everyone bounces onto sites they didn't intend to. We type too fast or click on something, and bingo, we end up on a site selling breast enlargement tools.

The problem was the magazine I'd found in John Talbot's dresser. Coincidences and me weren't the best of friends. In my mind, it equated to a pattern and thus was evidence.

People were free to engage in any activity they wanted to. My standard started at whether something was legal or not. I didn't understand the swinging thing. I mean, why get married? But the only thing I cared about was whether it had anything to do with Talbot's disappearance.

During my career, I'd asked more than my share of difficult questions. Not many people would describe me as shy, but the thought of asking Ann if they were swingers made me uncomfortable.

Was it because she was one of the better-looking ladies on the planet? I'd dealt with a lot of beautiful women, even dated quite a few of them, but this was giving me the willies.

Or was I afraid of being pulled into a dangerously different lifestyle?

7

———————

ANN WAS WEARING A SILKY NEGLIGEE THAT BARELY COVERED her thong. You wouldn't need kindling to start a fire. In a husky voice, she said, "Ready?"

"No, I can't."

Ann grabbed my hand. "Come on. It'll be fun."

She was leading me to her bedroom. Two men and a woman were laughing on the bed. They were naked.

"I don't know."

"You'll love it. It's going to be a great time." She turned around and pushed the straps off her shoulders. "Trust me, it's all good."

Her negligee pooled around her ankles. She stepped out of it and I followed her in. "Hey, everybody, this is my friend Frank. Isn't he adorable?"

I shot up.

"You all right?"

"Yeah, just a bad dream."

"The Barrow case?"

"Uh, yeah. Barrow, again." The homicide case had haunted me for years. It was a natural excuse.

MY THERMOS WAS JUST about empty when I saw Teddy walk out of Quarry Auto Parts. I was pissed that I'd wasted two hours watching the employee exit. It was a lousy way to make a hundred dollars.

Teddy got into a rust-colored Malibu and pulled onto Taylor Road. I stayed a hundred yards behind and followed him down to Radio Road where he turned into a community called Endless Summer. It was filled with RVs and mobile homes.

Coming up to an aluminum-sided trailer, Teddy slowed down, pulling onto a cement pad behind a pickup truck. I took a picture of the unit and jotted down the address as Teddy disappeared into the home.

A TV was playing. Putting my ear to the door, I tried to detect a female voice. Unsuccessful, I knocked on the door.

The door swung open. Teddy did a double take. "What do you want?"

"Carla Coyle. You show her to me, and I go away."

"She ain't here."

"Come on, Teddy, all the parents want is to know she's safe. I'm not going to do anything; besides, she's an adult."

"I told you today, and I'm telling you now, Carla's not here."

"You mind if I take a look around?"

"You want to come inside?"

"Yeah, I won't touch anything."

"Let me see your ID."

The kid was smart. "Here you go."

Teddy examined my license and handed it back. "All right, but make it quick. I want to get something to eat."

I stepped into the trailer. The kid kept a neat house. Was

that Carla's doing? There was only one coffee mug in the sink.

"What time do you go to work?"

"I'm in by eight."

"Oh, that's early. I need two cups of coffee before I leave the house."

"I'm a tea drinker."

I walked down a small hallway. The bathroom was to the left. "You have a cup before you go?"

"Yeah."

I pulled open the medicine cabinet. A single toothbrush along with men's deodorant and shaving supplies. Swinging open the door to the vanity, I saw toilet paper and a box of Stayfree feminine products.

"Whose are these?"

"They're old. Carla left them here."

"So, she was staying here?"

His shoulders sagged. "Just the first night. And don't tell her I told you; she'll be pissed at me. We had a big fight, and she took off."

"Where did she go?"

"She went with those wacky Koreshan people."

"Koreshan? Up in Estero?"

"Yeah, they're a frigging bunch of nutjobs."

"I didn't know they were still around."

"They are, but they're up somewhere past Babcock Ranch."

"And how did she get involved with them?"

"We used to go kayaking in the park, and one day they were having one of those farmers' markets, and we got something to eat. These girls were sitting at the next table, and they were saying they'd seen the ghost of the people that used to live there. Carla ate it up and was asking questions. She wanted to do the ghost walk they did. It was twenty-five bucks a head. I don't believe in that stuff, but Carla, her grandmother was one of those people that talk to the dead—"

"A medium?"

"Yeah, that's it. So we went, and all these people were dressed up like the old days, and it was nothing more than like a Halloween thing, but Carla, and she wasn't the only one, kept saying they saw things and heard whispering." He shook his head. "Then she started hanging around with people who said they were Koreshans and that the movement was still around, and they were trying to build a new paradise. I tried to tell her it was a cult, but she didn't want to hear it."

"You think she's in any danger?"

"I didn't like the leader guy, Eden. Most everyone else were girls."

My mind went to thinking it was a kind of sexual cult. "You get a sense the women were, uh, infatuated with him?"

"You mean like the Davidian guy with all the wives?"

"Something like that."

"I don't think so. Carla wasn't like that, and they preached celibacy. She and me, you know, we never did it. She said you had to be married."

The missing kid may have been off track in some parts of her life, but she had that right.

"You said you didn't like the leader. Why?"

"I don't know, he was weird, said he was like, a great-nephew of the guy who started it way back. He was a poser, you know, trying to be something he wasn't."

"But Carla was drawn to him?"

"He was part of it; she said he was a spirit. I tried to shake her up but . . ."

"You know how to get in touch with her?"

"I try calling her a couple of times a day, but last time she picked up was two days ago."

"Try now."

He did, waited, then shook his head and left a message for Carla.

"You said they're up around Babcock Ranch. Where exactly?"

"I don't know. That's what Carla said."

"I need the location before something happens to her and we risk never getting her away from them."

"Some of them do the ghost thing at the park."

8

———————

Instead of plugging their names into a search for criminal records, I Googled them first. I wanted to see what they looked like. It was childish, but I told myself that looking into their eyes would give me insight into the character of the men who'd slept with Ann Talbot.

I clicked to Tony Desmond's Facebook page. It said he was single and forty-two, but my guess was he'd shaved a couple of years off, like most people hawking themselves on social media. He seemed fit, like Ann's husband, and I hated to admit he was handsome.

There were several pictures of him on a sailboat, making me wonder if they'd met at the marina. Scrolling through a couple dozen of his posts, I didn't detect any sexual signaling. Combined with his single status, I didn't think he was a swinger.

I moved on to Miles Livermore. A picture of a serious-looking man surprised me. I hit the link to his Facebook page and was greeted with a profile picture of a bare-chested Livermore laying on a beach blanket.

It was an image a high schooler would use. This guy was

fifty. What did Ann see in this clown? I read several of his posts. They were all motivational, and several were actually quite good.

He was one of those optimistic people that drove me crazy. Every time I met one, I wanted to drag them to a couple of crime scenes and wake them up to reality.

Thumbing through photos, all meant to convey he was interested in amping up the envy, I felt my jaw drop. There was a picture of Miles Livermore and John Talbot seated next to each other.

I zoomed in. Livermore had his arm on the back of Talbot's chair. There was no doubt they knew each other. I scrolled down and found another one. This time they were standing, and the background was the shimmering Gulf of Mexico.

Did Ann meet her lover through her husband? Was she screwing one of his friends? Did they have what was called an open marriage? My heart sank. I've seen more craziness than most people, but the realization that people like this existed disheartened me.

I shook my head and did a background check on Livermore. I felt myself hoping something criminal would pop up, but there was no evidence of any criminal behavior.

Next up was Tony Desmond. The search produced two hits, both in Collier County. Twice, Desmond was convicted of battery. Ann's playmate liked to use his hands, and he had lied on his profile; Desmond was forty-five.

As a detective on leave, and with the sheriff interested in my rejoining the force, I had an advantage over the average investigator. As cautious as I was not to abuse the delicate information pipeline, this was a clear case to press my edge.

I grabbed my phone. "Hey, Sarge, it's Luca."

"What's going on, Frank? You enjoying the good life?"

"I hit a roadblock. Could use some help with information on a couple old cases."

"I don't know, Frank. Chester finds out, my ass is—"

"It concerns a missing man I'm trying to track down. I think it's going to turn out to be a homicide."

"What else you have?"

"They found his car up in Lee; it was stripped."

"That's it?"

"I just found out his wife was having an affair, with a guy with a temper—two battery convictions."

"You think it's him?"

"All I want is the case background on them. The who, why, and what he said his side of it was."

"All right. What's the name and dates?"

My PHONE VIBRATED. Dr. Bilotti was calling me back.

"Hey, Doc, how are you?"

"It's not the same without you, Frank. I'm getting so much more done without the interruptions."

"Very funny."

"How are you, Mary Ann, and Jessica doing?"

"All's good. Been busy as heck."

"Drink anything interesting?"

"I've been doing what you said, trying wines from undiscovered places in Italy. I had a really nice one from Puglia. It was a combo of Negroamaro, and I can't remember the other one."

"Primitivo?"

"Yeah, that's it."

"Primitivo is essentially zinfandel."

"Oh, that's right. I remember you told me that. Anyway, it

was nice, and just twenty bucks."

"Good. Play around with some of the wines coming out of Marche. There are some bargains, but some terrible ones as well."

"Will do. Say, I need a little help."

"What's going on?"

"I'm working a missing person case, and I think the guy might have been killed. His car was found up in Lee, but nobody wants to have forensics go over it."

"You left homicide here to work on it as an independent?"

"I know, anyway, the client has the money to do it privately. Can you tell me who you'd recommend for this?"

BILOTTI'S CONTACT was a retired man who had led Baltimore's crime lab. There was no doubt he had more experience than most. The three thousand he wanted was higher than expected.

Needing approval, I called Ann. She okayed it immediately and said she wanted to see me. I wanted to ask questions about the affairs she'd had but held back, pending the case files.

The feelings of urgency I'd had over John Talbot's disappearance had dissipated. At this point, I was almost sure that the only way her husband was coming back was in a dream.

That said, the best I could do for my client was to find her husband's body. That way, she'd be able to get on with her life.

I called the private forensic tech and told him to get moving. As I spoke to him, an email came in. It was the sergeant's private email. I opened the case files and shook my head.

9

EITHER THIS WOMAN WAS GUNNING FOR ME, OR ALL SHE HAD was clothing that was latex-like. This time it was a white pair of skin-tight, silky pants and a tank top that looked like one of Mary Ann's camisoles.

"Hello, Frank."

"Hi, Mrs. Talbot."

"Ann. Please don't be so formal."

"It's my training, ma'am."

She smiled and stepped aside. Music was playing. It sounded seductive. If it was Sade, I was leaving.

It was a TV commercial. She shut it off and handed me a check. "This is for the forensic tests and a thousand toward whatever I owe you."

"Thanks. I'm a little behind on billing." The truth was, I wasn't used to keeping time logs or making up invoices.

"How soon will we get information on John's car?"

"They're doing the collection tomorrow. I'm going to need a sample of your hair and DNA to rule out certain specimens."

"Okay." She grabbed a few strands of her hair, rubbed her fingers together and tugged. "Here you go."

I bagged her locks and took a DNA kit out. "Swab the inside of each cheek with separate Q-tips."

She smiled. "Glad I don't have to spit."

Pocketing the samples, I asked, "Who else would have ridden in John's vehicle?"

"Oh, I'm not sure. I assume his friends and possibly somebody from work. When we were together, we used my Cayenne."

That was a Porsche SUV, which in my book was an oxymoron. "The names you provided previously cover the friends?"

"Yes, it should, unless he had a girlfriend."

"You suspect he was having an affair?"

"Oh no. Just kidding around."

People said the strangest things. Especially if they were nervous or guilty. "Speaking of affairs, I ran background checks on the two men you advised me about."

Her smile faded. "And?"

"Well, Mr. Desmond has a temper issue."

"What's that supposed to mean?"

"He has two battery convictions."

"What? Are you sure it's the right Tony Desmond?"

"Absolutely. On separate occasions, one in a bar and the other over a parking space. Tony Desmond beat a man so badly he was arrested."

"Oh my God. I can't believe it. He had to have been provoked."

Desmond's lawyers claimed it was mutual combat and an effort at self-defense. "Well, he was the only one to plead."

"He went to . . . jail?"

"No. First offense was a thousand-dollar fine, and the second he got a year's probation."

"I can't believe it."

"In the time you were with him, you never saw him get angry?"

I took her shrug as a yes. "How did your relationship end?"

"I told him it was over."

"How'd he handle that?"

"He was upset. You know, wanted to keep things going."

I'm sure he did. "Did he ever talk about your husband?"

Another shrug told me I had to take a close look at Desmond. "I'm going to have to speak to him."

"Aw, come on."

"I don't have a choice."

"He never told anyone about us, and up to now, I didn't either. I don't want him to know I said something."

"I can tell him your husband hired me because he suspected something was going on. Where did you two used to go?"

"Usually La Playa."

It was one of the few beachfront hotels in Naples. "Okay."

"Can't you wait until you see what we get from the car?"

It was another day or so. "All right. I'll hold off."

LINDA COULDN'T DROP Derrick off because their baby was sick. I was up to my neck but knew he had to get out of the house.

"How you doing, buddy?"

"Thanks for coming, man. I hate to make you go back and

forth."

"No problem, pal."

"Get my laptop for me. It's in the kitchen."

"Hey, Linda, I'm leaving my keys on the counter. It's in the driveway. We'll see you in a couple of hours."

I rolled Derrick into the back of the Dicksons' van, secured the wheelchair, and headed to my house.

"Tell me about the telephone log."

"He's not a chatterbox. Most of the calls were a couple of minutes at best, but three of them were strange."

"How so?"

"All were under three minutes, and they were all female."

"How did Talbot know them?"

"That's the thing, none of the women remembered him. They all said it was a wrong number."

"Did you say they were under three minutes in duration?"

"Yes, they were from two to three minutes."

"That's way too long for a wrong number."

"I know, that's how I felt. They were cagey, but I didn't want to press them too hard."

"He could've been using an alias."

"Good point."

"What else was on the list?"

"A couple of people on the list of friends that his wife gave you, some calls to his office, and the rest were all businesses."

"All right, we get to my house, and you can chase down those women, see if they have anything in common."

"I got it."

The swinger lifestyle connection wasn't confirmed, so I never told Derrick about the possibility. He was good enough to pick up on it if it existed.

"Check to see if they're married."

"Sure, what are you thinking, he was looking for the husband or boyfriend or having an affair that ended badly?"

"You never know. Say, what do you know about the Koreshans?"

"When I came down here from DC, I never heard of them. Linda and me went to the park on a date. It was a pretty cool property, and the buildings were so well maintained you couldn't believe they were a hundred years old. I read the brochure, and it was a weird cult thing. The leader was from Upstate New York somewhere and said he was hit by lightning and God spoke to him."

"His brain was fried."

"Probably. Anyway, this guy settles down here with a bunch of followers and starts a community. They had some weird beliefs, like the universe was inside the earth, and the sun and stars were just reflections."

"I heard they were celibate."

"Yeah, and that you never died and would be reincarnated. When the leader died, they didn't bury him for like a week."

"In this heat?"

"The authorities forced them to, and they buried him at the beach in a bathtub."

"Nutjobs."

"I guess, but they never got in trouble. Just wanted to create their own little utopia."

"It looks like a relative is looking to revive the group. The missing kid's boyfriend said she got sucked into them."

"Where's this?"

"He said up by Babcock Ranch but knew nothing more than that. He gave me something to work with. Tonight, I'm going to see if I can run into one of the members at the ghost walks they do."

10

Derrick was settled in, and I was trying to figure out how to create invoices in QuickBooks. Mary Ann said it was supposed to be easy, but as usual, easy came after you knew how to do something.

Managing my frustration was something I learned from Dr. Bruno. She advised me to move on to something else for a bit, then come back to it. It was time to change it up, and I couldn't delay delivering bad news any longer.

I closed my laptop and was just about to tell Derrick I was going out when he lifted his head.

"You know, Frank, you don't know how good it feels to be working with you. It's just like old times sitting with you. I missed you, man."

"Me too. I'm going to try to build this up, and if it works out and you want to work with me, you can."

"Let's see how it goes. But you should think about going back on the force."

"We'll see. Right now, I have two cases that need solving."

"You're right, let's get to work."

While Derrick chased down info on the women Talbot had called, I decided I couldn't leave and would deliver the news by phone. I walked into the family room.

"Mrs. Coyle, this is Detective Frank Luca." Used to my old title, it just came out.

"Did you see Carla?"

"Not yet."

"Didn't you talk to Teddy?"

"Yes, I tracked him down. Teddy Delrio is his full name. I searched the trailer he's living in, but she wasn't there."

"He's lying."

"I believe him. She was there, but she left, and it looks like she joined people associated with the Koreshan group."

"What? Don't tell me she's living at that park in Estero?"

"I'm trying to clarify exactly where she is, and hopefully, I might know tonight."

"You will? What's going on tonight?"

"We're conducting an undercover operation."

"You're going to bring her home?"

"I don't believe so. The mission is predominately observational, though we hope to interact with the people she is staying with."

She sighed. "Oh."

"I'm going to do my best to reunite you with her, but you have to keep in mind that in the eyes of the law, your daughter is an adult. She'll have to decide on her own if and when to come back."

"I know, it's just . . ."

"Trust me, ma'am, I'm a father and know most eighteen-year-olds don't have what it takes to make sound decisions."

"My husband was just trying to do right by her. He's not her father, but he's a good man."

"What happened with her real father?"

"He took off."

"That's a tough situation for a child."

"She's a good kid but stubborn as they come."

Though teenagers weren't the smartest of God's creations, I said, "My dad always said, 'Don't stop talking to them. They may seem like they're not listening, but you can still reach them.'"

"I hope so. He was just getting too worked up. He didn't like Teddy and made it clear as you could. I told him to tone it down or it would backfire, and now she's gone."

"When it involves someone you're responsible for, it's tough to keep it in check. But look, I have to get back to work. I'll let you know as soon as I have something to report."

I said goodbye and walked into the den. Derrick said, "I couldn't get ahold of any of them. I heard you talking about the Koreshans and did a quick Google search. Take a look at this."

Though I couldn't believe what I saw, what scared me was the thought my memory issues were resurfacing. I hadn't even thought of doing a simple search about the group. Was it a legitimate oversight or chemo brain?

I scanned the search results. The first five visible on the screen all mentioned the reformation of the Koreshan Unity movement. "Open the top one."

"The second one is more detailed."

The headline of the piece read: "Koreshan Resurrection." The *Port Charlotte Times* article went on to say that Eden Grange, claiming to be the great-nephew of the founder of Koreshan Unity, was leading a new group. Grange called his followers an extended family and said they were guided by most of the beliefs of the original group.

I said, "New Jerusalem? That's what they're calling it?"

"It's the same name the original guy, Cyrus Teed, used."

"A new utopia. Guess that would put us out of jobs."

"True. I wonder what kind of, if any, crime they had in the original community."

"Good question. If it was such a paradise, why did it wither away?"

"You forgetting they were celibate?"

"I don't believe that for a second. It's an innate desire. I don't care how much praying you do, the hormones always win out."

"Exactly."

"Where are they building the promised land?"

"Off of Routes 31 and 74, by Babcock Ranch."

"Where they getting the money for it?"

"It could have been pretty cheap if they bought it before they started with that whole planned community thing."

"Supposed to be the first community powered entirely by solar, right?"

"Yeah, it's funny, we're the Sunshine State, but we hardly have any solar power because electricity is so cheap here."

"We'll see how it pans out. Look, it might be a good idea to find out where the money is coming from. We might need to leverage something to get this kid out."

"I'll dig into it."

My cell rang. It was Vincent Giri, Bilotti's forensics contact. "Mr. Giri, how are you?"

"Good. I wanted to let you know we processed the vehicle, gathering a supply of samples. I uploaded the raw genome data to GEDCOM and received a report with several direct and familial matches. I wanted to advise you before emailing them."

"Excellent. Thanks."

I hung up and fist pumped. "Looks like we have something to work with. Giri went over Talbot's vehicle. He sent samples to the public databases and is sending over the DNA hits they generated. Now, we're going to have to run them down, and see if we can find a suspect in them."

11

I LOOKED AT THE LIST OF DNA MATCHES. IF I WERE STILL with the sheriff's office, I would have known if any of the hits had been arrested or had records. These names had either asked about their ancestry or a family member had.

"How many names we got?"

"Seven."

"That's not bad. Can we eliminate any right off the bat?"

"Two are on the friends list, but we got to be careful, you never know."

"How many didn't match anything?"

"Three."

"That's not good."

"It's actually better than I expected."

Bottom line was very few lawbreakers submitted their DNA to discover their family tree. That meant if it was a criminal, we'd have to bank on a familial match.

"Give me a copy of the list. I'll start building backgrounds."

"Thanks. Since I'm going to the ghost thing later, let me

take you home so I can get back and spend some time with Jessie."

———

Jessie and her friend were in the pool. I kept an eye on them while Mary Ann, taking a head of cauliflower out of the fridge, said, "The checking account is getting low. When do you think you'll be able to put some money in?"

"I got the first check from Talbot but had to use most of it for startup subscriptions and fees. I'm behind with the billing."

"You have to stay on top of invoicing clients. Maybe you should get a retainer up front."

"That's a good idea. I've been thinking that I have to raise the hourly rate. At fifty bucks an hour, if I worked a normal forty-hour week, that would bring in a hundred thousand. More than I was making, but I got expenses now. Plus, Lew said I have to pay both ends of social security and Medicare taxes. That's over fifteen percent for those taxes alone. It's crazy."

"I don't want you working any more hours, so raise the rate to get you back to what you were making."

"Yeah, and we have to pay for our own health coverage."

"And save for retirement."

"I don't want to scare a customer away, so I was thinking to go up to seventy-five an hour. It would get us even and keep us at the high end of the competition."

"You don't have any competition, Frank. Not many private investigators have the experience you do. Go to eighty, that way you have a little breathing room."

"Thanks. I was starting to wonder why I kept you around."

"And all the time I thought it was my cooking skills."

I pressed into her from behind. "That too, and add being the sexiest woman on the planet."

"Frank, the kids are right there."

"All right. We'll finish this later."

THE SKY WAS TURNING from dishwater to black as I pulled off the dirt road. I was surprised by the number of cars. Slipping a Maglite into my pocket, I followed the signs for the ghost walk.

A lamp-lined path led to a clearing encircled by old wooden buildings. Most had wide porches lit by candles. People were gathered in front of the largest structure.

I stood at the edge of the crowd, watching as three people, dressed in period costumes, came out of the house. One of the women, in a floppy hat, welcomed the visitors and gave a quick background on the Koreshan community.

She pointed out several buildings, including an art hall, bakery, power plant, general store, and housing units. I was surprised when she mentioned that at its height, the community had over seventy buildings and owned seventy-five hundred acres.

As I smacked a mosquito on my arm, the guide said, "The Koreshans firmly believed in reincarnation. After his death, Master Koresh was awaiting his rebirth near the Estero River, just over there."

She pointed, and heads turned. "The authorities forced his burial near the beach, and a storm washed his physical body out to sea." She moved the candle in front of her face. "If you're attuned, you may encounter his spirit tonight."

Above the whispering and giggling, she said, "We're not

sure of the exact number, but at least twenty-five Koreshans are buried throughout the property. Most graves are not marked, but I don't think you'll have any problem feeling where they are."

Scanning the crowd, I wondered how many of them really believed in ghosts. The woman and her associates came down the stairs. "We're going to start by visiting the grave of Hedwig Michel. She was the last member of the Koreshans to live here."

A man on the fringe of the crowd shouted, "Not true. Hedwig wasn't the last. We are still here and growing. We're ready to welcome others. Come and talk to us; learn about our community."

The woman smiled at the man. "This park is dedicated to the original Koreshan settlement. Let's start the tour. We recommend you stay quiet and take one of the candles. Remember to be open to the spiritual signs we'll encounter."

As the crowd trailed behind the guide, I made a beeline for the man who interrupted her. He was wearing a long-sleeved white shirt and black Dockers. Was that his normal dress or his insect defense?

"How are you this evening?"

I stuck my hand out. "Good. Frank Luca, nice to meet you."

"Likewise. Morgan Creed. Would you like some information on New Jerusalem?"

With his blond hair and square features, I pegged him as Scandinavian. "Sure. I've always been interested in communal living."

"Then you'd appreciate our agricultural cooperative. Our production plans will generate more than current inhabitants can consume by the end of the year. We're planning to sell the excess to fund expansion."

"What's on the property now?"

"Currently, we have the gathering space and dormitories, as well as the food shed. Construction of a general store and livestock facilities have just begun. Master Eden has a grand vision, including a cultural center, that will exceed what Estero was at its height."

"How many members do you have?"

"We're forty-five in the core group, a handful in the middle group, and about ten nonbelievers who work for the community."

"What's the difference between the core and middle?"

"It's very similar to the way Teed structured his place. Core members are Pre-Eminent and celibate. Just below them is the Equitable Class. They can marry, but sexual relations are strictly for reproductive purposes."

Not much for fun, were they? "I heard it's up by Babcock Ranch. But where exactly?"

Creed explained where the community had put down its roots, finishing with, "I'd be happy to meet you up there and give you a tour. Are you available tomorrow morning?"

12

AFTER AN HOUR OF DRIVING AND FIFTY BILLBOARDS advertising Babcock Ranch, I saw the entrance to the community. I was curious about the place, wondering if the low home prices and the being-green thing would be enough to make people move to the middle of nowhere.

It'd be interesting to check the place out. Maybe Mary Ann would want to take the ride, I thought as I passed it and continued going east. The road slimmed to two lanes, and there was no trace of life in any direction.

As Creed advised, I slowed down ten miles after the end of the Babcock Preserve and saw a dirt road in the distance. Turning left onto it, my car kicked up dust until I reached a gate that looked like it belonged in Montana.

Barbed wire stretched from both sides of the gate in a triangular direction. Five minutes early, I stepped out of the car. The air was still, and it felt like a hundred degrees. Being so far from the water, I wondered how the people living in Babcock Ranch would tolerate the higher heat out here.

Unable to see anything interesting, I hopped into the car and cranked the air up. Staring out the windshield, I felt my eyes closing just as I saw a cloud of dust coming down the road.

I got out as Creed pulled a small school bus to the side. He opened the accordion doors. Standing on the bottom step, he said, "I'm really sorry to bring you all the way here, but Master Eden isn't permitting visitors today."

"Not even for a quick look?"

"I'm sorry, but he was firm."

"How about tomorrow or another day?"

"I'm not sure that will work."

"That's a shame, I have a lot of interest in your way of life."

Creed didn't respond. I'd been made. "Look, I'm just interested in knowing the well-being of one of your members, a Carla Coyle." I dug out a photo. "This is her."

Creed didn't budge.

"I'm not interested in what religion or lifestyle she leads; all I want to know is that she is okay."

"Everyone here is well and happier than in your world."

"So Carla is here?"

Creed went up the steps, closed the doors, and drove away.

Was the girl here? Why not acknowledge it? Either she was being held against her will, or they were insecure. Maybe whatever indoctrination members went through wasn't complete. I needed to understand what made people stay with these types of groups.

I had limited experience with gangs, but the last homicide case I worked on involved an El Salvadorian gang and was an eye-opener. More than one expert told me people were drawn to gangs the same way they were drawn to religious groups.

They told me most people were attracted by the sense of fellowship and community. Everyone wants to be a part of something, and these groups act as an extension of or replacement for family. It seemed weird to me.

There was tension between Carla and her stepfather, which could have been the catalyst, but her mother seemed caring. Besides my experience as a patient, I had zero credentials in the head-space game. There was a flicker of hope that if this kid was drinking the Kool-Aid, she might be easier to pull away before she got in too deep.

My phone rang. It was Mrs. Coyle. I'd dodged her call earlier, texting her that I'd reach out soon.

"Hello, Mrs. Coyle."

"Did you find Carla?"

"I think so."

"You think so? What the hell does that mean?"

"Take it easy, ma'am. Is Carla religious?"

"No. She was baptized, but we never went to church, except on the holidays."

"Did she have a lot of friends?"

"No, I told you already. She was pretty much a loner. But she was happy."

"She fought with her father?"

"My husband is her stepfather. Her biological father took off when she was two."

As a gold medalist in leaping to conclusions, I had to rein myself in. I needed firm proof she was a member of the new Koreshans before I told her mother. "I see. All I can say at this time is that I don't believe she is in any danger. It looks like she is living with a couple of girls in Punta Gorda."

"Punta Gorda? Who does she know up there?"

"I'm going to need you to trust me on this. It may take some time, but I'm close, very close to wrapping this up."

"You're going to bring her home?"

My phone vibrated, another call was coming in. "Only if

she wants to come back. If she doesn't, you'll at least know she's okay. From there, the rest is up to you."

"She has it easy here. I cook and clean, and she does nothing. That's why we wanted her to get a job . . ."

I pulled the phone away from my ear. Derrick was trying to reach me. "I got to go, ma'am. My partner is calling. Try and relax. I'll be in touch."

Derrick asked, "How'd you make out?"

"They wouldn't let me on the property."

"Why not?"

"He said Master Eden, the guy running this damn cult, didn't want visitors. I'm pretty sure they found out I was interested in the kid."

"Damn."

"Tell me about it. Between going back and forth, I wasted two hours. Anyway, what's up?"

"Maybe this will help. Apparently they got the money for the land from the foundation the original Koreshans set up."

"They had money?"

"Looks like it. They set up a trust called the College of Life Foundation. It's run by a Charles Dauray. I have his contact info."

"Great work. Hang on a sec, another call is coming in."

I looked at the screen. "Got to go, it's Ann Talbot."

"Hello, Mrs. Talbot."

She sniffled. "Hello, Frank."

"Is everything okay?"

"Tony, uh, Tony Desmond just called. He wanted to see me, but I said no. And he went ballistic."

13

———

"WHAT DO YOU MEAN BY BALLISTIC?"

"He was angry and starting cursing at me."

"Has he ever done that before?"

"No. Never."

She had previously told me she had no contact with him. "How often does he call you?"

"Not that much. I mean, he called a couple of times since John went missing."

"What were those conversations like?"

"It seemed like he wanted to, you know, start up again, since John was, as he said, 'out of the picture.'"

"And you think he may have something to do with your husband's disappearance?"

"I don't know what to think."

"It's time to talk to Desmond."

"Please, don't tell him I called you."

"No worries. I'll let you know when I have something."

I called back Derrick. "She's upset. Desmond called and freaked out on her."

"We got to speak to him."

"No doubt. Hey, If I'm not mistaken, the Verizon report covered both of the Talbots' cell phones."

"Yeah, it does."

"Do me a favor. Take a look at her call log. See if she's made any outgoings to Desmond."

"You think they're working together?"

"It's in the realm of possibilities."

I COULDN'T DO all this myself. Derrick was a huge help running things down and doing the necessary background work, but at this point I needed a foot soldier. He didn't want to get paid, and though I could use the money I was going to pay him to get an officer to moonlight, there was no way I could allow it.

Derrick was not only struggling with his physical injuries; his self-esteem had taken a beating. Losing most of his independence had perched him on the edge of depression. Asking anyone to work for free was beyond unfair and in Derrick's case immoral.

Flipping around options to cover both cases, I headed to see Desmond. The best solution was to solve one of them, but to do that I'd have to put all my effort into one. It made sense, but which one? I couldn't let the Coyle kid get sucked further in. Chances were John Talbot was dead, but with the possibility he might be held captive, I couldn't give up on him either.

One idea came to me as I waited at the traffic light entrance to Barrington Cove. The community was off Livingston Road, just south of Bonita Springs, and by the hordes of bike-riding kids, was a place for full-timers. Seeing a dozen American flags flying boosted my mood.

Tony Desmond lived in a beige, one-story home whose backyard faced the wall surrounding the gated community. By the looks of the landscaping, the place was new, maybe a year or two old.

When he pushed open the door, I got the sense Desmond was expecting me. I flashed my identification, and he didn't ask why I was there.

Desmond had a fresh haircut and was dressed in jeans and a button-down shirt. He was a good-looking guy, a touch of ruggedness to offset his meticulous grooming. He smelled like a smooth talker, but he wasn't making small talk.

The floor plan was completely open and dominated by a rug with a geometric pattern. It was so busy, I worried I'd get dizzy. We sat at a kitchen table. It smelled of Windex. Was Desmond a neat freak?

"I'm investigating the disappearance of John Talbot."

"What does that have to do with me?"

"You had a relationship with his wife, Ann."

"So? We had a little fling. That's all."

"When was your affair with her?"

"She told you about me, right? So why you asking me?"

"It's my job to ask the questions."

"Look, I don't have to talk to you. I'm only doing it to help Ann."

"You're better off talking to me than the guys I worked with at the sheriff's."

Desmond frowned. "I just said, I wanted to help her."

"You were upset when she broke it off with you."

"I moved on. There's no shortage of ladies down here looking for company."

That was true, but most of them were looking for men with money. "What do you do for a living?"

"I'm an architect."

It was the first architect I'd ever met. I wanted to ask how the homes down here had almost no bearing walls. When I Googled it, the answer that the roof supported everything made no sense to me.

"Big firm?"

"No, a builder, Imperial Homes of Naples, if you have to know."

"Did you have anything to do with the disappearance of John Talbot?"

He didn't miss a beat. "No. I didn't even know the man."

"Ann is an attractive woman."

He nodded.

"Isn't it true you wanted him out of the way so you could be with Ann?"

"People get divorced all the time."

"They sure do, but when they do, the money gets split up."

"I don't need her money."

"You have two battery convictions."

"So? It doesn't mean anything."

"It means you like to get physical, and you have an anger issue."

"Look, I learned a long time ago, somebody puts their hands on you, you have no choice but to respond."

"I spoke to Casper. He said all he did was ask you to pay him the money you owed him."

"That's bullshit. I didn't borrow anything. We were going into business together, and it didn't work out."

"What business was that?"

"A staging business, you know, to help sell houses when the owner moves out."

"What happened?"

"It didn't work out."

"You beat another man in Pelican Larry's. What's your side of that one?"

"I don't have to discuss this with you. I paid my fine and it's over. I don't look back."

"Perfect, let's talk about the present. You called Ann today. Why?"

"We're friends. Just checking in."

"She's one fine-looking lady. You want to get things restarted with her?"

"Not really."

"That's not what she said."

"Ann is lying if she said that."

"It looks like you're the only one telling the truth."

He shrugged.

"You lost it on the phone with her. She said you were yelling at her, pissed off she wouldn't see you."

"Not true. I asked her if she wanted to grab a drink at Hob Nob. She said no, and that was that."

"Where were you the evening of March second?"

"The second—th? I don't know. What day of the week was that?"

"A Thursday."

"Probably at Food for Thought, they have a nice little jazz trio playing that night."

"You go regularly?"

"Couple of times a month."

My phone vibrated and I snuck a peek. It was Derrick. I finished up with Desmond, hopped in my car, and called Derrick.

"What's going on?"

"I checked Ann Talbot's call log. She called Desmond five times."

"Five?"

"Yep, and that's not the troubling part."

14

"WHAT ARE YOU TALKING ABOUT?"

"Ann called Desmond March first and second."

"The day her husband left, and the day he disappeared."

"Yep. Maybe they cooked up a scheme together to get rid of the husband."

"What we know for sure is both of them are liars. What are they trying to hide?"

"It has to be the hubby."

"You got time to take a dive into Desmond?"

"What do you think, I'm training for a marathon or something?"

"You'll get there. You missing the running?"

"Oh yeah. But what do you want me to check?"

"This entire thing could be driven by money. See what you can find out about his finances. Nose around his job. Desmond works at Imperial Homes of Naples. We might learn something."

"I'm on it."

"Thanks. I'm going to talk to Ann Talbot. Let's see how she handles the calls."

"That should be good."

ANN WAS SITTING at an outdoor table in front of Delicious Raw. She smiled and stood as I approached. With the exercise pants she had on, the world would know if she had a mosquito bite on her thigh.

"Would you like something? They make fabulous juices here."

"I'm good, thanks."

She stuck the straw in her mouth, taking a draw of a beet-red liquid.

"Why do you go to LA Fitness up here?"

She put her drink down. "It's the newest one around; everything is clean. It's really not that far."

"I went to see Tony Desmond."

"What did he say?"

"He claims not to have gotten angry and was just touching base with you."

"That's not true."

"I'm confused. You were upset that he called you, right?"

"Yes, I was scared. He seemed out of control."

"And you thought he could have something to do with your husband's disappearance?"

"I don't know what to think anymore."

"What I don't get is you said you'd broken it off a few months ago. Is that correct?"

She hesitated. "I think so."

I flipped through my notepad. "That's what you told me."

"Who remembers? It's not like I put the dates on my calendar."

"But it's been several weeks."

"Yes."

"Why did you call Tony Desmond five times?"

"I-I was calling him back."

It was time to stretch the truth. "You do realize I can get Mr. Desmond's phone records and compare dates and times."

"I didn't call him back right away."

"Maybe not, but a pattern would emerge."

She averted her eyes, stirring the drink with her straw.

"What I find even more curious are the calls you made to Desmond on March first and second. I realize you're the client, but I deserve to know why."

She pouted. "I was a teeny bit lonely. John was out of town, and I needed company."

"I'm sorry, but I don't buy it. Your husband is gone one night, and you were looking for male company?"

"I know it sounds terrible, but we weren't going to do anything, just maybe get a drink or something."

"You know what I think? I think you never broke it up with Desmond. Now, I don't know why you wouldn't have told me."

"Because I knew people would think I had something to do with John going missing."

She had a point. "If you were looking to conceal the relationship, why did you tell me Desmond lost his temper?"

"I told you, I was scared. It made me think, maybe he did have something to do with it."

I told her I understood, but it was far from true. It seemed like Ann Talbot was playing it borderline. She had been a software engineer. I didn't know what that involved, but I was certain logic and organization were required traits.

Was this woman using her sex appeal and vulnerability to manipulate Desmond? Or was she working me? At this point, both of them were climbing the suspect ladder.

TONGS IN HAND, I opened the top of the grill. "The shrimp from Costco seem smaller than the last ones."

"It's the same bag."

"They're definitely littler."

"It's a beautiful night." Mary Ann got up. "Jessica is home."

"Good timing." I reached for a dish to plate the shrimp.

The slider opened. Jessie, in a tan uniform, and Mary Ann carried bowls of vegetables onto the lanai.

"Hey, Jess. How was your day?"

"Amazing. I really like the Girl Scouts."

"I was never into the Boy Scout thing."

Mary Ann held up three fingers and Jessie did the same. "I was a Girl Scout."

"You were? You never said anything."

"It was only for a year. But I had fun."

"How old were you, Mom?"

"Two years older than you."

"So, tell me, Jess, what do you like about it?"

"Our leader, Miss Rose, is real nice and teaches us a lot."

"What kind of things?"

"Like a sense of community. To remember we're spiritual beings and part of a greater universe."

"Spiritual beings?"

Mary Ann glared at me. "Jessica, tell Dad about the charitable work your troop is doing."

"We're not sure yet which one we're doing. Miss Rose gave us ten ideas and said all of them will make the world a better place to live."

"Tell Miss Rose if she wants to improve the planet, she should help the police."

"We're not allowed to do projects with law enforcement."

"That's ridiculous. Who the hell do they call when the shit hits the fan? The cops, that's who."

"Take it easy, Frank."

"Yeah, Dad. I don't know why you're being this way."

"Just forget it. Okay? I'm sorry, I have a lot on my mind."

After dinner, Jessie went to do her homework and we stayed outside.

"What was that all about?"

"I don't like all these groups; they act just like cults."

"The Girls Scouts are a cult now?"

"Damn right they are. Telling kids not to work with the police? It's mind control."

"The Girl Scouts don't do mind control. They instill good qualities in young women. What's got into you?"

"Nothing. I just want Jessie to make up her own mind about things. I don't want her indoctrinated."

"Indoctrinated? Come on, Frank, you're being a little dramatic, aren't you?"

"You know kids are impressionable. I don't want anybody controlling her."

"Unless it's you."

"That's ridiculous. I want her to be independent. And most of all, happy."

"She is and will be."

15

Turning off Pine Ridge Road, I meandered my way to a mixed community known as Pine Ridge Estates. Most of the lot sizes were huge by Florida standards, and the area was changing, like many of Naples' older neighborhoods were.

Passing three properties in various stages of construction, I pulled onto a gravel road leading to a faded yellow home. A black Labrador, laying in the shade, barely lifted its head.

Before I got to the entrance, Ernest Ray swung open the screen door. After the introductions, he said, "Why don't we sit out back?"

"Sure." I was always suspicious and disappointed when someone kept me out of their home. It was a missed opportunity to pick up information on the person.

The overgrown brush at the rear of the property obscured a view of the lake. We sat around a stone table I'd seen at Walmart.

"You been here long?"

"My daddy bought it back in 1960."

I was willing to bet the place had the original kitchen. "Great location."

"Yep, it's still quiet back here."

"It is. As I mentioned, I'm working for a family looking to locate their daughter. It appears she may be living on the new Koreshan settlement up by Babcock Ranch."

"They think she's following Eden?"

"That's what it seems. I tried to visit, but they wouldn't let me on the property."

"And you think I can get you on?"

"The family would appreciate it."

"I'm sorry to disappoint you folks, but I've never set foot on it, and they wouldn't let me either."

"But you're the president, the chairman of the College of Life Foundation."

"I am, but you see, I'm what they call a nonbeliever. Unless you're working for them in some capacity on the property, nonbelievers are not allowed on the compound."

"But didn't you give them the money to buy the land?"

"The foundation provided some of the funds, but Old Man Teed restricted disbursements in order to continue the mission to educate people about the Koreshans."

The last public filing, a year ago, showed the foundation had a million dollars in assets and generated income from investments. That was enough dough to keep the mission alive for decades.

"Why do you do what you do for them?"

"Income. I get paid a decent stipend, and I really don't do much for it."

"Carla Coyle, she's the missing girl, is an adult. All the family wants to know is if she's all right. They're not trying to make her quit the group at all. Given your position, would you be willing to call Eden and confirm she's there and okay?"

"I'd like to help you, but last year the mother of another

girl tracked me down like you did. She asked me to get involved, and I tried, but it went nowhere. I'm sorry, you'll have to find another way onto the property."

"Do the members leave the compound?"

"Generally not. They limit their interaction with the outside world."

"You know any way to sneak me on?"

"You might want to check with one of their suppliers. They're doing a lot of construction. Maybe a contractor could get you on."

The idea was one I had thought of myself. The problem was the undercover nature of it and the time required. My identity was known by at least a few of them. A secretive organization might distribute pictures to its members. And then it might take days to snoop around. I couldn't just walk in, search, and leave.

AFTER DINNER, I plopped onto my recliner. "Let's watch a movie."

"I'll be right there."

After navigating to Comcast's free movie section, I started scrolling. Mary Ann was cleaning up. "Find anything worthwhile?"

"Not yet."

"Don't forget, day after tomorrow, you have an appointment with the oncologist."

I didn't need a reminder. "I know. Hey, what about *Witness*? It's been ages since we saw it."

"Sounds good."

As soon as the movie began playing, a horse and buggy

came on the screen. I said, "I can't believe people still live like this."

"There's a couple of Amish communities. Most are in Ohio, Pennsylvania, and Indiana."

"Living without electricity? And no cars or trucks? It's insane."

"It's their way of life."

"I feel bad for the kids. They're trapped."

"I wouldn't call it trapped. They can leave if they want to when they get older. I think eighteen or so."

"After that many years, they're brainwashed."

"I read an interesting article about a year ago. It said that the kids in Amish communities are at least as happy as other kids in America."

"I find that hard to believe."

"It's true. Overall, the Amish are happier than your average American."

"Well, somebody should study how happy the people who leave these cults are."

"The Amish are not a cult. They're religious people with a strong sense of community. Just because you don't agree with their lifestyle doesn't make them some weird sect."

"What about the Koreshans?"

"They had their beliefs as well."

"Yeah? And what about if Jessie got mixed up with some group like them?"

"I probably wouldn't like it, but if she was happy, I'd be okay with it."

"That's crazy. I'd never let her live on some commune like a hippie."

"Just because she wouldn't end up living the life you wanted doesn't matter. If she's happy, I'm happy, and you should be too."

Mary Ann stormed out, leaving me with a sink full of dirty plates and a mind reeling.

COMING BACK FROM THE BATHROOM, I checked the time: 1:28 a.m. I slid into bed. It never failed; since my bout with bladder cancer, every doctor's appointment was a marker that could change my life.

I kept most of my fears to myself. It was tough to buy Mary Ann's line that because I was being monitored if the cancer came back they'd catch it early. She'd said that was a benefit other people didn't have. I said most people didn't have a bladder fashioned out of their stomach. She batted that away as pessimism.

It's not that she didn't care; she did. And I'd agree with her if we were talking about somebody else. But we weren't.

I turned on my side, forcing my mind onto the Carla Coyle case. Visualizing a map of the property, I wondered about an access point from an adjoining property when an idea hit me.

I swung my feet off the bed. This could work.

16

Sunlight filled the den. As I tried to get the wireless printer to work, my phone rang.

"Hey, Derrick, how you doing?"

"Good. I got something interesting on Desmond."

"Feed me."

"Take a guess."

Playing games in the morning was never fun. "Just tell me."

"Well, number one, he's not working for Imperial Homes anymore. They cut him loose two weeks ago."

"The lying bastard."

"And he's got a big-assed mortgage on his house to go along with a lien filed by Abbey Flooring for thirty thousand."

"The guy's got money problems."

"He might be using Ann Talbot to dig out."

"I'll bet there's a big, fat insurance policy on Talbot."

"We could call the state insurance commission."

"We'd need her to make the request."

"We can look through his checkbook and bank statements. It's not foolproof if the money came out of a trust or something."

"I'm going to ask to see their financial records. She can't say no. Maybe we can grab the last two years or so."

"That would cover it. This woman is smart; she wouldn't set off a flag by insuring her husband too close to knocking him off."

"If she did it."

"Just speculating. When you get them, shoot them over, and I'll comb through them."

"Thanks. Look, you know anybody that owns an insurance appraiser that does homes?"

"Funny you should ask. One of my neighbors has an outfit right off Wiggins Pass. Petey came over for a brew last night."

"Still drinking beer? What do I got to do? Drag you to a vineyard?"

"I like it all. What's going on?"

"Remember the Everglade City surveillance?" As soon as it came out of my mouth, I regretted it. After being shot on the case, Derrick landed in the hospital.

"Uh, refresh me."

"We used drones to keep an eye on things. If we could get one up over the Koreshan property, we might spot the missing kid."

"I like the idea. Let me ask Petey if he has one."

"They use them all the time to do roofs and things. Just make sure the camera is good enough from a couple of hundred feet high."

Ann Talbot's lips seemed more than capable of talking men into things. Needing to play it cautiously, I called her instead of going in person. She consented to turn over the last two years' worth of financial records.

The speed with which she agreed had me considering if she was going to cherry-pick accounts. Though I wanted to drive straight over, the day was melting away. I needed to talk to Desmond now because of my doctor's appointment in the morning.

I swung into Barrington Cove, parking in front of Desmond's home. The other neighbor's flag was still flapping in the breeze, but Ann's boyfriend had taken his down.

Desmond was perfectly groomed again. He was a neat freak. I considered asking to see how his garage looked, but time was precious. I asked, "What happened with your flag?"

"It was fraying."

Trying to throw him off, I hit him with, "You lied to me."

"What?"

"Your job. You claimed to be working, but you were let go two weeks ago."

"It's embarrassing. Besides, technically I'm still working because they gave me a month of severance pay."

Now I knew why he and Ann had hit it off; they both had answers for everything.

"It's still a lie. Tell me about the lien on your house."

"What are you talking about? There's no lien on this place."

"Abbey Flooring filed one for thirty thousand—"

"That's bullshit. I paid those bastards before I even moved in."

He could be telling the truth. Some contractors filed liens when they started a job, forgetting to remove them after payment.

"You better dig out the proof."

"I'll get the file. I keep track of everything I put into the house for tax purposes."

I followed him into the den. He pulled out a thick file with D.R. Horton - America's Builder, on it. Desmond fished through it. "Here it is. See? They stamped it paid."

"You should call them."

"Damn right I will."

"You having financial issues?"

"No more than the next guy. I lost my job, but there is plenty of work for architects in Naples."

With all the building and renovating, I was sure he was right. Unless he had a bad reputation.

"You have a large mortgage on this house."

His nostrils flared. "That's none of your goddamn business!"

"Did you and Ann get rid of her husband for insurance money?"

"Get out! That's it. I tried to be helpful, but I'm done with this bullshit."

The outbreak seemed genuine, but I had to keep in mind that Desmond was smooth. It could be an act to cover his tracks.

As a private investigator, I felt I had an edge by not revealing the two decades I spent as a detective. What I didn't know was if Ann had told him about my background. If they were working together, I was certain she'd have said something.

Intelligent people, like Ann and Desmond, usually believed they could outsmart private investigators. It was a mistake in this case.

While I no longer had the resources of a police department to draw upon, I was confident my training, experience, and instincts made up for it.

MARY ANN and I were watching some mindless reality show. I said, "Who watches this crap?"

"I don't know. Most of these shows are terrible. I'm tired anyway, let's go to bed."

"Go ahead. I'm going to do a little work."

"Now? It's eleven."

"I know. Just a little restless, that's all."

"You're worried about the doctor's appointment?"

"No, not at all."

"You sure?"

"Yeah, I'm sure. Go to sleep. I'll be in soon."

I went to my den, mystified how she always knew what was on my mind. Going to the doctors made me uneasy. It was impossible to quiet the whisper in my head that kept saying it wasn't *if* but *when* the cancer was coming back.

This time, my inner voice was shouting that the intermittent pain in my gut meant it had returned. I told myself to take it easy and pulled up the attachment containing Talbot's bank records.

I went through fifteen pages of single-spaced expenditures before my eyes started blurring. Two payments interested me, one to Prudential Insurance Company and the other to State Farm. I printed the pages they appeared on and headed to bed.

17

Most of the guys in the waiting room were twice my age. Going to the urologist as often as I did made me realize how many men had problems with their Johnsons.

I thumbed through *Gulfshore Life*. The magazine always had cool-looking homes and interesting design ideas. The coastal contemporary look was spreading fast, and I liked the fresh style.

Our place was more Tuscany than Miami, and I began reading about inexpensive ways to transition to a more modern look when my name was called.

Dr. Torino shook my hand. "How are you, Frank?"

"Pretty good, but I've been having pain every now and then, right here." I pointed to my abdomen.

"When did this begin?"

"Uh, about two weeks ago."

"Describe the pain."

"Kind of sharp."

"Pinching?"

"It's hard to describe."

"Let's take a look."

He pointed to the exam table. I'd done it a hundred times, but I was still uncomfortable unbuttoning my pants and lowering them.

Torino began kneading my gut like he was making a pizza.

"Ouch."

"I'm going to do it again."

I gritted my teeth. "That's it."

"Roll on your side."

Torino probed. "Feels okay?"

"Yeah, nothing."

As he checked the other side, I said, "Is it the plumbing?"

"It's tough to say, it's just above the surgical site."

I swallowed. "Is the cancer back?"

"Don't let your mind run away here. There could be several causes of the pain, so just relax."

Relax? I loved the way doctors told patients not to worry. Did they realize how silly that was?

"What's next?"

"We're going to need to do an ultrasound." Torino picked up the phone and made an internal call. He hung up.

"The first opening is day after tomorrow, nine a.m. Does that work for you?"

"Can't we do it now?"

"They said they're completely booked."

"Jesus, I can't sleep as it is."

He put his hand on my shoulder. "Hang on a minute. Let me see what I can do."

I waited for Torino, regretting not telling Mary Ann about the pain. Stress was bad for her MS, and the last thing she needed was to experience another flare-up.

Torino came in, trailed by a nurse rolling in an ultrasound machine.

"Thanks, Doc."

"Glad I was able to squeeze you in."

He may have been happy, but the nurse was as cold as ice. I didn't give a crap that she was inconvenienced.

She smeared my stomach with gel, and I held my breath as she picked up the device.

18

———

As soon as I left the doctor's office, I called Mary Ann.

"How did it go, Frank?"

"Pretty good, but I got gallstones."

"Gallstones? How did he see that?"

"Did an ultrasound."

"Why he'd do one?"

"Just precautionary. Does one every now and then to check the bladder they made."

"What are they going to do?"

"Nothing. They're not big, so hopefully they won't bother me. Torino said to stick to a low-fat diet."

"I've been telling you that. What did he say about drinking? I heard it's not good for that."

"Torino said wine was fine. He even said alcohol could help but not to overdo it."

"I'll go on the internet and research gallstones; maybe there's a supplement that will help dissolve them."

Dr. Google to the rescue. There was no doubt everyone was better informed on an overall basis about illnesses.

However, there was no shortage of rabbit holes to go down and an abundance of hucksters hawking cures. Though doctors told us to stay off the internet, it was impossible advice to follow, and many times it prompted questions that improved outcomes.

"Thanks. I'll see you in a bit. I'm going to swing by and pick up Derrick."

"I'm going to the mall and then Publix."

As I wheeled Derrick into the den, he said, "My own desk?"

It was a plastic thing I picked up at Walmart. "It's temporary."

"It's perfect."

"If this all works out, I'll rent a real office, and you'll get a desk and your own office."

"Don't do anything on my account."

I wondered if Derrick knew how guilty I felt about him getting shot. It was something I believed I could have prevented. Seeing him in a wheelchair only ramped up my feelings of culpability, and I was overcompensating.

"It's not just for you, brother. I could use a little space away from home."

"I thought you wanted to keep an eye on Mary Ann?"

He was right. With her MS, I wanted to be around to help her out and remove any stress I could. "She's doing fine. Let's get to work. Anything stick out on Talbot's banking records?"

"Yeah, a couple." He pulled out a document. "At the top of the list is a five-thousand-dollar payment to TransAmerica Life Insurance in November."

"Just five months before he vanished."

"I checked the previous year but couldn't locate a payment. It looks like it might be a new policy."

"If so, it could be big. Good catch. Anything else?"

"There were two wires to a Jeremy Costello, five thousand each, in January and February. It made me think there might be some kind of blackmail going on."

"Interesting. Why not root around, see if we can identify Costello before we confront her?"

"I already did. Couldn't find anything that made sense in Collier or Lee. Facebook was no help either."

"We have three different payments to insurance companies and the wires to Costello."

"Man, I'd like to see what she has to say about them."

"You know what? Let's go see her now."

"Me too?"

"Why not?"

"I don't know. It's weird being in a wheelchair. Nobody does that type of thing."

"We ain't nobody, brother. Let's get going."

For Derrick's sake, I was hoping Ann was dressed in something flattering. When the door opened, she didn't disappoint. A flash of concern melted into a bright smile, matching an electrifying low-cut red dress.

"Why, who do we have here?"

"Derek Dickson, ma'am."

She bent down, giving him a cleavage view. "Nice to meet you."

"Derek is working on the case with me, and we had a couple of questions."

"Come on in. Oh, let me get the vacuum out of the way."

This woman cleaned house dressed like that? Tipping the wheelchair back to clear the step into the house, Derrick turned his head, whispering, "Wow. I bet food doesn't even stick to her teeth."

"Amen."

"Come in the kitchen. I dropped a pod, and the coffee grains went everywhere. Would you boys like an iced coffee?"

We declined.

"Do you have news about John?"

"No, ma'am, but we're following a couple of leads and need your help."

"Sure. Whatever you need."

"Who is Jeremy Costello?"

"I don't know. Why?"

"Two checks, each for five thousand dollars, were written to him."

"By John?"

"I imagine so."

"I have no idea who or why he would do that."

"You're sure about that?"

"Absolutely. That's a lot of money, and John should have told me."

"Okay. We'll look into it further."

"Is that it?"

Derrick said, "No, ma'am. There were also two payments to TransAmerica Life Insurance. What were they for?"

"Oh, John wanted more life insurance, so we got it."

"So this is a new policy?"

"Yes. I'd have to check, but it was about two years ago."

"What's the face value of the policy?"

"I think it was three million dollars."

And three million reasons to kill her husband. I said, "Did you have an accidental death rider?"

"I'm pretty sure."

Make that six million incentives.

"Like I said, John wanted it. I didn't see the point. After all, we don't have children."

"What was his rationale, then?"

"For charities."

"What other life insurance do you have?"

"Wait a minute. You think I had John, uh, killed, for money?"

"We have to look at everything."

"But I hired you. The cops did nothing. Can't you see it doesn't make sense?"

Homicides rarely made sense to anyone besides the killers. "It's part of the overall investigation. There could be a policy or beneficiary you're unaware of."

"That seems unlikely."

"Do you have any other policies?"

"No."

I dug out the sheets I'd printed. "What are the payments to Prudential Life Insurance and State Farm?"

"State Farm covers our cars and homeowner's insurance. But I don't know about Prudential."

"You don't have any idea?"

"No. I don't."

"We must look into it. I'm going to need you to request a copy of the check. Do you bank online?"

"Yes."

"We should be able to get a copy immediately. Can you log in?"

"Now?"

"Yes, ma'am."

I could see the wheels in her head turning as Ann logged on and navigated to the checks. She printed copies of them. They both had the same number in the note section. Prudential would be able to tell us what it was for.

"I guess I'll hear from you?"

"Yes, ma'am. But we're going to need a copy of the TransAmerica Life Insurance Policy as well."

"It's in the bank safe-deposit box."

"How quickly can you get it?"

"Is this some kind of emergency?"

"No, but the sooner the better."

She looked at her watch. "The bank is still open. If you want to follow me, we can go now."

"Perfect. Let's go."

19

We were sitting outside Florida Integrity Bank in Derek's van. He said, "What do you think? She did it?"

"I don't know. Things weren't adding up before. She's too together, too upbeat. The lady's not putting on an act over how distraught she is about her husband. Every other time, spouses are falling over themselves trying to prove their love."

"You're right, but maybe she can't help herself. You know the joke where a husband keeps calling the doctor who told him his wife had died? After the third time, the doctor asks him why he continues to call, and the guy said he liked hearing she died."

I laughed. "That could be it. She was screwing around on him, and he had money."

"Here she comes."

I got out as Ann approached. A man walking into the bank turned his head, watching her sway toward me.

She held out a thick file marked TransAmerica. "I looked it over. There's nothing out of the ordinary that I can see."

"We'll need to go over it. You want to make a copy?"

"I believe I'm okay. I took a picture of the declaration pages."

"Excellent. Have a good afternoon."

"You too."

I climbed back in the van, and Derrick said, "Man, this lady is really put together. And she's what? Like fifty?"

"Late forties, like me, and by the way, being fifty doesn't make you old."

Derrick pulled onto Tamiami Trail. "Oh, I know, just saying."

As he drove, I slipped the life insurance policy out of its sleeve. "It's three million, like she said."

"It has that rider that doubles it?"

I paged through. "Yep."

"That's a lot of motive."

"Uh-oh."

"What?"

"It's a second-to-die policy. The insurance only pays out after both of them are dead."

"There goes that smoking gun."

"We still have the Prudential and Jeremy Costello payments to follow up." I pulled out the sheets we printed. "I don't know much about insurance, but ten thousand dollars has to buy a lot of it. What bothers me is the round number. That seems unusual."

"But the number on the check was long, like the ones they use for policies."

"Could be." I stared at the entry below Prudential. It was for fifty dollars and was paid to Spice Publications. "When you went through the disbursements, did you see any made out to Spice Publications?"

"Yeah, I think there were about ten of them. Figured it was some kind of subscription. Why?"

"Not sure."

It could have simply been a cooking magazine, but I tied the swinger publication I'd found in Talbot's closet to it. I plugged it into my phone's search bar.

The first line was a student publication; the second was interesting, as it led to a Facebook page for models. I navigated around the site. It was filled with young kids posing. I hit the back browser, and my eyes drifted down, stopping on Spice Publications for Adults. I clicked.

The website touted two BDSM magazines: *Bondage Erotica* along with *Dominance and Submission*. I shuddered at an image of a woman hog-tied while being suspended. Another had a masked man in a leather getup holding a whip.

I closed the browser wondering who was interested in this sexual subculture? Was it him? Her? Or both of them?

I replayed my visit to Talbot's home. My search was limited to John's things, but nothing I'd seen spoke of this type of behavior.

"I could be way off, but there may be some kind of sexual angle to this thing."

"What makes you believe that?"

"I found a magazine for swingers in John Talbot's closet, and it looks like someone might be into or exploring BDSM."

"Bondage stuff?"

"I don't know, but that's what Spice Publications seems to be."

"They could just be into kinky stuff with each other. Reading magazines doesn't really mean anything."

"You're probably right, but she's had numerous affairs."

"I know, but infidelity is rampant these days."

"Unfortunately, you're right. The images on the Spice site creeped me out. You should have seen them. I can't believe people are into that crap."

"Oh yeah. You see that show *Billions*?"

"I bailed out when I saw Giamatti doing that dominance stuff. Too weird for me."

"It was wacky, but they backed off with that crap. It's a pretty good show."

I'D ASKED to speak with the missing girl's stepfather at least five times. The mother claimed he was too depressed about the situation to talk to me. Originally, I'd let it slip because I was sure it would be hell being in his position.

But now I was uncomfortable with the attempt to dodge questioning. If it were my kid, I'd also be distraught, but I would do anything to find my daughter.

This was my second pass at a surprise visit. Yesterday I'd swung by after dinner, figuring both Coyles would be home at that time. There were no cars in the driveway, and no one answered the door.

As I approached the house, a young man who looked familiar came out of the garage. He looked both ways, put his head down, and walked to his car two doors down. I parked, trying to recall who it was.

Walking to the door, it hit me. It was Teddy, Carla Coyle's boyfriend. He must have been checking if there was any news on the missing girl.

I rang the doorbell, and Mrs. Coyle opened the door applying lipstick. She was in a nightgown and not happy to see me.

"Oh, I thought you were, uh. So how are you?"

"I was looking to speak to your husband."

"He's not here."

"I just saw Teddy leave. He checking on Carla?"

"Uh, yeah. He's very concerned about her. He's really a good person."

"Seems like a nice kid."

"He is. What happened with the Koreshans? Did you go back?"

"I'm actually going there tomorrow. We're deploying a surveillance tool that may be informative."

"Oh God, please. I hope it works."

"We'll see. Anyway, I'd appreciate it if you told your husband I want to talk to him. He can't keep avoiding me. It's starting to make me wonder."

20

THE FIRST TIME GOING TO THE KORESHAN PLACE BY Babcock Ranch, I noticed two dirt roads. According to the aerial view on Google maps, one led to an abandoned structure and the other to a track for dirt bikes and ATVs.

I chose the one leading to the dilapidated house. Even though it was a quarter mile farther from the Koreshan compound, the likelihood of running into someone at a place with no roof in Florida was low. Between the sun and rain, walls were less important than something over your head.

The area was deserted. Derrick's friend had come through with a drone. The downside was it didn't have the range or flying height of the kind the sheriff's department used. On the plus side, since it was used to assess damage to a home, its camera took higher resolution video.

I set up the drone, syncing it to an app on my laptop. The software to control it was similar to what I was used to. Hitting lift, the drone shuddered and rose. It seemed quieter than the ones I'd flown before.

For the initial flight, I was going to fly high, near the four-hundred-foot ceiling the FAA set. No one on the ground would know it was up there. If they saw anything, they'd assume it was a bird.

That height would enable me to get the layout of the compound. Once the vertical climb reached the regulatory maximum, I piloted the drone east. The view was nothing more than a big-picture orientation. I lowered the drone to three hundred feet.

I wasn't sure where the exact boundary was, but seeing a large clearing with several structures meant it was the target property. I could just about see people walking. A dozen cars and the bus I'd seen earlier were parked to one side, near the largest building.

A handful of people were working on two construction sites, and there was a penned-in area with livestock. I circled past the compound and hovered out of sight. Lowering the height to two hundred, I made another pass.

Even though it flew a hundred feet lower, unless the clothing was revealing, determining if it was a male or female was impossible. I slowly brought the drone down to just over a hundred feet.

Though chances were no one would notice it, a snake circled in my gut. It was going to be challenging to identify Carla. I'd need to have a good sense someone was her, then swoop down to around fifty feet to verify it.

If I was wrong, they'd be on guard, and I'd be screwed. Plus, there was a chance they'd shoot it out of the sky. I made a couple of passes and brought it down to around eighty feet to check how distinctive it was. It was good but not great. I quickly climbed higher when I saw three men coming out of a building. I circled to the northern end of the property where there appeared to be a wall.

After determining it was nothing more than stacked

building supplies, I brought the drone back. Loading the device into the back of my Explorer, I got a strange feeling.

Turning around, there was a dust storm being kicked up by three pickup trucks. They were speeding in my direction. Keeping a hand on my holster, I stepped to the side as they skidded to a halt.

A clean-cut thirty-year-old hopped out of his car holding a rifle.

It was illegal to brandish a firearm. "Hold on, now, there isn't any need for a weapon."

"Don't you worry about me. What are you doing out here?"

"Just having some fun, flying my drone around."

"This is private property. You shouldn't be here"

"Really? I thought this was owned by the county."

"It's not. And don't you be flying that thing over our compound either."

"You part of the Koreshan community?"

He put the rifle in the crook of his arm. "You should get on your way."

"Just asking, as I did the ghost walk a week or so ago. Real interesting people."

"Go on now."

I wanted to ask about Carla, but it would end any chance of them buying me as a drone hobbyist. Using aerial surveillance was a long shot but was worth another try. If it were going to work, I would need a slew of pictures of the missing kid and some video to pick up something identifying in her gait.

"Sorry to disturb you. Have a good day, fellas."

I kept my eyes on the rearview mirror as I drove off. Through the dust, I could see the pickup trucks following behind. Half of me wanted to call this into the sheriff. You weren't allowed to openly carry a firearm in Florida. He may have had a permit for the rifle, but as soon as he took it off his property he was breaking the law.

Giving up on trying to figure a way to go along with the sheriff to locate Carla, I called the missing kid's mother. She didn't pick up. I left a message.

Getting onto 75 South, an idea hit me. Kids were always taking selfies and videos of every little thing they did. I was betting that Teddy probably had more recent footage of Carla than her mother did. I checked my watch. By the time I got back to Naples, Teddy would be home from work.

Driving along Radio Road, I pulled into the Endless Summer RV Park. I was halfway down the lane Teddy's trailer was on when a car passed me. I slammed on the brakes and looked behind me as the vehicle exited the park.

It was her. What the hell was going on?

—————

21

WHAT WAS MRS. COYLE DOING AT TEDDY'S? WERE THE TWO of them—no, there couldn't be some kind of cougar-Mrs. Robinson thing going on. I replayed seeing Teddy leave the Coyle house the other day. He was guarded, but I'd attributed it to the rocky relationship he had with Mr. Coyle.

As I thought it over, my feeling was based on what Mrs. Coyle had said about it. I should have asked Teddy directly. And I would.

As soon as he answered the door, I had my answer. Teddy had a six-pack that had me sucking in my gut. Barefoot, with the top button of his jeans open, he smiled sheepishly.

"Just saw Mrs. Coyle leaving. Did what I think happened, really happen?"

Teddy shrugged.

"How long have the two of you been, uh, seeing each other?"

"About two months."

I felt my head shaking.

"I didn't want to, you know, with Carla and all, but the lady, she kept coming on to me."

"Let me guess, Carla found out and took off."

"Yeah. I felt real bad and all."

"She tell her stepfather about it?"

"I don't know, but I don't think so."

"I get the allure, my friend, but if you don't know by now, what you're doing is wrong. She's married, and Carla took off, possibly putting herself in danger."

"I know, like I said, I feel bad about everything."

"But you're still screwing around with her."

"She won't leave me alone. I tried to end it after Carla ran away, and—"

"You went to her house the other day. If you want to end it, stop going, stop seeing her, tell her it's over."

"I will, man, I will."

"Do you have any recent video of Carla?"

"Yeah, we shot a lot of stuff when we did things."

"I'm looking for some that show her walking and standing."

He took his phone out. "I definitely got some like that."

As Teddy scrolled through his gallery, I tried to process what I'd discovered by chance. Though my instincts had been dulled by chemo, they were still good. Was it my traditional background that blinded me to the possibility?

It was hard to believe. Teddy was a twenty-year-old, and Mrs. Coyle was in her forties. She was squarely in the average group in looks and body, but I knew it didn't dampen the excitement factor for him. By itself, it was a disturbing dalliance by a married woman.

Maybe she no longer cared about her husband, but her unconventional excursion drove her daughter to run. I was hoping her inability to contain her sexual urges hadn't endangered Carla.

Teddy sent me a series of texts with videos of Carla, and I

drove home, wondering how widespread relationships like this were. Though I couldn't imagine anyone I knew stepping out with a twenty-year-old, I knew I was wrong.

It was another example of unintended consequences that people never considered as they pursued selfish interests. Bemoaning the fact society had redrawn the lines of acceptable behaviors and forgotten to clue me in, I stepped off the soapbox.

I'd cheated repeatedly on my first wife. Breaking the same bond that Mrs. Coyle had led to a divorce. Though I'd kept my romantic escapades to women my age, it was still wrong.

While it was happening, it was easy to rationalize. Though we met when I was studying criminology at John Jay in NYC, my ex constantly fought me over the job.

Looking back, it was clear that I used the badgering to block any feelings of guilt. I felt bad about it for a couple of years. Being a homicide detective, I'd seen my share of good people getting killed by sociopaths.

Those upsetting experiences killed any chance of me believing in the karma thing. But when I got cancer, a part of me felt like the universe was evening things up. I never considered myself a bad person. Hell, I spent my career putting my life on the line for others, but I made a conscious effort to be better than I was.

A couple of minutes from home, I pulled into a shopping center at the intersection of Pine Ridge Road and Airport-Pulling Road. I went into a small shop run by a guy from Brooklyn.

"Wow, who are those for?"

I handed Jessie a bunch of purple tulips. "For you."

"They're so pretty. Thanks, Dad."

As she pecked my cheek, I asked, "Where's Mom?"

"In the bathroom."

I set the roses on the counter and took a bottle of pinot noir out of the closet. Popping the cork, Mary Ann came into the kitchen.

"Roses? What for?"

"Just because. I don't need a reason, do I?"

"What's going on, Frank?"

"Nothing. You like them?"

"They're beautiful. I'm just surprised." She kissed me.

"You want some vino?"

"Sure, but not until we eat."

My cell rang. "Hey, Derrick, what's going on?"

"Wanted to update you on the Prudential Insurance checks. You got time?"

I headed to the den. "Sure. Was it life insurance?"

"No. He has an investment account with Prudential."

"Damn."

"I know, but there may be something strange with it."

"How so?"

"The account holder was John Talbot. His wife isn't on it, and the address he used was his office address."

"Hm. Any recent withdrawals?"

"None."

"What's the value of it?"

"Just over a million."

"That's a lot of money to hide from your wife."

"No doubt. Maybe he was planning to run or split up with her."

"Running is possible but not a divorce. A lawyer would find that money in a heartbeat."

"True."

"There has to be a reason he kept it secret."

"A lot of couples keep their money separate."

"He might have designated someone other than Ann as the beneficiary of the account if he died."

"Could it be Jeremy Costello, the guy he paid five grand to?"

"Exactly what I was thinking. Tracking him down is priority number one. We're going to need Ann's help in getting the bank to provide details on who and where the checks were cashed."

22

My mind was occupied with trying to find a way to talk to Carla Coyle. I'd set up a camera, observing remotely from my laptop, across from the entrance to the compound. It wasn't exactly legal, but all I wanted to know was if she left the compound.

Getting the opportunity to talk to her was one challenge. The other was what to say to convince her to leave. I was going to tell the kid to go to her aunt's. It was safe, and from there her mother would have to find a way to repair the damage to their relationship.

The wild card was whether she'd agree. From everything I knew about her, she was a loner and had been betrayed by her real father, mother, and boyfriend. The kid had to feel alone, and the Koreshan community probably offered her a sense of belonging.

It wasn't going to be an easy sell. I hunted around the web for dirt on the Koreshans. But besides wacky beliefs, like the earth was hollow and contained the universe, there was scant evidence of a scandal.

One of the tools I often used was embellishment. I had no

qualms about using it with the criminal element because they lied all the time. Maybe it was because I was a father, but the thought of enhancing a rumor or making something up to save Carla didn't give me any bad feelings.

Even so, it was dangerous. I only had one shot at gaining the kid's trust. If she didn't buy it, I was done.

My phone rang.

"Hey, Derrick, how you doing?"

"Good. I'm going through the extra two months of Talbot's calls you asked for."

"I hope you find something; we need a break."

"I'll let you know."

"You'll never guess who I ran into at physical therapy."

If Derrick was back to playing guessing games, he was close to a full recovery. "I don't know. Who?"

"Dr. Bilotti."

Dr. Bilotti and I had worked on so many homicides I'd lost count. He was more than a medical coroner. His thoughtful demeanor helped to not only sort out cases but bumps in my personal life too.

"What was he doing there?"

"He took his neighbor. The woman broke her hip."

"Bilotti is about as perfect a man can be on the planet. Plus, he knows his wine."

"He looks good and said to say hello."

"You just gave me an idea. I'll talk to you later."

IT WAS GOING to be a good day. Dr. Bilotti was sitting at a table in the shade. There were eight wine glasses but only two place settings.

We embraced. "It's good to see you, Doc."

"Same here, Frank. How is Mary Ann and Jessica?"

"Doing well." I knocked on the table. "Mary Ann's MS has been quiet."

"Wonderful. Sit down. Have you been here before?"

"No. But I like the vibe."

"Food is a B, but they have a lot of interesting wines by the glass. Barbatella uses a Cruvinet system to keep open bottles fresh."

"Nice. Where'd they get the name from?"

"Barbatella roughly translates to the branches that develop off the shoot of a vine."

"Cool, I hope I remember that. All these glasses for us?"

"I figured we'd have a tiny taste of a couple of Rosso di Montalcinos."

"Brunello?"

"No. They're from the same region, but think of Rosso as Brunello's younger cousin. They don't have to be aged for four years, are drinkable immediately, and much cheaper."

"I'm dying of thirst."

"I'll take care of that. You in the mood for pizza? Maybe one with sausage and the other with chicken? They'll pair well with the Rosso."

"I'm in your hands, Doc."

Bilotti signaled the waiter and after ordering, said, "How's the new enterprise going?"

"Good. It's a little weird being out on your own and tougher without the resources I'm used to."

"I'm sure it is. If I can help you, let me know."

"Since you mention it, I'm stuck on a case; maybe you have some ideas."

Bilotti agreed as the waiter poured two of the wines. "I think you'll like these. They're made from Sangiovese grapes."

I remembered what he'd said when trying wine; tip the glass and look at the color first. Then swirl the wine around and smell the aromas. I closed my eyes and tried to pick out what I smelled before taking a small sip, letting it coat my mouth. "That's nice. Is that cherry I'm tasting?"

"Exactly." He took a sip. "They're lighter and not as complex as Brunello but a nice value. Tell me about the case."

I brought him up to speed on the Coyle kid.

"It's a shame. These kids are susceptible to, well, I don't want to call the Koreshans a cult, but any group with a charismatic leader . . . Try the second wine."

He didn't know it, but Bilotti had already given me an idea: Check into Eden; maybe there was something in his background. The next glass was a shade darker. "It seems to have more body."

"You're learning. So where are you right now?"

"I'm looking for an angle to get onto the property so I can make sure it's her and talk to her."

"You said the kid surprised the mother and boyfriend when she came back from the doctor."

"That's what Mrs. Coyle said."

"We could have something if we knew why she'd gone to the doctor."

"I thought so too. I asked the mother, but she said something about bloodwork for her thyroid condition."

"Sounds like the kid might have Hashimoto's disease."

"Yeah, she said that. What is it?"

"A condition where the immune system attacks the thyroid. Patients need their hormones monitored. She was probably getting bloodwork. It's tricky to regulate the dosage to keep everything in balance. Especially for women with their cycles. Weight gain and exhaustion are frequent symptoms."

"Maybe if I find out when she goes to the doctor, I can intercept her."

The waiter poured two new wines and left. Bilotti lowered his voice. "I have an idea. But let's enjoy the vino first."

23

THE ONLY THING FLORIDA INTEGRITY BANK TOLD ANN WAS that the check was cashed by a Bank of America branch in Stamford, Connecticut. Though we had the account number on the back of the check, the cashing bank wouldn't give me the time of day. Since there were only three Jeremy Costellos in the area, it wouldn't take long to track down the right person.

"Mr. Costello, my name is Frank Luca. I'm a private investigator, and I'm working a case on behalf of John Talbot."

"I'm not sure I understand. What is this about?"

"Do you have an account at the Stamford branch of Bank of America?"

"Yes, but what does that have to do with anything? Who gave you my number?"

"Did you cash a check from John Talbot in the amount of five thousand dollars?"

"I don't know anybody named Talbot, and I certainly didn't cash a check from whoever he is."

"Are you sure? Because we served the bank a warrant,

and I'll get this information in a couple of hours, and wasting time really pisses me off."

"I swear, I have no idea what you're talking about."

I was skeptical of the invocation of "I swear" with a true suspect, but it appeared this guy was genuine.

"All right, sir. I may have the wrong Costello. Sorry about that."

I dialed the next number. A man with a smoker's voice answered, "Hello?"

"Mr. Costello?"

"Yeah, who's this?"

"Detective Luca." It just came right out. "Uh, I'm investigating a missing man, you know, John Talbot."

"I dunno nobody like that."

"You cashed two checks from him, each one for five thousand bucks. Remember now?"

He hesitated. "I don't know the guy."

He had no idea where I was, "You want to do this over the phone, or you want me to haul you in?"

"Look, I didn't do nothing. I was helping a buddy out."

"What was the money for?"

"Like I said, I was helping Johnny out. All I did was cash them, and he gave me two hundred each time."

"Why'd he pay you to cash the checks?"

"I didn't ask questions, man. I needed the dough."

"What's Johnny's last name?"

"Daugherty."

"Give me his number."

His story sounded like a dodge, but this case was getting weirder by the hour. I took the number, promising to get in Costello's face if he was lying.

Dougherty's phone went straight to voice mail. It wasn't

unusual; everyone swiped away calls from unknown parties. I left a message, mentioning Talbot and Costello.

———

WHEN MRS. COYLE swung open the door, she looked different —younger, more vibrant. As we said our hellos, I tried to identify what had changed. Walking into her house, I knew she was the same, but my perception of her had been turned upside down.

The way she made small talk as we sat in the kitchen told me Teddy had said something to her. I declined an offer of coffee and said, "It's time to come clean."

"What do you mean?"

"You and Teddy is what I mean."

She averted my eyes. "I didn't think it would help find her."

"You wasted time making me track down Teddy while you were . . . You knew where he was and that she wasn't with him."

"I had to . . . my husband, he doesn't know and—"

"You want to make excuses? When your daughter is possibly in danger? If she was a minor, I'd call Child Protection Services, that's what I'd damn well do."

"I'm sorry. I really am."

"What else aren't you telling me?"

"Nothing. I swear."

There it was again. It was almost as bad as saying, "to be honest with you."

"Carla ran off because you crossed the line with her boyfriend. Is that right?"

She nodded.

"Unbelievable."

"It just happened. I didn't mean to. He came over when Carla was out and he—"

"I don't want to hear it. I got half a mind to walk away from this frigging mess."

"Please don't. I need your help. Please, will you find her?"

"All right. But I find out you're holding back or lying, I'm gone."

"Okay, okay."

"You have any brothers or sisters?"

"Me? No. Why?"

"How about your husband?"

"He has a sister, Lara. She lives in Winter Park."

"Have you checked with her?"

"Yeah, but she's not there. I checked right away because they really get along."

"Does Carla have any health issues?"

"What do you mean?"

"Like diabetes?"

"She has problems with her thyroid. It runs in the family. But her doctor has it under control now."

"Is that why she went to the doctor right before she disappeared?"

"Yes. She goes every couple of months for bloodwork."

"Who's her doctor?"

As soon as I got back in the car, I called Derrick.

"Hey, Frank, glad you called. Just got some good news."

"What's up?"

"Doc says I can ditch the wheelchair. Going to use arm-brace crutches for a while."

"Fantastic. Man, I'm so happy to hear this."

"Yeah, and he said two weeks or so more of PT, and I might be able to go with a cane."

"Way to go! What he say about driving?"

"Wants to wait a week more, but I know I'm ready."

"Don't push it, bro."

"Don't worry, I won't. So what's going on?"

"You're not going to believe what I discovered."

After filling him in on the sexual escapades of the missing girl's mother, he said, "Bingo, that's why the kid ran."

"No doubt."

"What's wrong with people today?"

"I guess they like chasing forbidden fruit."

"The kid's not even half her age, and he's her daughter's boyfriend, for God's sake. She must be starved for attention."

"Or sex. Don't forget, men hit their prime when they're twenty to thirty."

"Just when I'm getting back on my feet. I'm going to be over the hill in five years?"

"I'll trade ages with you." Another call was coming in. I looked at the screen. "I got to go. The guy, Daugherty, who got the five-thousand-dollar checks, is calling."

24

Derrick and I got off 75 and headed east toward Babcock Ranch. He said, "You never told me what Daugherty said."

"That's because I never talked to him."

"But he called you back."

"He hung up before I could answer."

"Sounds like he's dodging you."

"That's what I think."

"You want to go see him?"

"If he doesn't call today, I'll see if I can find someone to pay him a visit."

"Sounds good."

"Close your window. We're here." I turned onto the dirt road I'd taken before.

"How far up?"

"There's a clearing a quarter mile up."

I kept my eye on the rearview mirror, trying to see through the dust if anyone was following us.

"I see the house. Man, there's a tree growing in it."

"Been abandoned a long time. But if Babcock Ranch takes off, it might bring the whole area up."

"Good time to speculate."

I slowed, parking near the structure. "Not a bad idea, but I don't know how big a negative being next to the Koreshan property is."

"Who knows, they grow, we could sell it to them."

"Stay in the car. The ground is uneven here."

"You sure?"

Grabbing my laptop, I said, "Yeah, I don't need any help."

Within five minutes, the drone was three hundred feet high. I piloted it to the Koreshan compound. A car was driving up the access road. There were fewer vehicles parked on the property than the last time. It made me wonder whether a bunch of members were outside the community.

A group of people came out of the largest building. There were four of them, and they appeared to be wearing long dresses. I panned the camera. No one else was out. It was time to swoop down and get a close look.

The drone descended toward the women. As it approached, they turned, looking toward the sky. I brought it down close, to fifty feet. The girl to the left, who appeared to be the youngest, fit the age of Carla Coyle. I brought it closer and they began running.

Eyes on the youngest, I followed behind. It was tough to recall, but her gait reminded me of the video Teddy had provided. As they ran to a red building, a man stepped outside. He had a rifle.

He waved the girls to the side and aimed the firearm. I heard a distant blast, and the camera went dark.

I tapped the keys. No response. They'd shot down the drone. I turned toward my car. A rising cloud of dust was coming our way. Snapping the laptop shut, I opened the hatchback and stuck it in my knapsack as two pickup trucks skidded to a stop.

Three men, all with rifles, got out of the vehicles. I said, "Take it easy, fellas."

"We warned you to stay away."

"Did you shoot down my drone?"

They approached in a triangle formation. The lead man, built like a linebacker, said, "Damn right we did. Why are you messing with us?"

"I'm just out for a little recreation."

He raised the rifle. "Stop with the bullshit!"

"Put the guns down! Now!"

I turned around. Derrick, his back leaning against the Explorer, had a pistol in one hand and his badge in the other.

"Who the hell are you?"

"Detective Dickson, Collier County Sheriff's Office. Put your weapons down, or I'll haul all of your asses in."

"What are you doing here?"

"Put your weapons down, or I'm calling for backup."

The lead guy nodded, and the rifles were lowered. He said, "You a cop too?"

"Don't worry about him. Now, get in your vehicles and get out of here." The men stared at him. "Get moving, now!"

After watching the pickups head down the road, I helped Derrick get back in the SUV. "Sorry to make you get out."

"No problem. I was watching the rearview mirror, and when I saw the dust, I figured I better get moving. When the shotgun went off, I knew I made the right call."

"You sure did."

"You get anything?"

"Yep, I'm pretty sure it was the kid. When we get back,

we'll review the footage. The problem is going to be getting access to her."

"But I thought the job was to find her, make sure she was okay?"

"Yeah, but I have to try to get her home or at least out of a place like that. She's too young to join any group. Her mother may be a jerk, but we got to give the kid a chance at a normal life."

WE HAD JUST SAT down for dinner when my phone rang. I had a no-call policy in place for suppertime, but I pulled my cell out. Mary Ann glared at me as I stood. "Mr. Daugherty. Thanks for calling back."

"Sure. What do you want?"

"As my message said, I'm looking into the disappearance of John Talbot. You two were friends."

"Yeah, we were tight way back when, but his old lady, she didn't like it, and, you know, she had power over Johnny Boy."

"But you still kept in touch?"

"Not so much."

"Why'd he send you two five-thousand-dollar checks?"

"I needed help. Johnny was the only guy with money I knew to bail me out."

"You were arrested?"

"No. My trailer burned down, and, you know, I didn't have enough insurance. I lost everything."

"John Talbot gave you ten thousand to help you?"

"Yeah, he's good people."

"He kept it from his wife."

"He told me he wasn't gonna tell her."

"Why doesn't she like you?"

"She told him he was, like, my slave or gopher, I think she said. It was bullshit. Johnny and me was close. He always wanted to help me, that's all. It was no controlling shit."

It didn't make sense. Talbot was educated, an engineer. It was hard to believe someone like Daugherty could control him. It had to be Ann didn't want her husband around him. She probably had some snooty class thing against Daugherty.

Checking the story out would be easy. He gave me his trailer's address to verify the fire, and though John Talbot wouldn't like it, I had to ask Ann about Daugherty. The problem I was having was what other secrets Talbot had hidden.

25

My stomach growled at the smell of garlic sautéing in oil, which drifted into our makeshift office. Wondering what Mary Ann was making for dinner, I popped a name into a search engine.

"Bingo."

Derrick said, "What did you get?"

"Doing a background check on the Koreshan leader, Eden. He changed his name. Used to go by the name of George Waterson."

"Could have a record he's looking to hide."

"I know, but I'm not coming up with anything."

"Maybe he's got a record as a juvenile."

"We'd need somebody on the force to check on it. I can't keep going to Gesso."

"Let me check with O'Brien."

"You sure?"

"No problem."

Derrick dialed a number. "O'Brien, it's Derrick . . . All's good. Look, I could use a favor . . . Thanks. Can you run a juvi inquiry on a George Waterson?"

Derrick flashed a thumbs-up. "What's the date? July fifteenth, 2001. You think you can dig further, pull the arrest records? I'd love to know what he was up to." Derrick frowned. "I understand. No problem. You've been helpful, and I appreciate it. Be well, brother."

He hung up, saying, "He wouldn't go any further, said they're watching everything, and he's afraid they'd trace the inquiry back to him. It requires a sign-in."

"I get it. I wonder what the hell Eden did."

"It could be anything."

He was right. But Carla didn't know that. If I was careful, the info would plant a seed of doubt in her mind.

"We can't wait. The longer the kid is enmeshed in the group, the harder it will be to extract her."

"You're going with Bilotti's plan?"

"It's all we got."

I RANG THE BELL, wondering what Ann would be wearing. Would it be red, again? I heard her singing as she came to the door. Was Ann one of those people who could compartmentalize? Or was she simply unable to contain her glee after getting rid of her husband?

She had another huge smile on to go with canary-yellow pants, a white linen top, and bright red wedges. On anyone else it would have looked silly. On her, it was sophisticated.

"Nice to see you, Frank."

"You have a minute?"

"For you? Anytime. Come in."

It wasn't easy reminding myself that no wife with a missing husband should act so casual or dress as she did.

Walking into the home, it struck me why she was pursuing a private investigation rather than a public appeal.

She simply didn't fit the narrative of a woman in distress. Within seconds of the cameras being turned on, she'd be convicted of being involved in her husband's disappearance.

Ann sat, her smile vanishing. "Do you have any . . . news on John?"

"Not yet."

Her face relaxed. "What brings you here?"

"Johnny Daugherty."

She frowned. "What about him?"

"Tell me about him and your husband."

"They were friends well before I met John. I don't like to say it, but I didn't like Daugherty from the moment I met him."

"Why?"

"I'd rather not say; you'd think I'm a snob."

It was apparent she was part of a crowd I was unfamiliar with, but snob wasn't the word I'd use. "No worries, ma'am. I prefer things unvarnished."

"He was a loser. Typical big talker who never amounted to anything. Daugherty was a leech, and there was no way I was going to let John get bossed around by someone who didn't even graduate high school."

I was dying to ask, if the guy was a Rhodes Scholar, would it be okay to be bullied by him? "Remember the checks to Jeremy Costello?"

"Of course. What does that have to do with Daugherty?"

"It appears your husband wrote them to Costello to hide the fact he was giving money to Daugherty."

"John did what? Why?"

"It seems Daugherty's trailer caught fire, and John was helping him out."

"Oh, I'm not happy he hid it from me, and I'm not saying he shouldn't have done it, but John just couldn't refuse whatever Daugherty would ask him to do. It frustrated me."

"Was, uh, is your husband easily manipulated?"

"I wouldn't use that word, but John is a people pleaser. He has a hard time saying no. He wants everybody to be happy, and he'll do just about anything to keep it that way."

My phone vibrated again. I snuck a peek. It was the second call from Derrick in half an hour.

"Have you heard from Tony Desmond?"

"No, uh, well, kind of. He called to apologize."

She was lying. Maybe they had some sort of makeup sex. "And that was it? You didn't see each other?"

"I realize you're just doing your job, but I fail to see the relevancy of my relationship with Tony or anyone else, for that matter."

"Considering any male as a rival to your husband clears the bar for me."

"It has nothing to do with it."

"Do you and your husband have an open marriage?"

She shook her head. "No, we don't."

My cell vibrated. "Okay. I've got to be going."

Walking to my car, I hit redial.

"Sorry, I was talking to Ann Talbot. What's going on?"

"I think we have something."

"What do you got?"

"Going through the phone records, I ran across a Brittany Bradshaw. Her DNA was found in Talbot's car."

"Holy shit. This could be the break we need."

"That's what I'm thinking."

"Who called who and when?"

"Actually, there are two calls. Talbot called her twice. But they were short calls, under thirty seconds each, one February first and the other January ninth."

"You got her contact details?"

"Yep."

"Send them to me. I'll ask Ann if she knows her. If not, I'm going straight there."

26

THE HUMIDITY WAS AWFUL. IT FELT LIKE I WAS WALKING through wet cotton as I approached a coach home in Vasari. Though I'd made three calls to Brittany Bradshaw, leaving messages each time, she hadn't responded.

Desperate for a break, I took a ride to the community sitting on the Bonita side of the border with Naples. The homes in the neighborhood, named after the Italian artist, were brown and too close together for me, but I'd always heard they had nice, open layouts.

I rang the bell, hoping to speak to someone who might have seen Talbot right before he vanished, plus see the inside of the units I pegged at three to four hundred thousand dollars.

After another ring, I pounded the door with a palm and looked through the blinds hanging over the sidelights, but all I saw was a short flight of steps.

A woman stepped out of the home next door. She looked at me with a frown and shook her head. "Excuse me, ma'am. Do you know where Brittany Bradshaw might be?"

Scurrying inside, she said, "No."

It was as cold a reception as I've ever had in Southwest Florida. It couldn't be me, it had to be Bradshaw. But it meant nothing. For all I knew, she could have had a dog that barked or did the thing that seemed to piss people off without exception: park in front of their house.

At this point, I needed to talk to her before letting my mind run. Going to my car, a woman came out of the house across the street. She was walking a little ball of white fur. I waved. She nodded but no smile. This was a tough neighborhood.

Approaching her, I said, "That's one cute dog. What is it?"

"A Maltese."

As the dog licked my hand, I said, "I'm looking to speak with Brittany Bradshaw. Do you know her?"

"We're not close."

"Well, here's my card. If you see her, please ask her to call me."

MY PHONE SAID it was Sheriff Chester calling. I hadn't spoken to him since the week I took leave. He was almost as pissed at me as I was at him. My split from the department wasn't openly acrimonious, but I had made it clear the harassment by internal affairs and the lack of support from the sheriff were what drove me away.

"Sheriff Chester?"

"Yes. How are you and the family, Frank?"

Ever the politician, he nearly sounded genuine. "We're all good, sir. And you?"

"All is well. We're in a quiet spell, thank goodness, but the department misses you."

"Good to hear."

"I understand Detective Dickson is working with you."

I wondered if that was a violation of some kind. "Yes. He's going out of his mind sitting at home."

"That's good of you. The two of you make a great team."

"We work together well. I'm happy his recovery is progressing nicely."

"Yes, we've been keeping in touch with him. It's wonderful news."

Derek hadn't mentioned anything, but the department may have been in contact with his wife. "It's been a long road for him."

"It was an unfortunate set of circumstances. I wish we could go back in time, but we're looking forward to having him back."

"That would be nice."

"And how about you?"

"Me? What about me?"

"The department needs you. Are you ready to come back?"

"I'm not sure I ever will, sir."

"Look, I know you were disappointed in the way you thought the investigation was handled, and I certainly don't want to rehash it now."

"There's no need to, sir."

"I thought we had a good professional relationship, but I'm not going to be here forever. And the fact is, I've been offered a position at the state level that I'm seriously entertaining."

"Congratulations, sir."

"I care deeply about Collier County, and if I decide to take the assignment, I'd have to be comfortable the department is operating at peak performance."

"I'm sure it will be fine."

"With your solve rate, Frank, it'd be more than fine. Will you do me a favor and think about it?"

"Sure. I can do that."

After he hung up, I had mixed feelings. Chester was on his way out. That was good for the department, but moving into a larger role? It was typical of government. He was a smooth talker, never took risks, and would do a world-class sprint away from taking a stand. How did that entitle him to a promotion?

It wasn't that he was a bad man, he just didn't stand for anything other than protecting himself. The department needed a leader who'd been on the street and had experience with making unpopular decisions. Someone who'd back officers but be tough on them when necessary.

I thought about who might replace Chester until my phone rang. Caller ID said it was a Mildred Lightner.

"Hello. Who's this?"

"I'm a neighbor of Brittany Bradshaw. You gave me your card when I was walking Salty."

Salty? As a dog's name? "Oh yes. What can I do for you?"

"Well, I didn't know who you were, and then I saw on your card you're an investigator. I really shouldn't be saying anything, but this is a respectable community, and she don't fit in here."

"What do you mean?"

"She engages in inappropriate behavior."

"What kind?"

"I mean, I don't care what people do in their bedrooms, but this woman crosses a line."

It sounded like a sex theme again. "I'd really appreciate some detail."

"I'm not comfortable discussing these types of things."

"I understand, but I'm investigating a missing man, and she had contact with him. I'm trying to understand the nature of the relationship."

"It was sexual."

"Bradshaw is a prostitute?"

"I don't know what you call those people who use whips and that sort of thing."

"Are you certain about this?"

"Yes. Molly and I, she lives next door to that woman, we saw her through the window wearing a leather costume. It was disgusting."

27

MARY ANN WAS CHANGING AFTER SWIMMING. BUTTONING her blouse, I asked, "You ready to play your part?"

"I'm only doing this because a child is involved."

"I know. It's the right thing to do."

"Jessica can never find out about this."

"Don't worry. It's just a phone call. Jessie will never know."

"She better not. I'd feel terrible."

"Don't forget to monkey with the caller ID."

After being forced to lose Mary Ann as a partner because of our relationship, she did a stint in the cyber-crime unit before taking leave. She knew how to mask the number when calling someone. She played with her phone.

"Okay, all set."

"Go for it."

I gave Mary Ann a number and she dialed it. "Hello, this is Mrs. Ball from LabCorp. Is this Carla Coyle?"

"Yes."

"I'm sorry to advise you, but we've had a malfunction at

the lab. All the results during the window of your samples must be rerun."

"I don't understand."

"The hematology analyzer's program went askew, spitting out the same ranges, regardless of the sample. Fortunately, we caught the problem within two days."

"What does this mean for me?"

"We're going to have to ask you to submit another sample for analysis."

"Really? It's a real hassle giving blood."

"We realize the inconvenience and are committed to making it as easy for our customers as possible. We've set up a special time frame, and you won't have to wait. No paper-work is required or anything. We'll just need your ID. Where are you located?"

"In Charlotte County, by Babcock Ranch."

"Um, let me see. Okay, we have a processing unit at the Walgreens in North Fort Myers, on North Cleveland Avenue. It's close by. I can fit you in between three p.m. and four p.m."

"Today?"

"Yes. You really should get this done today. To be honest, Doctor Vincent was very upset with us."

"All right. I'll be there."

"Thank you for understanding, and we're sorry to have to put you through this."

Mary Ann hung up, wearing a frown. I said, "Maybe not an Oscar, but I'd give you a Golden Globe."

"I'm not doing anything like this again."

"Don't worry. I'll see you later."

Her strong moral character was something I loved about Mary Ann, but in the world I operated in, propriety was made out of Silly Putty.

I WAS on the exit ramp for Route 17 when the phone rang. It was Mary Ann.

"I'm almost there. What's up?"

"The bank just called. The Coyle check bounced."

"What? The one we got yesterday?"

"Yep, the one for fifteen hundred."

"I can't believe it. Let me call her."

"And we're going out on a limb for her?"

"It's for the kid, not the mother. Let me call her before I get there."

I pulled into a Publix lot and punched in her number. "Mrs. Coyle, this is Frank Luca."

"Oh, hi. Did you talk to Carla?"

"Not yet. Look, the check you sent in for fifteen hundred bounced."

"Oh my God, I'm so sorry. We ran into a little problem. You see, Bill lost his job. It was a misunderstanding. They said he failed a drug test, but that's ridiculous. He's probably going to be back next week. Can you just give me a little time?"

This woman's life was a petri dish of dysfunction. "You should have told me about this. I have bills that money was going to cover."

"Sorry, I'm so embarrassed over this. I can send a new check for, say, five hundred. Would that help?"

"Send it. But I need full payment to continue on the case."

"Please don't stop looking for Carla."

"I have to go. Don't forget to mail the money. Today."

I drove along Cleveland Avenue trying to figure out if the check to pay for the shot-down drone was in danger of bouncing. It couldn't get more embarrassing; the guy was a friend of Derrick's.

Customers were streaming in and out of Walgreens. Between CVS and them, there was a pharmacy at every intersection. How did all of them stay so busy?

At 1:45 p.m., I backed into a space close to the store's entrance. Under normal circumstances, as a kid, Carla wouldn't be early, but I was betting that since she was getting a ride she'd arrive before the appointed time.

A red pickup pulled in. The driver was one of the men who'd confronted me over the surveillance. It looked like Carla in the passenger seat.

Lowering my baseball cap, I pretended to reach into the glove box as he stopped in front of the doors. It was Carla. He pulled away after dropping her off.

I hustled into Walgreens. Carla was steps from the pharmacy counter.

"Excuse me, miss."

Carla turned around. "Me?"

"I knew it was you. Carla, right?"

"Yes, I'm sorry. Do I know you?"

"Oh, it's been a long while. I'm a friend of your mother's."

"And your name is?"

"Frank Luca. I'm a detective with the Collier County Sheriff's Office." It was risky, but I'd decided to use my old title, figuring it would reduce the chances of her thinking I was some kind of pervert.

She smiled. "Nice to meet you, uh, I guess, again."

"Your mom is really worried about you."

"You can tell her I'm fine."

"I found out what she did with Teddy, and you have every reason to be upset." I lowered my voice. "Look, you got to be careful with the Koreshan people, not all of them, but the leader, Eden. He's not who you think he is."

"What are you talking about? People think it's a cult, but they're not. Everybody there is super-nice and friendly—"

"Eden changed his name to hide the fact he was arrested."

"What for?"

"The records are sealed, and I can't reveal details without breaking the law. But trust me, and I'm speaking as a dad now, I have a daughter a couple of years younger than you, and there's no way I'd let her get anywhere near that man."

"What are you saying?"

"What I'm about to say is not in any official capacity. Do you understand?"

"Tell me."

28

"EDEN'S REAL NAME IS WATERSON. HE WAS ARRESTED FOR sexually molesting two girls."

"Oh my God. That's horrible. I can't believe it. Are you sure?"

I pulled my phone out and hit dial. "Here, ask your Aunt Jenny."

"You're calling her?"

"Yep."

Carla put the phone to her ear, and her eyes welled up. The plan was working. I looked down the aisle, afraid her chaperone would throw a wrench into things. He was nowhere in sight.

When her aunt agreed to help, I told her we'd need to keep the conversation short.

"It's crazy, Aunt Jen, he's seems so nice."

"Let me talk to your aunt."

I took the phone and said, "If Carla's willing, I can drive her up to meet you like we discussed. We can be in Sarasota in under two hours." I gave the phone back to Carla. "She wants to speak with you."

I kept my eyes on the entrance. When Carla said, "Okay, as long as you don't mind, I'd love to stay with you," I nearly fist pumped.

"I'm proud of you, Carla. You made the right decision. Come on, let's get on the road before—"

Walgreen's doors slid apart, and her driver stepped into the store. He looked in both directions, and I said, "Get behind me and don't look at him or say a word."

The driver stopped in his tracks when he saw me and Carla. I put my hand behind my back, and when she took it, I guided her to my side.

"Carla, come on, we have to go."

"She's not going anywhere with you."

"Who the hell are you?"

"A detective who'll get you arrested if you don't move out of the way. Trust me, you'll regret it."

He stepped aside. "Where are you taking her?"

I made a beeline for the door.

As the door slid open, he said, "Master Eden is not going to be pleased."

We hopped into my car. I felt bad about what I told the kid, but the bottom line was the kid was going to stay with family. In a few years, if she wanted to live an alternative lifestyle, she'd have the maturity to make an informed decision.

Though I may have stretched the truth, I considered it a win. I suppressed the need to share it as I drove north on Route 75. I'd have to wait two hours. As soon as I handed Carla off to her aunt, I could do a little bragging. I'd make Mrs. Coyle wait until I called Mary Ann and Derrick with the news.

CARLA WAS quiet most of the ride. She played with her phone the entire drive, speaking only to ask how much longer the trip would be. It was an uncomfortable trip north, and I began to relax when we finally took the Sarasota exit.

We pulled into a Publix on Route 780. When I pointed out the electric blue Mini Cooper her aunt was driving, Carla said, "Cool. I really love those cars."

I liked the go-kart look as well, but I wondered how safe they were. "They're nice. I almost bought one last year."

"I hope she lets me drive it."

"She will."

I parked, and when she reached for the door handle, I said, "Give me a second first."

After checking the woman's ID, I waved Carla over. She ran to her aunt, and they embraced. Carla started sobbing, and I wanted to bail out as the aunt comforted her, repeating, "It's going to be all right, honey."

Digging into my pocket, I cleared my throat. "I got to be going. If you need anything, call me. Okay?"

Carla wiped her eyes and nodded.

I squeezed a hundred dollars into her hand. "This is from your mother."

It wasn't, but it just felt like the right thing to say. It even got a thank you from the kid. Walking to my car, I heard the aunt tell her they'd get something to eat and then go shopping.

Before I was out of the lot, I called Mary Ann. "Hey, just dropped the kid off with her aunt."

"It went good, then?"

"Yeah, better than expected. She didn't give me any trouble."

"Oh, that's good."

"Tell you the truth"—I hated when I said that—"I think the kid was glad to be off the reservation."

"Poor girl is lost."

"The aunt seems levelheaded, and they get along. I got a feeling this might work out."

"She should be with her mother."

"If the lady was normal, I'd agree, but after what she did, it's going to take time to get over, if she ever does."

"It's not only her mother. Don't forget, her boyfriend betrayed her as well."

"I know, and that's on top of her biological father abandoning her."

"I don't like to say it, but it's going to take her a long time before she trusts anyone again."

"I know, and her aunt understands the situation. She never had kids or got married, but she's a social worker, so she said she'd know how to handle things."

"Good. What time will you be home?"

"If there's no traffic, under two hours. I got to call Derrick and the kid's mother."

"You never called her mother?"

"No. It's not like she deserves it."

"Frank! The poor woman is going crazy. Call her now."

"I will. See you later."

I disconnected Mary Ann and made another call.

"Hey, Derrick, just handed off the kid."

"How'd it go?"

"Pretty smooth. The guy driving her tried to give me some crap, but I blew him off. The kid didn't really resist leaving the Koreshans."

"Then she must not have liked it."

"It's no place for a kid her age."

"You got that right. Look, I'm not sure if this means anything, but I found Brittany Bradshaw."

"You did? Where?"

"She's in NCH North."

"She's in the hospital? What happened?"

"Nobody knows. She's conscious but unresponsive. I couldn't get any details, but I got the feeling she has some kind of brain injury."

29

———

BEFORE I PUT THE BOWL IN THE DISHWASHER, I REGRETTING eating the leftover pasta. Anytime I ate more than a light lunch, I'd get tired afterward. It was something I usually avoided, but the macaroni had soaked up a ton of sauce and was impossible to resist.

As an antidote, I should have taken a walk, but I headed to the lanai instead. The sun was out, the humidity low, and a chaise lounge was calling. Opening a slider, my phone rang.

"Is this Frank Luca?"

"Yes, who's calling?"

"Miles Livermore. You left me several messages."

"I'd like to talk with you."

"Concerning what?"

"Ann and John Talbot. What time works for you?"

"I'm good the rest of the day. We live in the condos in back of Naples Bay Resort."

He sounded relaxed but that could be because he had been vacationing in Europe.

"I'll leave now. Should be there in twenty minutes."

"I'll be at the marina, on my boat, *Swing Hard*. It's the second one from the end."

Swing Hard? What kind of name was that? Was it effort related, or did it refer to a sexual lifestyle? People, including yours truly, liked to say everything was about money. But as a private investigator, everything seemed to be about sex.

Multicolored buildings encircled a small marina filled with oversized boats. It had a serene feel to it. Just two slips were empty. Most of the boats had people hanging out on them. These well-to-do people were using their yachts as backyards.

Livermore was shirtless and had grown a mustache. He was trim with no sign of love handles. The five pounds I'd lost from the dietary restriction Mary Ann was following had just about dissolved the flab on my sides, but it was a battle.

"Mr. Livermore."

"Yep. Come on board."

We shook hands. "This is a very nice boat. How big is it?"

"Forty-two feet with a fourteen-foot beam."

"Out of my league. What do you do for a living?"

"Investment banker."

"How do you know the Talbots?"

"We belong to the same yacht club."

"When was the last time you saw John Talbot?"

"Been a while. Let's see, I've been in Europe for ten days, so, two weeks or so."

"What day did you leave on vacation?"

"Uh, March, uh, fourth."

Just two days after Talbot vanished.

"How was your trip?"

"Amazing. There's nothing like the Amalfi Coast."

"I'd love to go. It takes some planning, right?"

"Nah, you want some tips, I can lay it all out for you."

"I might take you up on that. Do you know where John might have gone?"

"No. I have no idea, but we weren't that close, so I really wouldn't know."

I lowered my voice. "But you'd know about Ann, wouldn't you?"

"That was a long time ago."

"Not according to her."

He looked around. "It's been months. Look, don't bring this up. My wife finds out, and I'm sunk, man."

I just loved it when people crapped in their own backyard and wanted help cleaning it up. "Do you know anybody Talbot had a disagreement with? Anyone who'd do him harm?"

"John got along with everybody. He wasn't one to ruffle anyone's feathers."

"So I'm hearing. I understand he was friendly with another boater, George Slater."

"Yeah, George's boat is the last one down there." He pointed to the other end.

"All right. I don't have anything else at the moment. I'll see if George Slater is around."

"He is."

As I stepped onto the dock, a guy in white shorts and boat shoes on the next boat called out.

"Hey, Miles. How was the trip?"

"It was great, man."

"You never said you were going away. Was it a spur-of-the-moment thing?"

"Uh, not really."

I walked toward the other end of the dock wondering if

Livermore took off after killing Talbot. It could have been something that escalated, and Livermore panicked.

A bald man with a beer belly was spraying his boat with a hose. It was a much smaller boat that I pegged at twenty-five feet.

"Mr. Slater?"

"Yeah. What can I do for you?"

I introduced myself. "I'm looking into the disappearance of John Talbot, and I understand you were friends."

"Yeah, I can't believe it. John's a good guy, one of those people who tries a little too hard to be liked, if you know that type."

"He got along with everybody?"

"Yep. Never heard him say a harsh word about anybody."

"How about his wife, Ann?"

"She something, ain't she?"

I smiled. "Any trouble in their marriage?"

He turned his head. "I wouldn't really know."

"Is there anything out of the ordinary that you can tell me involving John and anyone else? Even something small, it may seem insignificant, but you never know."

"Have you talked to his other friends?"

I nodded. "Just spoke with Miles Livermore."

"You know, it's probably nothing, but about a month ago, the three of us went out around six. We had a couple of cocktails, and well, I really don't know what happened, but I went to the head, and when I came out, I heard John shouting for help."

"What happened?"

"John was in the water behind the boat and—"

"Where was Livermore?

"Just standing there."

"He wasn't helping?"

"Not at first, but then he circled the boat around, and John swam up to the boat."

"How'd he get in the water?"

"They said it was an accident. The two of them were horsing around, and he went overboard."

"And Livermore didn't immediately try to rescue him?"

"I don't know; it's hard to say. I mean, when I came out of the head, I was stunned myself. It took me a couple of seconds to process it."

As he said that, I saw *Swing Hard*, with Livermore behind the wheel, motoring out of the marina.

30

By the time I walked to my car, the sun had taken the chill out of me. Hospitals claimed that keeping the facility cold helped control bacteria, but based on the number of people who contracted ailments while there, they needed a better solution.

The only place cooler was the morgue. The ghoulish place made me think of Dr. Bilotti. Despite all the time he spent there, Bilotti was as warm as a person could be. I wondered what insight he could provide on what happened to Brittany Bradshaw.

The poor woman was out of it. My expertise wasn't medical, but Bradshaw reminded me of someone with brain damage. I tried to get a response out of her, but her glazed eyes had no signs of recognition.

"Hey, Doc, how are you?"

"Doing well, Frank. And you?"

"Good. Say, I wanted to ask you something."

"What's on your mind?"

"Someone related to the Talbot case, the man who's missing. This woman knew Talbot, and her DNA was found in his car."

"Witness? Suspect?"

"I don't know. Here's the thing, she's in the NCH and is unresponsive. She's up but doesn't seem to know what's going on."

"That's unfortunate. What happened to her?"

"I was hoping you'd be able to clue me in."

"Without examining her and running—"

"Just give me the likely possibilities."

"You said she was conscious, so chances are it's a brain injury or maybe a neurological issue of some kind."

"What would cause that? A stroke?"

"Yes, it could be a stroke or an aneurysm. When the brain is deprived of oxygen for a prolonged period, the damage is generally permanent."

"So she could have been strangled or suffocated?"

"Absolutely. She may have fallen unconscious, and whoever was assaulting her thought she was dead and left her. Were there any visible markings around her throat area?"

"Not that I could see. How long would they last?"

"Depends on the force used and its duration. But keep in mind that approximately sixty percent of the time there's no visible evidence."

"Trust me, I've responded to more domestic violence calls than I care to recall."

"If her injury was the result of asphyxiation, I don't believe a ligature was used, as they tend to leave distinct markings. If she could speak, you'd notice a change in her voice if she had been strangled."

"Nah, she's not talking."

"She'd also have trouble swallowing because of the neck trauma she'd experienced."

"Um, that might help."

"Why do you believe she is a victim?"

"I'm not sure she is, but everything about this case is strange."

My phone rang. It was Ann Talbot. Answering, I closed the den's door.

"Hello, Mrs. Talbot."

"Hi, Frank. Look, I want you to be honest with me."

"Of course, I've been. What's the matter?"

"Is John . . . is he . . . dead?"

"Well, the short answer is we don't know."

"You said you'd be honest with me. Now tell me what you really think."

"Chances are he's a victim of foul play. Now, there's a possibility he's being held captive, but it's a slim one."

"I thought so . . ."

"I know it's difficult, but we're working hard to find out what happened."

She sniffled. "I can't take this much longer. It's eating away at me . . ."

"I'm sorry. It's a terrible situation."

"I feel so helpless. Is there anything I can do?"

"Let me ask you something concerning Miles Livermore and your husband."

"Sure. What do you want to know?"

"I heard about an incident where John and Livermore, along with George Slater, were on a boat, and your husband ended up in the water and had to be rescued."

"I heard about that. But the funny thing was, John never said anything the day it happened."

"How did you find out?"

"We were at the annual barbecue, and everyone was there, and I think it was Bill who asked John about it. I was shocked, but John played it down, said he had been drinking and slipped reaching for a fishing pole. It was weird because John doesn't like to fish."

"This was a fishing trip?"

"Yes, Miles and George love to fish. John would go along whenever they invited him."

"Did you know anything about a trip to Europe that Miles took around the time John went missing?"

"Europe? Are you sure?"

"Yes. He went to Italy. To the Amalfi Coast."

"That's a surprise. Miles always made comments whenever we spoke of going to Europe. He'd say there was more than enough to see in America."

"You had no idea he went away?"

"No. But why would he tell me?"

"Wouldn't you have known through your friends at the marina?"

"Probably. Why is this important?"

"The timing and spontaneous nature of it raise questions."

"You think he—nah, not Miles. He's, I don't know, not violent. It doesn't make sense."

She was old enough to know you never really know someone. Just when you think you do, they stun you.

"You, uh, know him better than most people. What I need you to do is review your relationship and everything you know about him. Forget what you think of him, and examine him with a fresh look. See if you can find anything unusual or troubling in his behavior. Can you do that?"

"Yeah, I can, but I can't believe he's somehow involved."

I had to say it. "Of all the things I've learned in my career, the one thing that stands out is that you never really know someone. You think you do, but trust me, you don't."

31

———

I COULDN'T FALL ASLEEP. MILES LIVERMORE WAS KEEPING ME up. The way I saw it, if Livermore was involved in killing Talbot, we couldn't rely on finding the body to nail him. I was willing to bet Talbot was dumped somewhere in the Gulf of Mexico.

What we needed was motivation. The obvious answer was the love triangle. The problem was that even though he'd had an affair with Talbot's wife, it appeared to be over. Ann said Livermore was the one to break it off and hadn't contacted her since the end of the relationship.

If passion was out, it was either greed or an incident that devolved into a fit of rage. Though it was unclear how Talbot had ended up in the water, it could have been an attempt to kill him. That undermined the possibility an argument had spiraled out of control, leaving greed as the reason.

I swung my legs off the bed and tiptoed to the den. Rifling through the Talbot file, I pulled out the phone records. There it was. Livermore had called Talbot two times. Once on March first and again on the second.

Afraid Mary Ann would go nuts if I drove over to Livermore's at this hour, I padded back to the bedroom. Lying in bed, I thought about Livermore. Talbot considered him a friend, but a friend wouldn't screw around with your wife.

There had to be another connection. Was it business? Livermore was an investment banker. I didn't know much about what they actually did, but I knew they advised companies on things like acquisitions and helped them raise money. Was there some kind of deal involving Talbot? It didn't seem to fit.

Wondering if Livermore, like Desmond, had money troubles, the thought made me remember to call Coyle. She'd never replaced the bounced check, and I was about to fall behind in paying bills. If I dipped into our savings, Mary Ann would be sure to remind me I should have stayed with the sheriff's office.

I did a mental tally of how many hours I could bill Talbot. I'd sent her an invoice just a week ago. It'd be early, but she was good about paying, and I needed to fill the hole.

CARRYING a second cup of java to the den, I called Ann Talbot.

"Good morning. Sorry to call so early, but I have a question."

"It's fine. I'm not sleeping much these days. What's up?"

"Did John do any business with Miles Livermore?"

"I don't think so. Miles is a banker."

"Did he arrange any financing for a project that your husband was working on?"

"I'm pretty sure he did. John mentioned something about it. I think it was the Gulfshore Playhouse. They're building a new facility on Goodlette-Frank across from Bayfront."

I'd seen renditions of the new building. It was cool looking. "When was this?"

"It's tough to say. The project has been on the drawing board for years. They're a nonprofit, so even though raising money for the arts in Naples is easier than most places, it's still a challenge."

"Can you recall when John mentioned it?"

"A couple of months ago."

After hanging up, I Googled the development. The website for Gulfshore Playhouse had a tab called Next Stage Campaign. It didn't look like a groundbreaking was in the near future. I rooted around the site, but none of the information helped beyond educating me on their mission.

I was about to go see Livermore when my phone rang. "Mr. Luca?"

"You got him. Who's this?"

"Brad Pincher from Universal Insurance."

"I don't need any insurance. Goodbye."

"Hold on a second. I got your name from Sergeant Gesso. He's a neighbor of mine."

I had to be polite, but I still wasn't entertaining insurance offers. "He's a good friend."

"He said since you're a private eye, you might be able to help me with a situation."

"What's the nature of the situation?"

"Most of our business is insuring personal valuables—people's jewelry, art, and auto collections, those types of holdings."

"Okay."

"One of our clients just put in another claim for losing a diamond ring. He's a little too unlucky, if you know what I mean."

"You believe it may be fraud?"

"I think so. This is the third time they've done it. It can't be a coincidence."

He thought like I did. "They said they lost three rings?"

"No. Two rings and a Rolex. They claimed that one ring and the watch were stolen while they were in New York, and the other ring they said the diamond fell out."

That muddied the picture. "I'm surprised you didn't drop them after the first claim."

"We will, but to me it's the principle behind what I think is going on. If we drop them, they'll just move on to another carrier and do the same thing if we don't stop them."

He was right. If someone committed a crime and left no obvious evidence, they'd get away with it. But human nature being what it is, they'd be emboldened and would continue their criminal activity. Eventually, we'd piece it together, or they'd make a mistake.

"You got that right."

"Are you interested in looking into this? We're willing to pay whatever your fee is and a bonus if we recover any funds paid out."

The timing was right. I only had the one case, and I could use a quick infusion of cash. "My rate is seventy-five an hour, and I'll need a retainer of a thousand."

"That's fine. How much time do you think this will take?"

"That would depend on what you have for me to work with and how crafty the insured was in the scheme he concocted."

"I understand."

"Send me what you have on the client and jewelry in question."

32

———

A BOAT WITH A BLUE BIMINI TOP WAS BACKING OUT OF A SLIP when I rang Livermore's bell. The man piloting it couldn't have been more than forty. Instead of heading to an office, he was aiming for the horizon. Boats weren't for me. If had money, I'd be parked on sand somewhere.

Livermore was buttoning a crisp white shirt when he came to the door. It was 8:35 a.m. Bankers did have better hours than the average worker. I liked the spicy cologne he was wearing. "Good morning, I'm just about to leave for work."

"I have a couple of questions."

"I'm meeting a client at, uh"—I could see him doing math in his head—"ten, and I have to prepare for the meeting."

"Tell me about the day John Talbot ended up in the Gulf of Mexico."

"What?"

"George Slater said the three of you were out fishing, and when he came out of the bathroom, Talbot was in the water, the boat was moving away from him, and you did nothing."

"That's bullshit. When I realized he'd fallen in, I went to get a life preserver."

"How'd he end up in the water?"

"We'd been drinking and were fooling around."

"What happened?"

"I used to wrestle and was talking about a match I'd had, and John said he wrestled in high school or something and that he was undefeated. He challenged me, and when we grappled with each other, he slipped and fell overboard."

"But you said you went to get a preserver when you realized he'd fallen in."

"That's right."

"What is it? You found him in the water, or you knew he'd fallen in?"

"I was stunned for a second when he fell in. It was surreal."

"You didn't stop the boat."

"It was only a couple of seconds. You're making it sound like I left him behind."

"Mr. Slater said you were just standing there."

"I told you I was shocked by what happened. You're making a big deal of it. Nothing happened to John."

"You called Mr. Talbot on March first and second."

"And?"

"What were the calls about?"

"We were friends, for God's sake."

"What did you talk about?"

"We were going fishing, and I wanted to see if he wanted to come along."

"But he didn't like to fish."

"He liked to hang out."

"You called him two days in a row to ask him to go fishing?"

"I can't remember. Oh yeah, I called him the next day about a project I heard about, but he wasn't interested in it."

"What project?"

"A real estate development that we're raising money for. It's a multiuse project going up on Bonita Springs Road. A client of mine, the group that put up the Promenade years ago, assembled a huge parcel of prime property. It's going to be a combination of residential, commercial, and retail. I thought John might be interested in bidding for a piece of it."

"He said no?"

"Yeah. I was surprised, but he said he was too busy."

"But the project was a long way off, wasn't it?"

"Probably a year or more from breaking ground."

"How would he know he'd be busy?"

"I don't know. That's what he said."

"Tell me about the Naples Playhouse."

His face darkened. I'd hit a nerve. "What about it?"

"I understand you and John worked on this together."

"Look, we didn't work on anything together. I'm a banker, and he's an engineer."

"I understand that. But you tried to help each other, right?"

"Of course. Geez, don't friends do that all the time?"

I wanted to ask him if buddies screwed their pal's wife.

"Are you still involved with the new facility they're building?"

"No. Look, I have to go or I'll be late."

Livermore was like a jigsaw puzzle piece that just didn't quite fit. It looked good, but something was slightly off.

IT BOTHERED me when an email had more than four attachments. Information was key to an investigation but having to open them and print them was annoying. Opening the envelope the insurance agent sent me added to the admiration I felt for him.

Not only was a check enclosed, but the documentation covering the jewelry and the insured was excellent.

Moses Green, forty-five years old, was the suspicious client. He resided in an area known as the Moorings, on Gulf Shore Boulevard, and liked expensive jewelry. The receipt for the Rolex, a GMT Master model, had a price tag of thirty-two thousand dollars. Why would anyone need something like that?

The diamond ring he said was stolen at the same time in New York City was valued at twenty thousand. There was no receipt, but the two-carat ring had an appraisal issued by South East Gems.

The value of the latest loss, a diamond that supposedly fell out of its setting, was purchased from Tiffany's at a cool forty-three thousand dollars. I knew people had a lot of money down here, but to spend that kind of money on jewelry screamed show-off.

Just who was Moses Green? Gulf Shore Boulevard had some high-end high-rises. Using Google Earth, I zeroed in on his address. Green lived in a white, two-story condo unit that spoke of the 1960s. How could a guy who lived in an apartment worth four hundred thousand afford a hundred grand of jewelry?

I called Derrick, bringing him up to speed on the new client. He said, "What kind of scam you think he's running?"

"Not sure if he's collecting the money and keeping the jewelry, or maybe he's also selling."

"Secondhand jewelry gets tagged with a big discount."

"Yeah, but these are not something handed down by grandma. I looked around at secondhand Rolexes. The one he had, or still has, is worth thirty K."

"We used to rely on the pawnshops to tip us off when someone was fencing. That's not going to work with high-quality stuff."

"No doubt. There are more than a few high-end jewelers in town. But I'm not sure anybody would touch something like this."

"If there's enough money in it, they will."

"You're right. You want to make some calls, see what we can find out, what they'd buy, and who the players are?"

"I'm on it."

33

I PULLED THE REFRIGERATOR DOOR OPEN. "THERE'S NO milk?"

"I asked you to pick up a bottle yesterday."

She did? I wasn't going to challenge her because my memory had been spotty ever since they filled my body with chemo. "Sorry, I got so deep into trying to figure out one of Talbot's friends, it slipped my mind."

"Sounds like you think he might be involved."

Spying Mary Ann's almond milk, I wondered whether to have my morning java black. "They're supposed to be friends, but I think it's a one-way street. The guy was sleeping with Talbot's wife."

"That's terrible. Passion is a motivator."

I put as little almond milk as possible in my cup. "I don't think it's related to the affair. Something ain't right, but I can't put my finger on it."

"How do they know each other?"

I took a sip. It was terrible. "Through the marina."

"What's he do?"

"Livermore is a banker. He told me about a new project

going up in Bonita. It's a big development. Apparently, he raises money."

"What else has he been involved in?"

"He was supposed to be involved with the new home for the Naples Players, but something went wrong."

"You know Mindy's husband, Fernando?"

"Of course."

"He's really involved with them. She says he always loved the theater, and it's a way for him to pursue his passion."

"He's an actor?"

"No. I think he's the executive vice president or something."

"Hm. Maybe he'd know the inside scoop on what went on with Livermore."

"Maybe. Give him a call."

"I'm going to the 7-Eleven to grab some milk first."

"Fernando, it's Frank Luca, Mary Ann's husband."

"Hi, Frank. How you been? I heard you're not with the sheriff anymore."

"Yeah, I took a leave. Doing some private investigation work."

"How's that going?"

"Pretty good. In fact, it's the reason I'm calling. Mary Ann mentioned you're the vice president of the Naples Players, and it's come up in a case I'm handling."

"I'm the executive director. But how are we involved in a case?"

"Not the organization, but you were about to do business with a banker by the name of Miles Livermore."

"That's right, but we were able to obtain much cheaper financing from Fifth Third Bank at the last minute."

"Was there anything unusual about your dealings?"

"I know everybody has to make money; it makes the world go round. But we're a nonprofit, and we need to keep our costs as low as possible. The firm Mr. Livermore was with was charging a large upfront fee. Luckily, an engineer we were working with had a contact at Fifth Third, and we were able to avoid it."

"Any chance the engineer was John Talbot?"

"Yes. But I understand he's gone missing. It's a shame. He's a good man."

"When you backed out, how did Livermore react?"

"He was pretty upset."

"Can I ask how much the fee was?"

"Two hundred thousand."

"That's a lot of money. How much were you planning to borrow?"

"Fifteen million dollars."

"Still sounds high."

"Many institutions charge origination fees for these types of loans."

I finished the call and wondered how a banker like Livermore got paid. Was it like a life insurance salesperson, where the first-year premium went to pay the agent? Even so, was two hundred thou, if he received it all, enough to kill someone over?

Between where he lived and the boat, Livermore seemed to be doing well. Maybe it was a pride thing that set him off. Livermore was a poser, all about the image, but it was still a stretch to knock someone off.

It was time to dig deeper into Livermore.

34

Pulling open the door, I said, "Hey, man, this is a milestone."

Derrick smiled. "I never thought I'd be looking forward to driving."

"We take so much for granted."

"You're so right. I'm not going to sweat the small stuff anymore."

He was right, but I didn't want to rain on his parade. The truth was, we usually go back to who we were. Even after everything I went through because of bladder cancer, the surgery, the chemo, and the endless doctors' appointments, I reverted to letting minor things irritate me.

After the shock of the diagnosis wore off, I got depressed. Then as the outlook brightened, I was as thankful as I'd ever been. Little encounters were treasured, and a day at the beach was heavenlike. The problem was it didn't last.

There was no doubt the cancer changed me. Besides being scared, I paid a little more attention to the sunsets and appreciated my family, but I wished I could have permanently stayed in the gratitude zone.

Derrick was walking much better. I figured a week more and he'd be using a cane. "What did you dig up on the jewelry?"

"I figured tracking down the Rolex might be easier because they have serial numbers, but I learned something about diamonds."

"And you didn't have to get engaged to do it?"

"Oh, I remember the crash course when I wanted to propose. I think every guy goes through it."

"Yeah, my first time I was up in New York, and a buddy of mine took me to the diamond district. I was glad he knew someone because you're basically walking in there naked. They make you look through those little things and expect you to see the differences. The business is an entire world unto itself."

"If I thought I could get away with it, I would have gone with one of those fake ones."

"They look good these days."

"Yep, anyway, one technological advancement may be a big help. Diamonds have serial numbers now."

"They do?"

"Not all of them, but ones graded by the Gemological Institute of America. They found a way to engrave a serial number on them."

"Really? That's amazing. If the jewelers cooperate, it could put a dent in theft."

"Not going to be easy though. It's not like diamonds need to be repaired like a watch."

"True." I reached for a manila envelope. "Go through this. The insurance agent sent it over. See if you can grab the serial numbers from it. One of the diamonds was bought at Tiffany. It's expensive and was probably engraved."

"If they do, I'll start reaching out to the jewelers."

"The Tiffany rock is the latest claim, so he may not have fenced it yet." I picked up my phone. "I'm going to have another chat with Livermore."

"Hello, Mr. Livermore."

"Hi. Look, I'm in the middle of something and can't talk."

"This won't take long."

"I'm sorry, but I have a client waiting in the lobby."

"You want me to come down, or would you prefer we do this over the phone?"

"I only have five minutes."

"I understand you had a deal with the Naples Playhouse that got pulled at the last minute."

"What does that have to do with anything? Deals come and go all the time."

"I understand they went with a bank recommended by John Talbot."

"What's the relevancy of all this? I told you I'm busy."

"Losing that business cost you a big bonus, didn't it?"

"That's none of your business, Mr. Luca. Now, I've got to be going."

"Hold on, I have one more question."

"Make it quick."

"Did you get revenge for the lost commission by killing Talbot?"

"That's ridiculous. Goodbye."

Derrick looked at me. "He hung up on you?"

"Yeah. He didn't like me prying into his business. It makes me want to dig in even more."

"I can go to his place of work and start asking questions."

"We may have to. I have to think about this. All this talk about business makes me wonder what we'd find if we looked over Talbot's business accounts. There might be something to tip us off."

"We still don't know why he kept that separate bank account either."

"Let me call Ann to get access."

DERRICK and I were headed over to Talbot's engineering office when a call came in.

"Hello?"

"Mr. Luca?"

"Yes. Who's this?"

"Jimmy Reed. My wife and I are friends with the Talbots. We spoke at the tennis club."

I struggled to put a face to the name. "Oh, yes. I remember. What was your wife's name again?"

"Connie."

"Right. What can I do for you?"

"Well, it might be nothing, but I remembered something, and when I told Connie, she said I should tell you."

"What did you recall?"

"It was about six weeks ago. I can probably get the exact date because he was late for a match, and John is never late."

Why did so many witnesses need to be kept on track? "Tell me what happened."

"When John finally arrived, he was flustered. I asked him what was wrong, and he said he was involved in an accident."

"A car accident?"

"Yeah. He wasn't hurt or anything, and he said his car wasn't damaged, just a tiny scratch on the bumper."

"Why was he upset?"

"Because the other vehicle was a Lamborghini, and the

driver went off on John. He said the guy was very intimidating. He thought he was some kind of drug dealer, and John was scared."

"Did this person threaten him?"

"John wanted to call the police to report the accident, but the guy flipped out on him. He said he didn't want the police involved, and he'd kill him if he called them."

Maybe this person was carrying drugs and was known to authorities. "Sounds like a prince of a guy. I'm guessing Talbot didn't report it."

"Not that I know."

"Any chance he said anything about getting the guy's license plate number?"

"He didn't say."

"What color Lamborghini?"

"I'm pretty sure he said white."

"What kind of damage did Talbot do this guy's car?"

"He creased the side of it."

I'd seen criminals kill people over dirtying their sneakers. This could be another murder over a car accident.

I quickly made two calculations: the cost to fix the Lamborghini was probably ten grand, and the number of white Lamborghinis in the county had to be under a dozen.

35

HANGING UP, I SAID, "DERRICK, YOU GOT ANYONE AT THE DMV that would run a quick report?"

"Depends how detailed. What's up?"

"Talbot was in a car accident with someone driving a Lamborghini. According to what he told one of his friends, the guy was some kind of thug and threatened to kill him if he called the cops."

"People are frigging crazy. What are we looking for?"

"A white Lamborghini. See how many are in the county and if we can get a registration list."

"Okay, I think Manny Sokol can help us."

"Great."

I punched a number into my cell.

"Hello, Frank."

"Hi, Ann. Look, I learned that your husband was in a minor car accident a couple of weeks before he disappeared. What can you tell me about it?"

"It wasn't a big deal. John's car had no damage, and he didn't report it to the insurance company. John said he was going to pay to fix the other car."

"Did he say anything about the other driver?"

"Just that he was angry. John said it was an expensive Italian car. Not a Ferrari, the other one—"

"Lamborghini?"

"Yes. You don't see many of them on the road."

That was true, but it had nothing to do with the three-hundred-thousand-dollar price tag. The old, rich guys simply couldn't get in and out of them.

"And John never said anything more about it?"

"No. Just the guy was going to get an estimate, and since it was John's fault, he'd pay for the damages."

"He ever mention when or how he was paying this person?"

"No."

"We went through your financial records and didn't come across anything like that."

"I don't know, that's strange, but maybe the other driver never got back to John."

That didn't seem realistic, unless the driver took what was owed in blood.

BRIAN BLADE LOOKED like he'd aged since our first meeting. The reality that his boss wasn't coming back had sunk in. I had ruled him out, as by all accounts they had an excellent relationship, and there wasn't a motive. Blade didn't have the degrees or license to operate the firm, and the client base was made up of contacts Talbot had developed over the years.

After shaking hands, he said, "I still can't believe we don't know what happened to John."

"We're working on it." I didn't want to tell him his boss

had started the mystery by lying about which flight he took back to Fort Myers.

"This goes on any longer, I don't know how we'll be able to keep this place going."

It was another example that the actions of one person barreled into others. I'm sure Blade had thought of things that could go wrong but never considered his employer vanishing.

"I'm sorry."

"Me too. You can use that desk." He pointed to a secretary desk piled with ledgers. "I pulled the month-end reports for the last year and the bank statements as well."

"Thanks."

"I'll log you on."

"That'd be great. I know Mr. Talbot had at least one private bank account at Florida Integrity that listed this office as the address of record. Can you get those records as well?"

"I didn't know that, and I've never seen a statement from Florida Integrity."

"I guess he went paperless."

"Probably. Who wouldn't these days?"

Me for one. I banked online, but I still had statements mailed to me. If the world crashed from a hacker or some event in space, I wanted hard proof of my assets.

"Let me ask you something. Did John ever mention anything about a car accident he had?"

"No. I never saw anything wrong with his car, and we park next to each other most days."

"Okay. Let me get to work."

The first thing I wanted to look for was a payment that could be for the damaged Lamborghini. Unless Talbot had a hidden account somewhere, his business one was the last place it could have come from.

I started at the beginning of the year and worked my way

forward. I scanned the payees and amounts. My eyes drifted to a nine-thousand-dollar payment. The payee said Colby. It could be the other driver's name. I clicked to see the check. The full name was Colby Structural, but Talbot could have disguised the payee. I jotted the details down.

On February 4, a payment for fourteen thousand caught my eye. It was made out to cash. This had to be it. I wanted to see who endorsed the check, but the back of the check wasn't available online. I looked through the stack of envelopes containing bank statements but couldn't find the one from February.

"Excuse me, Mr. Blade."

"Yes? You need something?"

"I can't seem to locate a hard copy of February's bank statement."

He pawed through the same pile I had gone through. "Hm. Maybe Melissa put it in John's office."

I followed him into Talbot's office. A tray on the corner of the desk was filled with mail. Blade picked up the bundle. "Most of this is personal. Oh, this has to be it."

He handed me an envelope postmarked March 8.

"Great. I'd like to take a look at what came in the mail for him. You never know."

"Sure." He handed me the bundle and left the office.

I tore open the envelope and took out a pile of checks. Holding them like a deck of cards, I placed them down one by one. A third of the way through I found what I was looking for. I paused before turning the fourteen-thousand-dollar check over.

It was endorsed by Talbot himself. There didn't seem to be any way to trace who the money ultimately went to. I sat back wondering if the driver had accompanied Talbot to the bank. If so, the bank's surveillance system could help identify the man.

Noting the date it was cashed, I thumbed through the other checks. Nothing stood out. Trying to think of a way to ID the Lamborghini driver, my eyes drifted to the pile of mail, and I rifled through it. There was a piece from Spice Publications. Figuring it was an invoice for a magazine subscription, I opened it.

I was wrong, but that wasn't what shocked me.

36

———

I was looking at an invoice for a classified ad in *Cuter When Cuffed*. There was no way it concerned engineering services. So what kind of an ad had Talbot paid for?

This was a touchy subject. I didn't want to tarnish Talbot, who was likely dead, but sexual exploration of this kind had to be looked into. Besides finding out the details of the ad itself, I needed to know if this was a one-off thing or something regular.

I walked to Blade, wondering if the pain in my gut was related or from the gallstones. "I hate to bother you again, but where do you keep the backup for bills that you've paid?"

He pointed to a row of filing cabinets. "They're filed alphabetically. Each drawer is marked. You looking for anything in particular?"

"Just want to check one of two. I got it, thanks."

I opened up a drawer marked M, dug out a folder, rummaged through it, and put it back. Two drawers lower was the target. Sliding it open, I felt weird, almost like a Peeping Tom. There was no folder labeled Spice. I found what I was looking for in the miscellaneous file: two other invoices, one from last year in December, and another in January of this year. Talbot had advertised for three months in a row. But for what? I took the check numbers written on the paid invoices and pulled them. All checks had Silverman in the note section.

I made copies of them and of the check made out to cash and resumed examining the rest of the records. An hour later, I thanked Blade and left with more questions than I'd bargained for.

ELBOWS ON THE TABLE, I wasn't in the mood to eat. My belly was killing me. I was hoping it was the gallstones.

"Dad, you all right?"

"Yeah, stomach is a little upset. But it'll be okay."

"You sure, Frank? You look pale."

I bolted out of my chair and ran to the bathroom. I hugged the bowl and vomited. The pain dissipated somewhat.

"Frank, let's go to the hospital."

"No! I'm fine. Just leave me alone."

"Daddy, why don't we go to one of those emergency clinics?"

"I'm okay, hon." I got off the floor and turned the sink on. "Go finish eating. I'm going to lie down for a minute."

I changed positions on the couch trying to get comfortable. Mary Ann opened a slider. "How you feeling?"

"Better."

"How much better?"

"At least fifty percent. Maybe I passed a stone."

"Why don't we go to a walk-in?"

"It's just the gallstone thing."

She lowered her voice. "With your history, we can't take

a chance."

"I know. It's not related. Finish dinner, save me something for later."

I wasn't the only one living in fear that my cancer would return. Anytime a serious illness hit someone, the entire family was affected. We were just one of millions of families facing health issues, but my goal was to avoid stressing out Mary Ann, which could cause her MS to flare up.

Not wanting Jessie to worry, I got off the couch and sat at the kitchen table. I didn't want to risk grabbing my laptop, so I used my phone. I opened my email, and there was one from Derrick.

The subject was Lamborghini. I clicked open the attachment, and a spreadsheet from the DMV opened. Scanning it, I noted there were eleven white ones in Collier County, raising my spirits.

I went straight for the registrant column. No surprise, they were all male. I clicked on the first name, Robert Johnson, and his driver's license record appeared. The guy was seventy-one. I hit the browser's back button.

Though it was something I expected, it was disappointing that there wasn't an owner under seventy. The driver could have come from Lee County, or more likely, given the possible drug connection, Miami.

Who knew how many Lamborghinis were tooling around in Miami? Whatever the number, it was bound to be a multiple of what we had in Collier. Googling the number of used ones on the market in Miami, Jessie came off the lanai. "How you feeling, Dad?"

"Much better. It was a stone. When you pass them, it can be painful, but it's not dangerous."

"You should still get it checked."

"I will."

"You want to eat now?"

I didn't want to, but said, "Sure, thanks."

I hit the search icon. There were sixty-two used Lamborghinis for sale. As I contemplated how it could translate into the number of white ones, Jessie set a plate and cutlery in front of me.

"Thanks, honey."

"Enjoy. I'm going to take a shower."

Mary Ann came in with an armful of dishes. I rose to help her, and she said, "Stay put, I got it. You feeling better?"

"Yeah. What do you know about bondage and submission?"

Mary Ann looked as if I'd levitated. "The sex stuff?"

"Yeah, I'm not sure what was going on, but Talbot was placing ads in one of those magazines."

"From what I know, it's an underground thing. Is his wife into it?"

"I don't know for sure, but I don't think so."

"He might have been looking for a partner."

Talbot was married to a Victoria's Secret model. If he was advertising for a woman to have sex with, he had bigger problems than I could solve.

"You know anyone in the sex-crimes unit that owes you a favor?"

"What kind of a favor?"

"I hate to admit it, but I don't know yet. We need to know what the ad was for. Someone may be out there preying on people who put ads in. Who knows? There could be other missing or dead people who placed ads."

"A serial killer who gets his victims from a BSDM magazine?"

"Why not? I'm sure people keep that kind of behavior secret."

37

Between the dull pain in my gut and trying to figure out how to tell Ann about the classified ad, I didn't get much sleep. I drove down her street. The Park Shore neighborhood was starting to grow on me. We'd never be able to afford living here unless the private investigation business exploded.

When she opened the door, I was afraid to step into the house. "I was reading by the pool." Barefoot, her bright red bikini revealed too much of her fine china. "I thought you were Marilyn. She was supposed to stop by."

I stared at my shoes.

"Come on in."

She closed the door behind me, and a sharp pain hit my belly. I gasped.

"What's the matter?"

"Gallstones."

She reached for my stomach, and I backed away. "I'm okay. It's passing."

"You sure?"

I nodded. "Yes. I have something to discuss with you."

"Let me throw something on. Feel free to sit outside if you'd like."

I hit the lanai before she left the room. The yard was simple but nice—a rectangular pool, bordered by a low hedge. The sound of water flowing from the spa into the pool calmed my nerves.

As I pulled a chair away from a dining table, Ann came out. She wore a silky robe, red, naturally, and was tying a bow with its belt. "Would you like anything?"

"No, ma'am."

"Ann, please call me Ann."

"Okay. Look, I'm not sure how to say this, so, I'll just come right out with it."

Her face crumpled as she grabbed the back of a chair. "You . . . found—"

"No. Something different."

"Thank God."

I wasn't so sure she'd say that after I told her. "Maybe you know about this, but your husband was placing classified ads in a bondage and submission magazine called *Cuter When Cuffed.*"

Her face pinched up. "You mean, like being tied up when you have sex?"

"Something along those lines."

"But why?"

"I was hoping you'd shed light on it."

"I'm . . . trying to process this. Was he looking for a partner?"

"We don't know. I need your help getting the details from the publisher. They won't give me any information because of privacy laws."

"Okay."

"I wouldn't ask if I didn't think it could help the investigation."

"I understand. What do you want me to do?"

"You're going to need an attorney to represent you and contact them. They'll know how to frame the request. I assume you have a lawyer you can reach out to."

"We do, but . . ."

"I know it's delicate, but they're legally bound to keep whatever it is confidential."

Her eyes welled up. I wanted to run. "It's going to be all right. I can recommend someone if you'd like."

She shook her head. "That won't be necessary."

My phone rang. It was Derrick. "I've got to get this. It's another thread we're following."

"That's okay."

I answered, telling Derrick to hang on, and left Ann sitting at the table. I felt bad for her. The news unsettled her.

I closed the door behind me and said, "You got some timing, pal. You saved me."

"What's going on?"

"Ann took the bondage news hard."

"Who wouldn't be shocked?"

"And disgusted. What's happening?"

"I did some digging into Livermore, like you asked. You'll never guess what I found."

I let the guessing crap pass because he saved my ass with the call. "I got no idea."

"What are the chances two guys fall off a boat?"

"Spit it out, bro."

"One of Livermore's old neighbors, guy named Gunther, ended up in the water just like Talbot did. And it was a guy he sued a couple of years before."

"What was the beef about?"

"Property lines. The guy had one of those concrete pool

enclosures, and one side encroached on Livermore's property. Nobody knew it until Livermore wanted to put a pool in and the survey revealed it. The neighbor refused to do anything, and Livermore couldn't go forward with the pool."

"But how could he get away with not doing it?"

"It had been there for years, and since it was never challenged, it essentially became the neighbor's property."

"Yeah, right, I've heard that before. It's some version of squatting."

"I don't think that's what they call it."

"I'm pretty sure the legal term is adverse possession, but it doesn't matter. How long after the court case did the incident happen?"

"About two months."

"Any witnesses?"

"Just Livermore and Gunther."

"I don't like Livermore. The bastard thinks he's smarter than everyone else."

"It's a pretty good way to get rid of someone. No witnesses, no DNA traces, maybe not even a body if he weighed it down."

"In the incident with Talbot, there was a witness. Another one of their friends, George Slater, was on board. He's the one who told me."

"If he could fool the witness, it would strengthen the cause as an accident."

"It bothered me, but now, with another one, Livermore just elevated himself to the lead suspect."

"You want to go see him?"

"Not yet. I'd like you to sniff around his workplace a bit more. Make it known. Maybe we'll force Livermore to make a mistake."

"I'm on it."

I TORE open the envelope I picked up from Florida Integrity Bank.

Taking out a thumb drive, I plugged it into my desktop. Navigating to the day Talbot cashed the fourteen-thousand-dollar check, I clicked to see the bank's entrance video.

The quality of the surveillance was excellent, as it should be. The branch opened at ten, and a dozen seniors, who'd probably been waiting outside for thirty minutes, streamed into the bank.

I fast-forwarded, stopping when I saw a figure entering the bank. The increase in online banking kept the cyber-crime unit active and reduced in-person visits, making surveillance easier.

After a minor rush during lunchtime faded, I sped the tape up. I hit pause when I saw two men entering. The time stamp was 1:28. Zooming in on the image, my heart raced. It was Talbot. The other man was both larger and younger. Who was he?

38

———

I HIT PLAY. TALBOT AND THE MYSTERY MAN WALKED IN. They waited in the teller line but didn't appear to talk to each other. The mystery man put a phone to his ear and left the line.

Talbot went to a teller. From behind, I could see him put the small bag he was carrying on the counter. Two minutes later, he turned around and walked out of the bank. A minute later the mystery man also left the bank.

I jotted down the times, went back to the menu, and clicked to open the parking lot video. Talbot walked to his white Genesis parked a few spaces away from the entrance. The mystery man walked toward the far end of the parking lot. He appeared to give a thumbs-up to someone before disappearing off the screen.

Talbot backed out and headed in the direction the mystery man went. He stopped where the man vanished. The rear end of Talbot's vehicle was visible. After a minute, Talbot backed out and left the lot.

I replayed the footage, slowing it down to a crawl. There was another man, one in a baseball cap, standing next to a black Escalade. He didn't move but looked in the direction of mystery man when he exited the bank.

Zooming in on the unknown man who came into the bank with Talbot, I noticed he had a goatee and what looked like an earring. Wearing oversized sunglasses, he was dressed in white and appeared muscular. I pegged him as six feet and a hundred and ninety pounds.

Running a private investigation meant I had no lab to enhance a picture of the man who might have killed Talbot. We also had no access to a facial recognition database or software to identify the man.

Derrick was miles better in the tech area than I was. I'd ask him to clip a couple of pictures from the video. There were plenty of professional photographers in Naples, and we'd get them to help make a picture we could pass around to try to ID the man.

I WAS JUST ABOUT to hang up when Derrick said, "I forgot to ask you, what's going on with getting the ad copy?"

"Haven't heard from Talbot's wife. Let me call her now. I'll talk to you later."

"Hello, Mrs. Tal, uh, Ann. How are you?"

"Okay, Frank."

"I'm just checking on where you're at with the lawyer and the magazine."

"Oh. You know, I'm not sure."

"Why don't you give him a call. I'd like to see what this is about."

"Do you really think it's worth it?"

"Yeah, you never know."

"With all due respect, Frank, it seems like a waste of time, a wild-goose chase."

"Not necessarily. It may open a new line of inquiry."

"I doubt it. Look, I'm sorry, but I'm meeting someone and have to run."

I hung up and replayed the conversation. Something was going on. Ann was usually bottled sunshine and now she was just okay? And why the sudden disinterest in finding out what the ad was about?

Was it sinking in that her husband had a secret and wasn't coming back? Or was she trying to hide something? Maybe she knew about his deviant tendencies, or she was into it as well. The most important question was whether it was related to his disappearance and she needed to protect the information.

The last thing I wanted to do was keep an eye on Ann Talbot, but I had no choice. I couldn't move the case forward if I didn't know if my client was involved.

Saying goodbye to Mary Ann, I hopped into the Escape. One of the reasons I used for a leave of absence had been by working from home I could keep an eye on my wife. I'd make sure she avoided stressful situations that were bad for her MS. But the reality was I wasn't home much more than I used to be working for the sheriff.

It was 11:15 a.m. when I turned onto Willowhead Drive. Half a dozen cars were parked outside of the house two doors down. Thankful someone was having a get-together, I pulled behind a green SUV, pulled a Red Sox cap on, and kept my eyes on Talbot's home.

Where was Ann Talbot going? Was she having another affair? Had Tony Desmond weaseled his way back into her bed? Maybe she wasn't going anywhere; someone could be coming to see her.

The sun was heating up the left side of my face. Leaning

away, I dialed up the air as a tan Volvo turned onto the block. I watched it go up Talbot's driveway, trying to recall what car Desmond drove.

A woman in a long skirt got out and approached the door. Before she got there, Ann opened it. The first thing that hit me was her dark pantsuit. My client wore red almost every time I saw her.

The two women embraced and stayed that way for a full minute. It appeared they hadn't seen each other in a long time. Maybe the woman was family. They disappeared inside. Was Ann hosting a luncheon?

I called Mary Ann to burn time and then Derrick.

"Hey, what's going on?"

"Sitting outside Talbot's house. How about you?"

"Been talking to a few of Livermore's colleagues."

"Anything come of it?"

"He's not exactly the most likable guy, but nothing more. Hey, looks like we got a line on the insurance scam."

"What do you got?"

"Just got a call from Naples Jewelers in Pavilion. He said a man who said his name was George White dropped off a diamond that matches the serial number of the Tiffany stone."

"I can't believe it. He's looking to fence it?"

"No, the guy wanted him to make a necklace out of it."

"The balls on this guy."

"I know. I'm heading down there to show them a picture, make sure it's Moses Green."

"Good."

"What's going on there?"

"Zippo. Some woman just went inside, but I think I'm going to take off."

"All right, I'll see—"

"Let me go, they're coming out of the house."

39

I FOLLOWED THE VOLVO ONTO BELAIR DRIVE. WHEN IT MADE a right onto Neapolitan Way, I figured they were heading onto Route 41. Though the women were dressed conservatively, I couldn't stop thinking they could be going to some sort of sexual encounter.

Surprised as they made a quick left onto West Boulevard, I stayed a quarter mile behind. The possibility they were going to lunch somewhere loomed large, but why pass up spots in Venetian Village with killer views?

Stopped at the light on Seagate Drive, the destinations were endless. I was betting it would be Waterside Shops. When two girlfriends, especially those with means, got together, there was a 50 percent chance shopping was involved.

The light turned green, and the Volvo made a left, away from Waterside Shops, and then a puzzling right turn. I passed them and made the next right, circling the block into the parking lot's rear entrance.

Ann and her friend got out and walked into St. Williams Church as the bells tolled. They were going to midday Mass.

I waited a minute, then followed a man with a walker to the entrance.

Waiting for the man to make his way in, I noticed a sign on an easel proclaiming today as the Feast of St. Anthony of Padua. I knew people prayed to St. Anthony when they'd lost something and went over to the display.

Reading a short paragraph, I learned St. Anthony was also the patron saint for missing persons. I picked up a card with a prayer for the missing and recited it. As music began playing, I left, hoping the collective prayers of those inside would work.

As soon as I got home, I went straight to the fridge. I'd remembered there was a tray of leftover zucchini and a turkey burger I'd grilled for dinner last night. Mary Ann came into the kitchen as I popped the dish into the microwave. She was towel drying her hair.

"Hey, you took a shower?"

"Yeah, the chlorine is killing my hair."

"Maybe we should get one of those salt systems for the pool."

"It'd be nice, but I think they cost two thousand dollars."

"I know, but you're swimming every day, and chlorine is not good."

"Let's see how things go with the business first."

Did she realize she was putting pressure on me? "I'll start making calls and see what the numbers look like. You want some leftovers?"

"No, I'll make a salad. Let's eat outside, it's perfect out."

We settled around the lanai's dining table. I speared a sliver of zucchini. "You'll never guess where I followed Ann Talbot to."

"You're tailing the client?"

"It's kind of a long story, but I have some doubts about her."

"The 'Always look to the spouse' protocol."

"Yeah. Her and a friend went to Mass this afternoon."

"That's nice."

"It's St. Anthony's Day. I knew you prayed to him when you lost something, but he's also the patron saint for missing persons."

"You didn't know that?"

"No. I'm telling you, this tastes better than last night."

"It soaked up all the juices."

"Amen to that."

"That's not funny."

"Do you believe in praying to a saint?"

"Why? Don't you?"

I shrugged and shoved a piece of burger in my mouth.

"Praying to a saint amplifies your request to God. It's like asking a friend that knows somebody you need for a favor."

I got the way it was supposed to work, and I guess it never hurt to have a saint asking God for help, but I was skeptical. "Why couldn't God just hear you?"

"It's not exactly the same, but remember the story you told me about your hearing? I'm sure you and your mother were praying for help, but it took going to a special priest at a healing mass to fix it."

She had a point, but I'd prayed my cancer wasn't as bad as they said it could be, and it was. Then I prayed it would go away, and it didn't. Then I prayed Mary Ann's MS would disappear. "It did seem to work that time, but other times . . ."

"Our prayers were answered with Jessica, weren't they? She is healthy and perfect."

"Amen."

MARY ANN DIDN'T LIKE TAKING the shells off shrimp. The frozen ones we bought at Costco were hit-and-miss it seemed. Sometimes they'd come right off, others you'd lose half the meat removing the shell.

Working the last one off, my phone rang. It was Derrick. I dropped the shrimp on top of the others in the strainer, rinsed my hands, and answered.

"Frank, you got a minute?"

Wiping my free hand on my pants, I said, "Sure, what's up?"

"Two things, one is Naples Jeweler said it was Moses Green who dropped off the diamond."

"Good work. Let Gesso know when he's going to pick it up, and they'll nab his ass. What else?"

"Livermore."

"What about him?"

"I don't think he's our guy."

I rinsed the shrimp and put them in a Tupperware container. "Why is that?"

"The trip. He told one of the secretaries that he was going a week before."

"Is she a hundred percent positive about the time frame?"

"Yep, she remembered because it was her last day before she went on vacation for two weeks. By the time she got back, Talbot was already missing."

Sliding the container into the fridge, I said, "Are we sure about this?"

"Yes. I even checked with one of her coworkers. She verified the dates."

"Damn. But good work, Derrick. I don't like to say it, but

I wish we would have found something on Livermore. He's a bastard, in my opinion."

"You're not alone, bro. Sleeping with your buddy's wife? How low can you go?"

"You ain't kidding."

"What happened with watching Ann Talbot?"

I filled Derrick in on following her to St. Williams Church, and another call came in. "Speaking of the devil, that's Ann Talbot buzzing in now. Let me go."

"Hello, Mrs. Talbot."

"Hi, Frank."

"What's going on?"

"I wanted to let you know that my lawyer will have copies of the ads in the morning."

"Oh, that's good. I know it was, uh, uncomfortable for you, and I'm sorry I had to ask."

"No need to apologize. We all need to know what he was doing."

40

"DAD, UNCLE DERRICK IS HERE."

Mary Ann looked at me over the top of her coffee mug. "I guess you want me to take Jessica to school this morning?"

I got up. "If you don't mind. We got kind of a big morning."

"Sure." She smiled. "How are you, Derrick?"

"Good morning." He kissed Mary Ann's cheek.

"Grab a cup and let's go to the office. Have a good day at school, Jessie."

Walking to the den, Derrick said, "Totally different vibe in your house. I can't imagine sending my baby off to school."

"It's scary at first, but don't worry."

"Oh, it's too late, I already am."

"That's another thing we have in common, buddy."

"What's your gut telling you about the ads?"

"Even though I'm leaning that Ann isn't involved, in the back of my mind I got a bad feeling the two of them might have been looking for some twisted BDSM swinger thing."

"It doesn't fit. She's had affairs that seem normal."

"We don't know that." But we should have. Why hadn't I dug around Livermore and Desmond to see if there was anything there?

"I wasn't looking for it, but nothing anybody said about Livermore was out of the mainstream."

"Most people would keep this type of stuff away from the office."

"True. I think this guy had some fetish but didn't want his wife to know. I mean, you wouldn't want to turn off a woman like her."

"Can you imagine if Ann couldn't get him going? He'd have to be dead down there."

"Agreed, but I hate to tell you, there's plenty of people who can only get their rocks off doing something weird."

"Keeps the sex toy industry going."

"How about those piercings?"

"Ew, I can't even imagine—" I reached for my phone. "It's her."

"Hello, Ann, how are you?"

"I've had better days."

"I'm sorry about all this."

"Not as sorry as I am."

"Was the lawyer able to obtain the ad copy?"

"Yeah, I don't want to discuss this. It's extremely upsetting."

"I'm really sorry."

"Promise me you won't share this with anyone."

"You have my word. I will only use it to inform the investigation."

"Thank you. I'll email the file over. It's protected by a password. I'll text you the code to open it."

"Okay. Thanks, and I'm sorry about this whole thing."

I hung up. "I feel so bad for her. She's sending the file over by email. It needs a password."

"It's a tough thing to learn about your spouse."

I kept my eyes glued to the in-box. A ping sounded and there it was. I opened the email. Ann hadn't written a word of text. My finger hovered over the attachment. What was inside? I dropped my finger and a dialogue box opened.

It needed a password. I grabbed my phone, checking my texts. There it was. I plugged in the code, and a cover letter from her attorney opened. It was brief, referring to four documents enclosed. I scrolled to the next page.

"Derrick, take a look at this."

I read it again. Derrick peered over my shoulder, saying, "This is crazy."

Fit, intelligent and brave fifty-year-old, seeking woman who will claim and collar me. 239-044-1234 John Silverman

A vision of a nude man on a leash and on all fours popped into my head. "He's using Silverman as an alias. Let's see what other surprises await."

The next ad was worse.

Handsome male, will submit mind and body, willing to do everything and anything to please my Mistress. 239-004-1234 John Silverman

"This guy is frigging nuts."

"I sure as shit don't want to know what everything and anything is."

"People get their rocks off doing this crazy shit?"

Instead of answering, I moved to the next classified.

Submissive, white male, attractive and loyal, would enjoy being leashed, collared and owned by a Mistress. 239-004-1234 John Silverman

There was that picture of a man playing dog again in the back in my mind. "Let's see what the last one looks like."

Trim, white male looking to be collared and please his dominant Mistress. Anything she wants to do, I will. I like it rough. 239-004-1234 John Silverman

It was more of the same. Processing what we had, Derrick said, "You think this is connected to his disappearance?"

"It certainly could be. I don't know enough about this submissive sex stuff, but maybe one of their sex games went wrong, and Talbot ended up dead, or there was fear he or his partner would be revealed, or maybe somebody refused to play a role, and things escalated."

"Did you see *Fifty Shades of Grey*?"

"No, I don't watch that crap."

"Me neither, but I heard it had a lot of bondage in it."

"We need to understand this stuff, what drives people like Talbot, what these relationships look like."

"There has to be a ton of stuff on the internet."

"I'm sure there is." I picked up my car keys. "I might know somebody that can bring me up to speed. You're welcome to stay here, but if you want to do your research at home, go for it."

"I think I will."

"Okay. We'll talk later." I headed out the door before Derrick could ask me who I was going to see.

I struggled to keep a flood of disturbing images out of my head. People did what they wanted. Just because I thought it was strange and unsettling, they had a right to get their sexual pleasure any way they wanted. The key being if it was consensual.

There were plenty of sex crimes on the books, and there were cases where dominant role-playing had resulted in injuries and death. The legal system didn't care if it was consensual or not. If bodily harm took place, charges were going to be filed.

Turning onto Hibiscus Lane brought me back in time. Dr. Bruno had helped me through some difficult times. It was fifty-fifty whether I'd be a father if I hadn't talked with her.

Life is funny that way; I'd resisted talking to a head shrink. I didn't think they worked, and I can say it now, I was afraid of the stigma. It was stupid, especially the stigma part. People needed help with their mental health, and we needed to support them in getting it.

Society needed to treat a mental issue the same way they did a physical illness. There was no shame in getting cancer, and there shouldn't be any with mental illness.

41

———————

Dr. Bruno looked ten years younger dressed in jeans. She had a serious look on her face.

"Hi, Doc. Don't worry, everything's good. I'm doing fine."

"Glad to hear that. What's the nature of the visit?"

"I'm working a case and needed some background information on, uh, a certain behavior. I know I should've called, but I remembered you didn't have office hours on Wednesday."

"I see."

"I'd appreciate the professional courtesy if you can give me a couple of minutes. I'll pay your normal rate, no problem."

"No more than half an hour, okay?"

"Sure."

She stepped aside, and we settled into the same gray club chairs that we discussed Derrick's shooting in.

"Tell me how I can help?"

"This is a touchy subject, kind of embarrassing, actually."

"There's nothing that anyone should be embarrassed over."

I could come up with a list but said, "Tell me what you know about people, focusing on men who engage in submissive behavior, particularly sex acts."

Bruno didn't flinch. "A submissive person has a service-oriented personality. They willingly submit to the authority of another. It's easier for them to take direction than to make decisions."

"Anything else?"

"They enjoy pleasing others. When something goes wrong, they assume it was their fault and work to correct whatever transpired."

"What about in a male-female sexual relationship?"

"It's important to note, in healthy relationships, where one is consensually in charge, the submissive partner does not feel threatened as to their value as a person. They are equal but have decided to give decision-making to one partner."

"If someone is submissive, are they that way in all their relationships?"

"It's a strong personality trait."

"My case involves a sexually submissive man who actively seeks to be dominated by women. Why would he do it?"

"There could be a myriad of reasons, but he may enjoy a helpless role as a form of escapism. He would have no responsibilities other than following the wishes of a dominant woman."

"Any other reasons?"

"The feeling of being under the power of a strong, controlling person may evoke feelings of the safety and protection he felt as a child."

"It goes way beyond that, Doc. This man is placing ads

looking for someone to do anything and everything to him. He said he likes it rough."

"He may be a sadomasochist, using pain, often extreme pain, as a sexual stimulant."

"Pain? What's this world coming to?"

"It's been around for a long time, going back to ancient Egypt. It used to be considered a sign of mental illness, but today, as long as it's consensual, it's not considered a psychological problem."

"Geez, we're normalizing everything these days."

"Well, keep in mind there are different classes of sadomasochism. A class one is someone who has fantasies but doesn't act on them. Class two involves some pain, but it's not necessary to achieve an orgasm. Where it gets complicated is where pain or humiliation is vital to have an orgasm, like classes three and four, the important distinction being that class threes are able to have a romantic attachment, where the next class of people are unable to form romantic relationships."

"So, it's all about the need for pain to satisfy themselves sexually?"

"That's an oversimplification."

"How the heck does someone get this way? Are they born like that?"

"No. Most of us in the field believe that experiences in early sexual development can have a large effect on a person's sexuality. However, a lot of these, uhm, desires, can develop at any age. Some have these tendencies before puberty, but others discover them well into adulthood."

I was good at keeping a poker face, but hearing that shocked me. It must have shown, as Bruno said, "I have to end this. I have a hair appointment."

"How much do I owe you?"

"Payment is not necessary."

Thanking her, I made a mental note to send her a check covering her normal fee. It was not only the right thing to do, but it was almost guaranteed I'd need Dr. Bruno either professionally or personally in the future.

A weird feeling of dizziness hit me as I sat in my car, gripping the steering wheel. Had I lost my center? My willpower and moral lines were as hard as anyone's, but I was human. I was as susceptible as the next person to things like addiction and acquiring unusual behaviors.

During my career, I'd seen too many murders, drug dealing, and thefts, but not once had I worried that I might cross over to a life of crime. This was different, but was it contagious?

I forced myself to think of the job I was being paid to do. It was my responsibility as a professional to look at the facts and keep emotion out of it. It wasn't about me; it was about John Talbot.

Pulling out of her driveway, I had to quell the urge to go straight to see Ann. Was that the best tactic? As uncomfortable as it was, questioning her on the sexual nature of her relationship with her husband was important.

I parked at the top of the street and thought it over. There was no doubt—whatever they did was private. It was also clear that clarifying if sex played a role, it would go a long way into defining the balance of the investigation.

In solving a homicide, the who, where, and how played large roles. We had no *where* to work with. Without a body, we had no *how*. The sexual angle might point us in the *how* direction while revealing more on just *who* John Talbot was.

How was I going to start this discussion? I've had my share of uncomfortable conversations, but this had to top the list. There was no way out. I had to do it. I put the car in drive and drove as slowly as I could.

42

I HIT THE BELL HOPING ANN WASN'T HOME. THE SOUND faded and my hopes rose. Rather than ring it again, I turned on my heels. Before my foot hit the ground, the door swung open.

"Sorry, Frank. I was in the little girl's room."

She looked different. No makeup and looking tired. "Oh, that's okay. If you're busy, I can come back another time."

"No, come in. I'm just reading."

Instead of a red dress, she had on jeans and a T-shirt with a picture of the Colosseum on it. "You sure?"

"Absolutely."

I stepped into the foyer.

"Are you here about the ads?"

She was braver than me. I nodded. "I'm sorry, but it might lead us somewhere."

"I understand."

"This is not the easiest stuff to talk about."

"No, it's not, but as much as I try, I can't accept something like this."

"I'm sorry."

"It's not your fault. John's the one who . . . forget it. Let's sit here."

We took chairs around a glass-topped kitchen table.

"Please don't take offense at any of this. I just want to get to the truth."

"I'll try not to. Go ahead."

"You and others described your husband as a people pleaser. Was he always like that?"

"When we met, John was successful and kind of the go-to guy. But as time went on, he was under a lot of stress and began to dislike responsibility. When I'd talk to him about social events, he'd say, 'Make a decision and tell me where I have to be.'"

"He was sick of being in charge?"

"He has a very demanding job; everyone depends on him."

Instead of saying he should hire a damn assistant, I said, "When did he start to feel overwhelmed?"

"I'd say it's about ten years now."

"Did you know of your husband's, uh, tendencies?"

"Assuming you're referring to his submissive sexual needs, the answer is no. I find it repulsive."

"How was your sex life with him?"

"It was good."

"Then why did you feel the need to go outside of your marriage?"

"It had nothing to do with it."

"Come on, Ann, I need you to be honest with me. What was going on?"

"It wasn't that it was bad, but John was having some ED problems. It happens to every man when they hit fifty."

Did she know what she was talking about because fifty

wasn't that far away? "These, uh, problems, did he ask you to do anything to, uh, help him along?"

"No, he was kind of embarrassed about it. I told him there was no need to be, but he'd close down and wouldn't want to talk about it."

"Did he ever ask you to engage in anything like BDSM?"

She flinched. "Bondage?"

"Yes, anything along those lines or anything out of the ordinary?"

"No. John was straightlaced."

Was had to be the operative word, otherwise she was living in an alternate universe. "Now, think about this before answering. And it does not have to be sexually related."

Ann blinked.

"Have you ever noticed any bruises on your husband? Something he may have made an excuse for?"

"Like he was hit or in a fight?"

"Yes. Maybe on his back or somewhere not easily visible?"

"No, nothing like that."

"Did John seem to take pleasure in receiving or causing pain?"

There was that flinch again. "Pain? I'm not sure I understand."

"I'm not sure, myself, how it works, but from what I'm told, some people enjoy inflicting or receiving pain, you know, sadistic or masochistic."

She shook her head. "No. No, that's not John, it can't be."

I wanted to ask her how he came to want to be collared, but either she was in denial or truly didn't know her husband's tendencies. Whether she admitted to it or not, I was forming the opinion she started having affairs when her husband went off in another sexual direction.

Talbot's secret orientation could be a rabbit hole we'd get lost in. But other than the fender bender with the Lamborghini, we had nothing else concrete to pursue.

———

As soon as I turned onto Park Shore Drive, I dialed Dr. Bilotti's number. "Hey, Doc, how are you?"

"Good, Frank. What's going on with the missing-man case?"

"Pretty sure it's a homicide now."

"Sorry to hear that. The sheriff's not involved?"

"No. There's nothing hard yet. I'm sure Chester doesn't want to leave with an open case."

"I'm hearing an announcement he's leaving may be coming soon."

"I told you he wanted me to come back."

"And you should. We need you."

"We'll see. Look, something came up in the case, and I wanted to bounce it off you."

"Sure. What do you have?"

"The missing man, his wife said he was having ED issues, but the guy is only fifty-three. How can that be?"

"He certainly could have. The general rule of thumb on dysfunction is about ten percent per decade. So about fifty percent of men who are in their fifties have issues, and sixty percent of sixty-year-olds."

"Really? That seems way high."

"It's pervasive and the reason why the little blue pill is so popular. You having any issues?"

"Me? No. I'm only asking because of the case. Say, we should get together and have a glass of vino or two."

"Anytime. I've been trying a bunch of wines from Ventoux. I think you'll like them."

"Where's that?"

"The Rhone Valley. Mostly Grenache, and they're wonderful buys."

"I like them already. I'll call you in a day or so."

Driving north on Route 41, I pondered the stats Bilotti recited. It wasn't a pretty picture. It was not an *if* but *when* I'd start having problems. To change the subject, I called Derrick.

"Hey, I just left Ann. She claims to be in the dark about her husband's freaky desires."

"Tell you what, I did a bunch of reading, and this crap makes me sick. I mean, some of these people got to be frigging crazy. I saw some pictures of people pouring hot wax on their private parts."

"What? Are you kidding?"

"Wish I was, bro. You think this has something to do with it?"

"We got to check it."

"You want to put an ad in mirroring what Talbot was looking for?"

"It's not a bad idea, but it'll take too long, and who knows if these people have some kind of code when they talk."

"True. What do you want to do?"

"Talbot put his cell number in the ads. You came up with a couple of calls, like the Bradshaw woman who may have responded."

"Yeah, you said the neighbor said she was kinky, but she's almost a vegetable."

"I know, but I was thinking he either had another cell phone or he made arrangements from his office. I'd like you to cross-check a month of outgoing calls from the office, see if any of those wrong numbers pop up."

"I'll head down there now."

"Thanks. I'm going to pick up the images of the mystery man at the bank. Maybe somebody will recognize him."

43

THE CLERK HELD OUT A FOLDER. "HERE YOU ARE, MR. Luca."

"Thanks." I emptied the file, spreading the photos on the counter. The pictures from the bank were good. I hoped the larger images would help identify the man who was at the bank the same time Talbot withdrew fourteen thousand in cash.

I picked up the third one, studying the man's face. Large sunglasses were always a good way to hide your face. If this guy was a thug, he'd worn them on purpose. But the guy was big. His broad shoulders and narrow waist were admirable, and I hoped it'd trigger something in someone's mind.

"Can you make me four copies of these two?"

"Sure. I'll need five, ten minutes max."

"Perfect. I'll be outside"

I stepped into a strong breeze and tapped my phone.

"Hello, Carla. This is Frank Luca, the detective friend of your mother's."

"Oh. Hi."

"I was just checking in to see how you were doing?"

"I'm doing good."

"Sarasota is nice, isn't it?"

"Yeah, I like it up here; there's more young people."

"That's good. How's things with your mother?"

"About the same."

"I know it's hard to forgive her, but she loves you; she really does."

"I know."

"Keep the lines of communication open. That's the smart thing to do."

"I'll try."

"Good. Okay, just wanted to check in with you."

"Thanks, and by the way, I know you're not a detective any longer."

"I used to be."

"Don't worry, I didn't say anything."

The kid was smarter than I thought. She'd be all right. "Thanks, I'll see you around."

I paid for the photos and hopped in my Escape.

TWO OF THE outdoor tables at the marina's café were occupied. The smell of espresso had me considering getting a cup before showing the picture around. It was 4 p.m. I couldn't take chances of ruining what little sleep I got.

"Excuse me, folks." Two men in shorts and boat shoes stopped chatting.

A guy in a T-shirt with a sailfish said, "What can we do for you?"

I held out three photos. "Any of you know this man?"

"What's this all about?"

"I can't say, but it's important we locate him."

"He do something wrong?"

"We think so."

"Who's we?"

This guy had to be a damn lawyer. "It was a hit and run. Took off on an old lady, and she was hurt."

He peered at the picture. "Bastard. I wish I knew who it was."

His friend said, "I've never seen him. This happen around here?"

"Yeah, thanks anyway."

I went to the next table, where a woman and man were just getting up. "Hold on a second." I offered the pictures. The woman didn't take one, but her partner did. "I'm looking to see if anyone knows this man. He was involved in an accident, nearly killed a woman, and took off."

The lady said, "That's terrible. How could he do something like that?"

"Do either of you recognize him?"

The man tilted his head. "He looks a little familiar, but I'm not sure."

She took the picture. "Let me see. You know, he reminds me of a guy I've seen at Campiello's a couple of times."

"He works there?"

"No, hangs out at the bar."

"How often you go there?"

"Not too much. It's not my favorite, but a friend likes to go there."

"By any chance, when you go, is it the same night of the week?"

"Not really. But I'm not sure it's him with the sunglasses."

"That's okay. I appreciate your help. Here's my card. If you see him, give me a call."

———

THERE WASN'T a parking spot open on Third Avenue because the early bird diners were out in force. Some people made fun of the older folks going out with their canes, but they were living their lives, and I liked seeing them having fun. Down here they went out as much as the young kids did, just at a different time.

The outdoor tables were all full, but the bar just had one customer, a guy whose hair was dyed so black it looked silly. A lone bartender was working the service bar and keeping his eye out for any clients. He nodded to me and scurried over.

"What can I get for you?"

"Just a seltzer, no lemon or lime."

He grabbed a glass and the soda gun, and I said, "You work nights?"

"Six days a week from four p.m. till closing."

He put down a glass, and I handed him a picture of the mystery man. "I understand this guy comes to the bar."

After a quick glance he put the image down. "I don't know."

I leaned in. "This guy pushed himself on a young woman. Don't protect the slimebag."

"He did what?"

"Girl filed a complaint a week ago. We're trying to track him down. What's his name?"

He looked both ways. "I think it's Bebe."

"Bebe? What is he, Israeli?"

"I don't know, I thought he was Spanish."

"How often is he in here?"

"Every now and then."

"When was the last time you saw him?"

"Tough to say, the bar is packed during season. Maybe a week ago."

"He pay his bar tab with a credit card?"

"No. He carries a big roll of cash with him."

"I know it puts you in a tough spot, but think of the women who come here. You wouldn't want anything to happen to them, would you?"

"Of course not."

I slid my card across the bar. "Call me when he's in. He'll never know who tipped me off."

He walked away, stuffing the card in his pocket. I sipped my seltzer. We had a line on the Lamborghini driver. It was just a matter of time before he'd show up. I drained the glass and left.

Walking to the car, my cell rang. It was Derrick. "Frank, you were right."

That wasn't news. "About what?"

"I checked the telephone calls on Talbot's cell to the ones on his office line, and two of them match."

44

———————

"WHAT DID YOU HAVE, COFFEE THIS AFTERNOON?"

"No. Why?"

"You're fidgety."

"It's the Talbot case. Looks like we've narrowed it down."

"That's good." She handed me a bag. "Use up some of your energy slicing the zucchini up."

Grilled zucchini was a favorite of mine, but I hated putting it on the barbecue. Pieces would always fall through the grate, creating a mess. I took a cutting board and a chopping knife to the lanai.

I concentrated on cutting the first one, making sure my fingers were a safe distance from the blade. Slicing the second piece of squash, my mind went back to the Talbot case. Thinking about the chances the Lamborghini man was a known criminal, Mary Ann stuck her head out. "You need anything?"

"Nope, I'm good."

I watched her through the slider, wondering how devastating the news was to Ann Talbot. It had to be a blow on many levels, not just their relationship, but on her personally. Though she did her best, I could tell she was horrified about her husband's sexual leanings.

If word got around . . . I put the knife down. Had she learned about it and got so disgusted she did the unthinkable? A divorce would accomplish it, but there was the money to deal with, and if there was a prenuptial agreement, she could have been cut out.

She could have tried extorting him, threatening to expose the secret, but that would get ugly and possibly ostracize her. Did she believe killing her husband, with his reputation intact, was the only way to end the nightmare?

Sliding slices of zucchini into an aluminum tray, I couldn't discount the possibility. On the surface, most people would dismiss it. They'd say, just divorce him, and why be embarrassed? She didn't do anything, he did.

What the naysayers didn't know was that secrets, of any kind, kill. I'd worked crazy cases: a husband killed to keep news of an affair from getting out; a teenager murdered someone who was about to reveal he was gay, and a cross-dresser strangled a coworker who found out about his fetish.

THE DOORBELL RANG. I picked up my coffee mug and said, "That's Derrick. I'm gonna need you to take Jessie to school."

"All right, but promise me you'll be careful."

"No problem."

I went to the door, wondering what she was concerned about. We were doing background on two women. Maybe she confused them with the slab of granite that drove the Lamborghini.

We sat across my desk. "Before we get going, I want to make sure we stay open to the possibility that Ann offed her old man to make sure nobody would find out what he was doing."

"It's a stretch, don't you think?"

"Not at all." I explained how she'd reacted and recounted homicide cases that had similar motives.

"I guess it's possible."

"Just tuck it in the back of your mind. All right, what do we have?"

"Lisa Tess, thirty-seven-year-old, lives in Kensington, and Dawn Hill, forty-one, who resides in Wyndemere."

He slid pictures to me. Tess was a brunette with short hair and a Dolly Parton bust. Hill was a blond and had a slight resemblance to Talbot's wife.

"What do they do for a living?"

"Tess is a dental hygienist. Hill owns one of those decorator places in the industrial park off Airport."

"Any of them have a record?"

"No, but Hill had a massage place in Tampa before moving to Naples six years ago."

"At least that fits. And both of them claimed the calls they made to Talbot were wrong numbers, right?"

"Yep. So we got them covering up."

"Maybe they weren't covering up. We asked them about calls to Talbot. But they probably knew him as Silverman. And he always used his real first name. We should have asked about calls to both Talbot and Silverman. It could be an honest mistake on their part or a dumb mistake on ours."

"Either way, who do you want to start with?"

"Tess. Let's give the hygienist a little bit of the discomfort she gives her patients. Where does she work?"

"Gulf Shore Dentistry, but I checked, and she's off on Fridays."

WE TURNED off Immokalee Road into Kensington's entrance. It must have been considered grand when it was built. The community was about thirty years old, and though well maintained, it needed a face-lift.

Passing a handful of neighborhoods, we circled to Hamlet Drive. Tess lived in a ground-floor coach home that backed up to a large lake. The front door to the apartment was deep in the middle of the building and was too dark for me.

When Tess opened the door, I was hit with the smell of something frying. Tess was braless in pink jeans and a black T-shirt, exposing a thin strip of her belly. She was barefoot with pink toenails.

She had a decent smile. "Hi, there. What's going on?"

"We'd like to ask you a couple of questions about John Talbot."

"Who?"

"There's no use in playing dumb, ma'am. We know you've talked with him on several occasions."

"I have no idea who you're talking about. You sure you have the right house?"

Derrick said, "He uses the name of John Silverman."

"Oh. Right. Why don't you come in?"

There was no foyer to speak of. I counted doorways. The unit was small. I figured two bedrooms and baths. What it did have was a great view. A huge lake was steps from the lanai and beyond that the golf course.

"Why don't you sit right here." She showed us to a

Tommy Bahama kitchen table. "I'm going to get some shoes on."

We watched her walk into her bedroom. Curious, I discounted the idea to peek into the other bedroom, wondering if there were telltale signs of her activities.

The thwacking of her flip-flops sounded her return. She pulled out a chair. "Sorry."

"When was the last time you saw the man you knew as John Silverman?"

She pursed her lips. "Must be about a month and a half."

Derrick jumped in. "You called him—February twenty-sixth."

"I returned his call. He wanted to get together, and I had another commitment."

I asked, "Another date?"

"No, my sister was in town. She lives in Panama City, in the Panhandle. It's a hell of a drive."

"Are you aware that he's gone missing?"

"Really? No, I had no idea."

"You sure about that?"

"Yeah, how would I know?"

"How did you meet him?"

"Through his ad."

"Where would you meet?"

"Right here."

The place looked too normal. And it was a first-floor unit without blinds on the sliders.

Derrick said, "You're a dominatrix?"

She smiled. "No."

"Then why respond to his ad?"

"Look, I don't have to get into this with you. It's people like you that give role-playing a bad name."

"Role-playing? Is that what you call it?"

"Yes. People have been doing it forever. It keeps things fresh, makes the old new and exciting."

Pictures of women dressed as French maids popped into my head. Years ago, men considered it some kind of a turn-on. I didn't get it. Was it the outfit or the forbidden nature of screwing around with the help?

"What kinds of games did you and Mr. Silverman play?"

"These are private interactions, and really, it's none of your business."

Derrick asked, "How much did he pay for each of your, uh, sessions?"

She hesitated. "That's not what it was."

It was a mistake to infer prostitution. I said, "Got it. I'm interested to learn why Silverman would advertise a desire to be collared."

"It's a common thing. It's no big deal."

"Did he enjoy being in pain? Did it arouse him?"

"I'm not a sadistic person."

She didn't answer the question. "I didn't say you were. I'm interested to know if Mr. Silverman got any pleasure from being in pain."

"I told you I don't do that type of stuff."

She hadn't said that. "Did Mr. Silverman ever ask you to inflict pain or punishment on him?"

"No pain, but punishment is part of role-playing."

"Do me a favor and enlighten me."

She smiled. "It's very simple. If he was a naughty boy, I'd deny him." Her smile widened to something a jack-o'-lantern would envy. "I'd tease him so much, he'd be ready to burst."

I felt heat run over my face. "You'd taunt him?"

She nodded. "Yeah, I'd make him beg."

45

It was raining when we left Tess's home. Derrick started jogging to the car. I walked. The rain felt good; I needed a cleansing.

Climbing into the driver's side, Derrick said, "What did you think?"

I didn't know what to say. "It's another world, my friend."

"She seems nice enough. I can't see her involved in Talbot's disappearance."

"Maybe not."

"Why do you say that?"

"We don't know anything about this woman. We need to dig into her, see if any crap pops up."

"I'll start with the place she works at."

"Hold off on that. If she's clean, I don't want to raise flags where she works."

"It'd be interesting to talk with another of her men toys."

Interesting wasn't the word I'd use. "I don't know how much more I'd like to hear. What we need is video of March second. She said she hasn't seen him in a long time. Grab the entrance videos from that day."

"Good idea. We only need a couple of hours to see if Talbot visited her the night he disappeared."

"We're pretty close to Wyndemere. Let's run by and see if Dawn Hill is home."

"I've never been inside there."

"It's a nice place but backs up to the interstate. You know Mike Ditka, the Bears coach; he lived in there."

"Really?"

"Yeah, they have a nice golf course I hear. Some pro golfer lived there as well."

"How come you know so much about it?"

"A friend used to live in there. Everybody likes to brag about their neighbors, even if they didn't know them."

"The human condition, fame by association, no matter how weak."

Derrick was getting to be a little too much like me. Cynicism was something I didn't like about myself. I'd have to find ways to steer him away from it.

We drove along Livingston Road and Derrick said, "I can't believe how empty Livingston is."

"Nobody likes to come this far east. You know, Livingston is named after the same man who built Wyndemere."

"It'd be cool to have a road named after you."

I nodded and answered my phone. "Hello?"

"Yeah."

"Right now?"

"I'm on my way. Thanks, I appreciate it."

I swerved left, across the road.

"Whoa! Who was that?"

Making a U-turn, I said, "Guy from Campiello's said he was out running errands and saw the Lamborghini driver going into Total Wines on Pine."

"Let's hope he likes wine as much as you do."

We pulled into a maze of buildings known as the Carillon Shopping Center at the corner of Airport-Pulling and Pine Ridge Roads. Looking out for a Lamborghini, I weaved over to the huge liquor store and parked.

"Wait here and keep an eye out."

Entering, I looked right to the checkout area. No sight of the mystery man, but several cameras were keeping an eye on the registers and a wall of glass protecting high-end wines.

I walked across the aisles, looking down each but came up empty. "Can I help you with something?"

I waved off a salesperson with a cranberry apron and headed to the checkout area. A balding man was wiping down the conveyor belt.

"Excuse me." I flashed my ID. "I'm looking for someone, a big guy. He came in about ten minutes ago."

"Not sure it's him, but someone left about five, ten minutes ago."

I pulled out a picture. "This him?"

"Yeah, he's got expensive taste in Scotch. Bought two bottles of Dalmore King Alexander. They're two hundred and fifty a shot."

"He pay with a credit card?"

"No, had a big wad of cash."

"Damn it."

"Sorry."

"He a regular?"

"I don't think so. I ain't seen him before."

"I'd like to see the video, to make sure it was him. Can you get the manager?"

I signaled Derrick, and we both watched the camera footage. It was him. No one noticed a Lamborghini, and since they're hard to miss, he was driving something different, or somebody had driven him there.

The surveillance didn't catch him getting into a car, and I wasn't happy.

We got back in the Escape. Derrick said, "At least we know he's from around here."

"What do you mean?"

"He's got to be local if he's shopping local."

It was a valid point. "You're right, we'll catch up with him sooner or later."

"Give that bartender a call. Let him know we missed him."

Another good idea, but I had to force myself to dial the phone.

"Let's swing by Hill's place."

The guard waved us through Wyndemere's entrance, and we snaked our way past the clubhouse toward the rear of the community. Glen Meadow Lane, where Hill lived, was close to the highway.

Her one-story home had a green roof that was popular thirty years ago. I also didn't like that the garage faced the street. The front door was to the side and set back. It didn't make sense. Hill was a designer with a nice roster of clients, including a new development of contemporary homes. I expected something hip. Was this another case of the shoe-maker's kid going barefoot? Maybe she was just too busy.

A pair of motorcycles roared on the interstate as I rang the bell. I peeked in the sidelight, but there was no activity. I knocked on the door. No answer. "Let's get out of here."

The day was turning into a fat zero. I tossed the keys to my partner. "Why don't you drive?"

"Sure."

A golfer was lining up a putt when Derrick's phone rang. He talked for a minute and hung up.

"That was the security office for Kensington. They have the footage we asked for. You want me to drop you off?"

"Nah. Let's check it out."

"You sure? Because you seem a little . . . off."

Don't tell me he was getting a sixth sense like Mary Ann was. "I'm fine."

We pulled up to Kensington's gate and followed a man in a uniform to a cubbyhole plastered with five monitors.

"This here is what you were looking for." He pointed to a screen. "March second, right?"

"Yes. That's it. Let it run."

I sighed when I noticed the date stamp. "We were looking for March second. This is dated February twenty-seventh."

"Oh, yeah. Must be the short month February is. Let me get the right one."

As he dug into a filing cabinet, I elbowed Derrick. "Freeze it." It was Talbot's white Genesis.

"The plate matches. It's him."

<h1 style="text-align:center">46</h1>

WE LOOKED AT THE VIDEO FROM MARCH 2 BUT DIDN'T SEE Talbot's car. Leaving with a copy of the clip showing Talbot entering at 6:45 p.m. and leaving at 9:07 p.m. on February 27, I said, "Why would Tess lie about the last time she saw him?"

"I don't know. It's not like she could have mixed up the dates or anything."

"She claimed to have met Talbot at her apartment when they played their games. But we don't know that to be true. Who knows where they could have gone or who else may have been there?"

"You think there may have been someone else involved?"

"From what I read, this seems to be a tight-knit community."

"That's true."

"And the thing that's bothering me is, Tess is no Amazonian. How could she or most women move a body the size of someone like Talbot?"

"True, but why kill him?"

"It could have been in self-defense."

"That would make it easier to bring someone in to help with the body."

"It would, but with what we found out about Talbot and his likes, who knows? It may be a he."

"You think so?"

Truth was, I found myself once again unsure of what to think. "I'm willing to bet there's a whole other sector of nutjobs playing in that pool."

We took a ride by Tess's place, but she wasn't home, and I was too confused to do much more than call it a day.

MARY ANN and I were in the bathroom finishing the endless regimen to keep our teeth healthy. After using a Waterpik, I said, "If you come up with one more thing to do, we'll have to start at nine."

"You want to keep your teeth, don't you?"

"It might be easier to get dentures."

"It's not that bad."

"What's going on with Jessie?"

"Something has to be bothering her. She won't talk to me, and the way she snapped at you after dinner isn't like her. I'm surprised you let it go."

I shrugged. "That's the way my entire day went. I'm glad it's almost over."

"Poor Frankie had a bad day."

I tossed my hand towel at her, and she lowered a strap off her shoulder. "How about we end it on a good note?"

I felt a surge in my groin. "Now, we're talking."

We jumped in bed, and Mary Ann threw her leg over mine. I ran my hand over her thigh and between her legs.

Mary Ann worked my underpants off, and I shimmied her nightgown off.

We cuddled for a moment, but Little Luca wasn't responding. Mary Ann said, "I have to use the bathroom. I'll be right back."

I recalled what Bilotti had said regarding ED. Did I just join the 40 percent of men in their forties with problems? The last time I was fine. The time before that I made it, but it took a fair amount of prodding.

Wondering if I'd have to start taking pills, Mary Ann hopped back in bed. She ran her hand down my chest, but Little Luca didn't respond. No matter what she did, nothing happened.

"What's the matter?"

"Nothing, probably just tired or something. Can I take a rain check for tomorrow?"

She hugged me. "Sure. I might even give you two passes."

"Deal."

A minute later, Mary Ann's breathing deepened. I don't know how she was able to fall asleep so quickly. I stared at the ceiling stressing over whether I should see a doctor.

***

"WHERE'S MY COFFEE THERMOS?"

"Above the stove."

"I got it."

"You're taking one for the road?"

"Need it today. Didn't sleep last night."

"I thought you were tired."

"I was, but I don't know, just couldn't sleep."

"Come on, Jess. Let's get rolling."

My daughter put a piece of toast in her mouth and grabbed her backpack. "Don't need a ride. Beverly's mom is outside."

I peeked out the window and waved. "Make sure you have a great day."

"Bye."

She was barely a teenager, and already we were down to one-word answers. Shoving aside the thought it would get worse, I got into the Escape and drove to see Dawn Hill. Derrick had a doctor's appointment, and I wanted to catch Hill before she left for work.

Above the hum of morning traffic, I heard a TV playing and rang the bell. The click of high heels grew louder and the door opened.

Dawn Hill had a white skirt that outlined her curves. I wondered if she could sit wearing it. In person, she didn't quite resemble Ann Talbot, but the combo of her body and clothing were enough of a reference.

"Are you here about the roof?"

"No, ma'am." I showed her my ID. "I have a couple of questions for you."

She took a tiny step back. "About what?"

"John Talbot, but you know him as John Silverman."

There was a tick in her cheek. "I have to get to the show-room. Maybe another time?"

I took a shot. "I'd hate to drag you down to the station, ma'am."

Her eyes widened. "Okay, but make it quick. I have a client meeting."

Walking in, the place made sense. The floor was made of long pieces of ceramic tile made to look like wood. The main room had whitewashed beams outlining its cathedral ceiling, and the kitchen had a white quartz island with a waterfall.

"You have a beautiful place here. I got to say, you'd never know from the outside."

"Dealing with the homeowners' association is like dealing with the federal government. I just got the approval to redo the roof, but it took ten months."

A bank of sliders opened to a lanai with a liver-shaped pool and some kind of tile that looked like travertine. "I like what you did out there."

"Wait till I do the outdoor kitchen. They're giving me a hassle because I want to open up the wall to vent the barbecue hood."

"Just what we all need, another layer of government."

"You got that right."

She was nervous, but I liked this lady. She had great taste. I wondered how much she charged when she said, "I really have to get going. It's an important meeting. We're pitching to do six new models for a community going up in Estero, on Corkscrew Road."

Just what they needed, another community on a traffic-choked road. "Okay. When's the last time you saw John Silverman?"

"February thirteenth."

"How do you remember that?"

"It was the day before Valentine's Day."

"What, he bring you chocolates or something?"

Her phone rang. She answered, "Hey, Linda, I'm on my way."

I heard the other person. It was a male who continued to talk as she hung up. "Sorry, I got to go."

47

Turning off J&C Boulevard, I headed down Jane Lane and pulled into a tree-shaded parking lot. It wasn't much of a building, but the sign caught your eye. Coastal Contemporary Design occupied the entire space.

It looked like a furniture showroom. There wasn't a window in sight, but the feel of the place was light and airy. What was notable was the absence of any palm tree or dolphin designs, a rarity in Florida.

I asked one of two perky kids manning desks off the entrance to see Hill. She made a call and directed me to a room on the left.

Dawn Hill was seated at a table covered with books of fabric. I wondered if her dress had elastic in it. Hill stuck a yellow Post-it on a piece of pale-blue cloth and looked up.

I could smell her fear as I closed the door behind me. "Uh, what are you doing here?"

"Just wanted to follow up. I can't believe it, there must be over five thousand samples in here. How do you know what to look for?"

"Actually, there's almost ten thousand. But it's all about a client's style and the mood we want to invoke. But I really don't have much time."

I rolled a chair out and sat. "I need to know how you met Silverman."

She swallowed. "I answered his ad."

"How long ago?"

"I don't know, a few months ago."

"Did he pay you by the visit?"

"That's not what it was. John was a nice man, and he would show his appreciation for me. Not every time, but every now and then he'd leave me a present."

"Money?"

She nodded.

"What did he"—I fingered air quotes—"'appreciate' about you?"

"You're making me uncomfortable. I don't want to discuss this."

"Look, we know Talbot slash Silverman, was into being submissive. Did he enjoy pain?"

"Not that I know of."

"Did he need pain to get his rocks off?"

"I never did anything like that."

"Let me ask you, what do you get out of all this?"

"I'm going to have to ask you to leave."

"I just have a few more questions."

She picked up her cell phone. "I don't want to call nine-one-one, but I will."

Calling the police might have been a bluff, but I couldn't take the chance of using up any goodwill with the sheriff's office. I said goodbye and headed to the parking lot.

It was a broiler. I opened the driver's door to let some heat out and called Derrick.

"Hey, bud, do me a favor and get Wyndemere's entrance surveillance."

"I'm on it. You want March second, right?"

"Get the third and fourth as well."

"You got it."

"GULF SHORE DENTISTRY. How can we improve your smile today?"

"Hi, I want to speak to Lisa Tess."

"She's with a client now."

"What time does she go to lunch?"

"At twelve."

"Thanks."

"Shall I tell her you called?"

"Nah, I'll catch up with her tomorrow."

The place where Tess worked was in a shopping center anchored by a restaurant called Noodles. The place advertised sushi and Italian food, a combo that didn't sit right with me.

Tess stepped out into the sun wearing blue scrubs. I intercepted her on the way to her car. She did a double take.

"You're the one who called? How dare you come to my placc of work?"

"I didn't say anything to jeopardize your job. Didn't even say why I was calling."

"That doesn't matter. Leave me alone."

"I'm sorry, but that's only going to happen when you start telling the truth."

"I didn't do anything wrong."

"We'll see about that."

"What is that supposed to mean?"

"Let's start with your lie on when the last time you saw

the man you know as John Silverman. You said you hadn't seen him in a month and a half, right?"

"I don't remember exactly."

"As I recall, you were pretty specific when we questioned you about the call you made to him on February twenty-sixth. You said he wanted to get together, but you couldn't because your sister was in town. Do you even have a sister?"

"My family has nothing to do with this."

"Still sticking to your story?"

"I don't remember."

"Let me refresh your memory. You saw John Silverman on February twenty-seventh. Don't say no, we have the surveillance video."

Her shoulders sagged. "I didn't want you to think I had anything to do with what happened to him."

What happened to him? "How did you hear something happened to him?"

"I didn't hear anything."

"Come on, Ms. Tess, then how did you find out?"

"I just figured it out, that's all."

"You expect me to believe that?"

"Why else would you be asking questions about him? I'm not stupid, you know."

"I didn't say you were. You have to have a certain amount of smarts to become a hygienist, so you have to know I'm going to find out what happened to him. It'd be easier on all of us if you just tell me."

"I don't know, I swear. I don't know what to think of all this."

"You know what I think? I believe it was related to all this submissive stuff."

"You're misunderstanding what it's about. It's not dangerous."

"Really? Putting out a classified ad asking to be dominated by complete strangers could never lead to trouble, right?"

"The people that participate are just regular people."

"As a homicide detective, I can tell you most murders are by what you call regular people."

"I don't know about anybody else, but I would never let it get out of hand. If someone wants to do something risky, I won't do it."

"Did Silverman ever ask to do something you considered risky?"

"No. He was harmless."

"I know a lot of this domination involves things like whipping and inflicting other pain."

"John wasn't into that. He had a fetish for collaring. He just enjoyed being pushed around. That's all."

"Did he ever say anything about anyone else he was seeing?"

"No. Look, I only get a half an hour for lunch and got to go."

As Tess drove off, I kept rolling around our talk. Though she lied, I was leaning toward believing her. She didn't appear to be nervous. Was that because she was not involved, or was that a skill she picked up to protect anyone from knowing about her unusual sexual escapades?

48

———

I was loading the dishwasher when Bilotti called. "Hey, Doc. What's going on?"

"You free?"

"Uh, yeah, just finished dinner. What's up?"

"I'm about to open an older Barolo, from 2001. I thought you'd like to taste it with me. It's by Luciano Sandrone and highly rated."

"Sounds good. Thanks, I'll see you in a bit."

"You're going out?" Mary Ann asked.

"Yeah, why? You always say I'm not spontaneous."

"It has to involve wine."

"Bilotti is opening a special bottle and wants me to try it."

"Okay, have a good time. You could use some fun."

I stopped into ABC Liquors and asked the wine guy for a couple of Italian whites made with the Grillo grape. Bilotti and his wife liked to sip a glass of the expensive wine on weekends. I left with the only two they had.

Bilotti opened the door with a warm smile. "Come on in."

I handed him the bottles. He examined the labels. "Perfect for a late afternoon, predinner splash."

"I hope so."

"They will be. I opened the Barolo right after our call."

If a man had an interest in being someone else, they'd generally want to be a movie star or a big-shot businessman. I was comfortable in being me, most of the time, but Bilotti had an easiness to him that I admired. Though he was the smartest person I knew, he treated me as an equal.

Bilotti had not only mastered the world of wine but had achieved an enviable level of balance in his life. I never understood how he could be so committed to his job but avoid getting hung up on a case. I guess it was the number of autopsies he performed.

The wine was sitting on a silver tray on the kitchen island next to a pair of fishbowl-sized glasses. Bilotti handled the bottle as if it were a scalpel, pouring a quarter inch into each glass.

Tipping the glass, he said, "Check the color of the rim."

I followed as he said, "See how it's not quite brown but is losing its color? It's a good indicator of a wine's age."

I'd never had a twenty-year-old wine, but he was right. I mimicked his tasting routine, and he said, "That's near perfect. Makes me want to have a bowl of spaghetti Bolognese. It's one of life's great pairings."

"It's nice. The Barolos I've had were dry and thin."

"The tannins can be brutal in younger and mediocre ones. This one I can taste truffles, dried meats, and umami from mushrooms."

I was kind of with him until the last reference. What the heck was umami?

"Boy, you hit the nail on the head. I really appreciate the chance to taste this with you."

"My pleasure. Luciano Sandrone is a legend in Piedmont.

He started with nothing and helped put Barolo on the map. Enjoy it."

"I like it."

"What's the status with the man gone missing?"

I filled him in on the mystery man and sex angle. "It could be my hang-up about this whole submissive stuff, but that's where I'm leaning."

"We've both seen more than our share of drug-related corpses."

"But why not just off Talbot after the accident? These guys have plenty of money, so why make him pay if revenge is the motive?"

"Don't discount the twisted code these gangs operate under."

He was right. Rationale wasn't part of their protocol. "Amen. He could have been trying to teach his guys a lesson or something."

"But you're leaning toward a twisted ritual that went too far?"

I smiled. "I know I'm not supposed to say it, but it seems easier than nailing a drug kingpin."

"There's no doubt the thrills some individuals pursue can be deadly. I had a couple of disturbing cases in Virginia. Two young men, neither of them over twenty, who hung themselves."

"Damn shame."

"They both appeared to be suicides, but during the autopsies I discovered they died of heart attacks induced by asphyxiation."

"What's surprising about that?"

"They hung themselves accidentally attempting to heighten an orgasm."

I choked on a sip of wine. "What?"

"It's called autoerotic asphyxiation, and it increases sexual pleasure. Besides lowering inhibitions, depriving your brain of oxygen produces a sense of euphoria before you lose consciousness."

"Are you kidding me?"

"No, it's as real as it gets. We don't talk about it outside professional circles. We don't want to give kids ideas."

Whatever good I was feeling from the wine vanished. "What kind of frigging world is this?"

"As I mentioned, we don't talk about it much, but it's generally believed many suicides are actually autoerotic asphyxiation deaths. Most officers that respond either miss the signs, or the parents of the victim hide pornographic materials. Either way, nobody presses the issue given the shock and grief the parents experience."

It felt like someone was squeezing my heart. "I can't even imagine. This is the craziest thing I've ever heard."

"It's extremely dangerous. Even if you don't hang yourself, you're causing irreversible damage to the brain by denying it the oxygen it requires. It can also trigger a heart attack."

I drained my glass. "How widespread is this practice?"

"Impossible to say, but I'm aware of some use within the BDSM community."

"Would they use collars?"

"I've never seen that, but I'd imagine it's possible, though not the most effective method."

I envisioned Talbot being choked by a collar. "Would it leave a mark?"

"If tight enough, and it would have to be to constrict airflow, bruising would occur."

Even during winter, no one wore turtlenecks or scarves in Naples. Ann claimed she never noticed any marks on her husband. Was she being truthful? We needed to check with their boating and tennis friends. The clothing they wore on the court and water could be telling.

49

I DRANK TOO MUCH AND HAD TO TAKE A LYFT RIDE HOME. The upside was the wine had increased my libido. Mary Ann was washing her face. I gave her a squeeze from behind and brushed my teeth.

Sliding under the sheets, she said, "How was your night?"

"The wine was great. Bilotti is really a good guy."

"He likes you, Frank."

I threw my leg over hers. "Enough about the good doctor." I ran my hand up her belly. She was silky smooth.

"You missed me, didn't you?"

"Darn right I did." I humped her leg, but Little Luca wasn't interested.

Mary Ann reached down but still no response. I backed away.

"Give it some time. Maybe it's the wine."

"Nah, it's not the wine. It's what me and Bilotti talked about; it's turned me off."

It wasn't true, but it was the perfect cover. I told her about the practice of sexual choking. She was as horrified as I was.

She drifted off to sleep, and I was playing ping-pong with the idea of going to see a doctor. The issue was whether it was something physical or a mind game I was losing.

The vibration of my cell on the nightstand woke me up. It was 12:07. I grabbed it, whispering, "Hello."

"It's Ben from Campiello's. I'm sorry to call so late, but he's here."

"Try and keep him there."

"How am I going to do that? He'll know it was me. No way."

"All right, I'll be there in fifteen."

I hopped out of bed. Mary Ann said, "Where are you going?"

"Downtown. That mystery guy I've been trying to track down is at Campiello's."

"Stay away from the women."

I kissed her cheek. "You got nothing to worry about."

A LIGHT DRIZZLE pushed the partying to the inside section of the bar. The revelers were three deep. I caught the bartender's eye, and he tilted his head to the right.

His back to the bar, a man in a tailored yellow shirt had the V-shape of the man in the bank's video. I circled toward the service bar area. Mystery man was talking to a woman in a white dress that accentuated her ass. It was a big one that you'd think a gal would want to hide.

Eyes on my target, I tried making small talk to the other bartender, who was raking in the tips like a casino croupier. An older man with thinning hair stepped up to him and whispered in his ear. He shook his head and the friend walked away.

I watched his buddy retreat to a round table in the back. Two other men and a woman in a shoulderless dress were holding champagne flutes.

I jumped when someone tapped my shoulder. "Sorry. Are you waiting for someone?"

I turned around. A woman in a leopard top, skinny jeans, and a pound of makeup smiled at me. At least she had good teeth.

"Uh, no."

"Interested in buying a girl a drink?"

I held up my left hand. "No thanks, I'm married."

"So are half the men in here."

"That's not who I am."

"Tell your wife she's got a keeper. Good night."

Trying to understand the workings of a place like this, I saw my target step away from the bar. I figured he was rejoining his party, but he walked to the far left corner.

Setting my drink down, I pushed through the crowd. He made a turn into a small hallway where the restrooms were. Following a man into the bathroom was one of my least favorite tactics. I didn't like the optics, and it could lead to getting ambushed.

I hesitated and pushed the door open. He was alone, standing at a urinal. He turned his head to see who had come in and went back to staring at the wall. For a second my pride was hurt that he didn't consider me a threat.

I went to the sink, washing my hands as if I had tar on them. He flushed and took the sink next to me.

"Hey, I don't mean to be nosy or anything, but you're the guy with the Lamborghini, right?"

He looked at me, gave the slightest of smiles, and brushed past me. Counting to twenty, I followed him out. He went to the table full of friends and hiked a thumb. The men stood and followed him out.

Had I been made? Criminals had a sixth sense detecting a cop, but why leave so suddenly? I watched them leave and went over to the woman he'd been talking to.

"How are you doing?"

Her dress was made out of knitted material and was stretched far enough that her skin was visible. "Pretty good except for the rain."

"We're nice and dry in here."

"You're cute, almost like an older George Clooney."

It was tough to hear her over the music, but I got the old reference. Leaning in too far would send the wrong signal to her. Using my left hand, I pawed my jaw.

She said, "What a shame. You're married, and I don't date married men."

"That's a good policy. Look, you were talking to a man earlier, the big guy in a yellow shirt. I'm pretty sure his name is Bebe."

Her smile disappeared, and she took a sip of a red drink but said nothing.

"You know him well?"

"Not really. I mean, he comes in here a lot, but that's it."

"But you were talking to him? About what?"

"I don't understand . . . oh, I get it, you're a cop, right?"

Was it that obvious? "Not exactly, I'm a private investigator. What were you chatting about?"

"Nothing, just small talk. I was just being nice. He started talking, and I didn't want to speak to him, but you know, I couldn't just blow him off."

"Why not?"

"Let's just say he doesn't have the best reputation."

My opinion of the women who hung out here got a much-needed boost.

"For what?"

"I don't know, just that he's some kind of drug dealer or something. But I really don't know."

50

I told Derrick about my visit to Campiello's. He said, "We need to ID this clown. Let's keep eyes on the bar, then we can grab his plate number and follow him home."

"We don't have the manpower."

"There's two of us. We'll alternate nights."

"Linda's going to be okay with that?"

"No problem. It can't be more than a couple nights till he shows, right?"

"He goes regularly, but we don't have a pattern."

"It's okay."

"It closes around one a.m. But if he isn't there by twelve thirty, we can leave. We'll be in bed by one."

"You're the old man; can you handle it?"

"Watch it, wise guy. You give me a case to think about, I'll be up later than a teenager in love."

"Ah, the good old days."

"It's funny, I never look back. I feel the only time that counts is now." It was true, but what was also a fact was my inability to consistently be present when it counted.

"You're right, Frank. You want me to take tonight?"

"Only if you want to."

"No problem. Linda's been watching this lame series, and I need a break."

"Know the feeling, bro. And don't worry, you'll be on the clock. I'm billing Talbot for the time."

"All right, I'll talk to you later."

"What about the video from Wyndemere?"

"They gave me the privacy bullshit and wouldn't turn it over. I went to Detective Mendoza. He owes me a couple of favors. He said he was going to run by there today."

"The only thing good about these gated communities is the surveillance, and now half of them are pulling the privacy card."

"What the hell do they think we'd use it for?"

"Who knows? Cameras are cheap enough these days . . ."

It was a modern-day fact of life. People had cameras everywhere and walked around filming who knew what. Where was the video of Talbot disappearing?

It was Orwellian, but how easy would it be to catch criminals if all the video taken was uploaded to a database? Then we could run facial recognition software on the bank of faces and find our target.

Nah, that was even too creepy for a cop.

I CHECKED in with Ann Talbot and told her about the surveillance. She approved it but was less enthusiastic than usual. She had taken a quick look at the picture of Bebe that I'd shown her and claimed not to know him.

Now it made me wonder if there was some kind of relationship between her and Bebe. It was a crazy thought, but this case was as strange as it got.

I hopped in my car, rolling over the possibility the Talbot case might never be solved. The reality was far too many cases went cold. A large number could be closed, but the relentless onslaught of new cases made time precious.

My record was good, make that near perfect. I'd worked two cases that faded to the background and remained unsolved. That meant two families who would never know who took their loved one from them.

It was something I thought of from time to time. It bothered me, but I was hopeful technology would advance, allowing me a path to deliver justice to the two Collier County cases.

I pulled into the bank's parking lot. It was my second visit, but a teller and an assistant manager had been off the first time.

It was still surprising to see people waiting in line for a teller. Except to open the business account, I hadn't been to a branch in over two years.

The assistant manager was a young lady who went out of her way to be helpful but in the end wasn't. She hadn't seen Bebe before but took over for the teller I wanted to speak to.

I pinned Frank Moreno as a retiree looking to keep active. He had great posture and a crushing handshake for someone in his late sixties. This was a man intent on staying relevant.

"Mr. Luca, is it?"

"Yes. Frank."

"What can I do for you?"

"I'd like you to take a look at a picture of a customer and see if you can identify him."

"I'll give it my best shot."

I opened up the file. He picked up the first one and said, "Oh, this is Fabio Lovecchio."

Was he playing some sort of a joke? "Fabio Lovecchio?"

He fingered the second image. "Yes. Pretty stylish name, isn't it?"

The only Fabio I knew of was the long-haired, bare-chested one gracing romance novels. "Can you spell that last name?"

I jotted down the spelling. "When is the last time you saw him?"

"Must be a solid two weeks. I only work three days a week, you know, to stay engaged."

"You're smart. I hear Mr. Lovecchio uses a lot of cash."

He cleared his throat. "I'd have to get clearance to discuss a client's business."

"I understand. If you could give me his address, I'll be on my way."

"I'm sorry, but that information is private. I'm not sure even Ms. Fiorelli could reveal that."

"Okay. Well, you've been helpful, Mr. Moreno."

I hung around until Moreno took his position back. It was worth the shot to ask Fiorelli if she could provide an address. Her refusal was one the United Nations would be proud of.

It wasn't what I hoped for, but I still had a rush; we had a name for the mystery man.

DRIVING FASTER than I should have, I made it home in fifteen minutes. I flipped open my laptop and opened the DMV portal. I plugged Fabio Lovecchio in and sat as the hourglass circled.

When "No results found" popped up, I reentered the name, checking the spelling before hitting enter. Zippo again. Though the definition of insanity is doing the same thing and expecting different results, I did it a third time.

This guy was tooling around in a Lamborghini without a license? I did a registration search and nothing came up. I banged my head into the seatback. Closing my eyes, an idea surfaced.

I hit the archive tab and plugged in Lovecchio. The hourglass turned twice before spitting out a single result that stiffened me. It was tough to believe.

51

FABIO LOVECCHIO'S LICENSE HAD EXPIRED IN 1988. AT THE time, he was ninety-one. It appeared that our mystery man was using a name he'd pulled out of the cemetery.

It was an old trick that had lost its effectiveness as systems became automated. But as we learned, criminals were equally effective in deploying technology to cover their tracks.

My next move should have been a no-brainer, but since I wasn't with the sheriff's office, I couldn't pull over or question the unknown man. It was a serious and fundamental downside.

Being on my own had a lot of benefits, chief among them was the absence of politics. But the limited manpower, lack of a lab's resources, and the simple effectiveness of flashing a badge made an investigation miles harder.

There would also be the inevitable handover of the Talbot case if a body surfaced or evidence we'd collected left the sheriff with no other choice but to pursue the suspect we identified.

I didn't want to ask for help in pulling over the

Lamborghini to see what, if any, license the driver was using. It would be quick but make me look weak and dependent. We could burn a couple of days waiting for him to show up at Campiello's.

When he did, we'd grab the plate number and follow him home. Between the two prongs, we'd uncover who he was.

———

I PICKED up my phone for the hundredth time. Nothing. Setting it down, Mary Ann said, "Why don't you just turn on the notifications?"

Though the alert function was already on, I said, "Good idea," and fiddled with my phone. Derrick was at Campiello hoping the mystery man would show. I didn't want to sound foolish, but the tingling at the base of my skull was signaling something was going to happen.

I got out of my recliner, went into the den, and dialed my partner. "Hey, how's it going?"

"No sign of him so far. I'm going to have to go inside and use the bathroom."

"Go ahead. Just be careful. I got a feeling tonight's the night."

"Oh my God, I can't believe who just walked in the place."

"Our guy?"

"No, take a wild guess."

"Come on, man!"

"Dawn Hill."

"Really? Is she with anybody?"

"A woman with red hair. I don't know whose skirt is shorter."

"Keep your eye on her."

"Will do. You know, Mendoza never got us the video from her neighborhood. I'm gonna give him a buzz."

"All right. Look, I know you gotta take a leak, but don't go into Campiello. She might recognize you. Go next door to the Continental. The bathroom is in the back, to the left of the bar."

One of the benefits of having to relieve my bladder on a schedule was I knew where most of the bathrooms in town were. It reminded me of another benefit of carrying a badge that I was missing: getting to use a business's restroom was easy as an officer.

I grabbed a water bottle and plopped onto the couch. Mary Ann had gone to get ready for bed. The eleven o'clock news came on. As usual, it led with an ominous tease about some weather pattern that was forming thousands of miles away.

I knew hurricanes could be threatening, but just as dangerous was endlessly telling the public about possible storms that never materialized. Like they did with the continual shootings in inner cities, people tuned out the weather.

Flicking the remote, I switched to *Shark Tank*. There was fake drama, no shortage of oddballs, and too many food products, but the show highlighted America's entrepreneurial spirit.

A woman was making a pitch for her dog treats when a text came in. It was Derrick. Our guy had shown up with another man. Dialing his number, I went into the den.

"You got eyes on him?"

"Yeah. He's having a drink."

"You see the Lamborghini?"

"No, the two of them walked up from Twelfth Avenue."

"I'm coming down."

"Why? I got this."

"I'll keep you company. I can't stay here knowing he's out there."

When I told Mary Ann I was going, she shook her head. "Be careful, okay?"

I swept my pistol off the closet shelf and kissed her on the way out.

Parking behind Tommy Bahama's Restaurant, I met Derrick just off Broad Avenue.

"Tess and her girlfriend just left."

"Any chance she knew our guy?"

"They stood on the other end of the bar. It looked like they ran when a couple of older guys hit on them."

"Let's go in, we'll hang by the outside bar."

We walked south, and just as we entered the outdoor area, mystery man and his buddy were leaving.

I said, "Shit, man, I left my wallet in your car."

Derrick said, "All right, let's get it."

I kept eyes on our target as he walked toward Twelfth Avenue. Derrick's car was in the opposite direction. I said, "Pick me up," and crossed the street, following a safe distance behind.

The men turned east on Twelfth as I hopped into Derrick's vehicle. I scanned the street for a parked Lamborghini but came up empty. We pulled to the curb as they crossed the street diagonally. It looked like they were headed to The Bevy.

The lights on a gray Mercedes flashed, and the mystery man went around to the passenger side and got in. When they pulled away, we followed.

I jotted down the plate number of the Benz as they weaved their way to Route 41. We followed them north past

NCH Baker and the Coastland Mall. It was 11:45 p.m., and there was still a fair number of cars on the road.

"Where the hell are they going?"

"I hope not to Fort Myers."

"They would have taken Seventy-Five."

As we passed Pine Ridge Road, I said, "I hope they didn't make us."

"I don't think so. There's a Toyota and a Beemer that have been with us the whole way."

They slowed as we crossed Vanderbilt Beach Road. Derrick said, "They're going into Mercato. I bet they're headed to Blue Martini."

"They're a little old for that place, aren't they?"

"How would I know?"

They went down the main drag and surprised me by making a left across from Bravo.

"They're going in the resident's parking area. I'm getting out."

"Hold on a minute. We gotta be sure."

"We're going to lose them."

I grabbed the door handle, and the two men turned the corner, stopping in front of a pair of glass doors. Mystery man's friend punched the keypad and opened the door. I bolted out of the car.

52

———

I HUGGED THE BUILDING. THE TWO WERE STANDING IN FRONT of the elevator. When the doors slid open, they stepped in. As it closed, I went to the glass door and peered in.

The floor indicator counted to three, stopped, and they got off. But what did that tell me? I went to the parking area, ducking under the gate. I checked each floor, but the Lamborghini wasn't there.

I went back out and got in the car. "We frigging lost them."

"What floor they get off?"

"The third, but there's probably a good thirty apartments if not more on each floor."

"Do the buildings connect to each other?"

"I hope not, or we're looking at a bigger number."

"You think he lives here?"

"I don't know what to think. But we can pass some photos around, see if anyone recognizes him."

"We got the plate number; it'll lead us somewhere."

I didn't want to complain, but I was tired and about as

frustrated as I'd ever been. "We keep at it, we'll get him. Let's get out of here. I need to get to sleep."

"You want me to drop you off at your house? We can get your car tomorrow."

I hated waking up with something unproductive to start the day, but I was beat. "That's a good idea."

Derrick dropped me off, and I slipped into the den. Opening the DMV portal, I entered the Mercedes plate number. It was registered to an Emilio Chavez at an address on Daniels Boulevard in Fort Myers.

Scrolling to the registrant's driver's license, I threw my head back and groaned. Chavez was sixty-nine years of age and bald. Who the hell were these guys?

Slamming the laptop shut, I headed to bed. We'd continue the chess game in the morning.

I TOLD Derrick that the plate number looked like another dead end as he drove to my car. He said, "I couldn't sleep either and did some poking around. It looks like the Mercato residential buildings aren't connected."

"I wouldn't call that a break."

"I know, but I put a call into Lugert. They developed Mercato with the Collier family. I figured it'd be the easiest way to get the unit numbers. Then we can run them against the tax records and come up with the owners."

I didn't have the heart to tell him I was betting the ownership wasn't direct. "Good idea."

We rolled to a stop at the light on Moorings Line Drive. Derrick checked his phone. "Oh good. Looks like Mendoza sent the video from Wyndemere. I'll forward it to you."

"Sounds good. You want to grab a coffee?"

"Sure."

BESIDES TWO DELIVERY TRUCKS, Tommy Bahama's parking lot was empty. I pulled onto Third Street and my phone rang. It was Brian Blade.

"Hello, Mr. Blade."

"Morning, Mr. Luca. I just wanted to be sure you got my message yesterday."

"I did, but it was a heck of a day. I'm glad you reminded me."

"It's probably nothing, but there's a couple of pieces of mail that came in for John that look personal. I didn't want to open them."

"I'm a few minutes away. I'll stop by now if that works."

"Yes, that's good."

I parked in the lot for John Talbot's engineering business. The coffee had boosted me, but when I stepped out of the car, the soft breeze and warm sun had me longing for a towel on the sand.

Closing my eyes, I turned my face to the sky and took several deep breaths. Making mental plans to take the family to Wiggins Pass Park this weekend, I walked into the offices.

I shook Blade's hand and he said, "The mail is sitting in a tray in John's office."

Following him to the private office, I caught a glimpse of one of Ann's lovers, the one with a record, coming out of a restroom. I froze. "What's he doing here?"

"Ann hired him. We needed someone with credentials to keep this place going. She said Tony Desmond was perfect. He not only was an architect but was between jobs and could start right away."

It felt like someone had poured Red Bull into my brain.

"Are you all right?"

"Uh, yeah. I shouldn't have had that burrito for breakfast."

"Ugh."

I paged through the envelopes but was too distracted to have the senders register.

"Anything there?"

"I don't think so, but I'll have to open them to be sure."

"Knock yourself out. I got to run to a meeting."

I tore open each piece of mail. The only item unidentified was an invoice from the Starfish Group. It was for a flat eight hundred dollars for services rendered. The vague description didn't sit well with me.

Stuffing it into my pocket, I tried to make sense of Desmond being here. Was this part of a grand scheme by Ann and her lover to not only get rid of her husband but to take over his business?

Had I miscalculated her cunningness, or was I blinded by her beauty? I recalled the touch points concerning Desmond, dwelling on the threatening phone calls.

Was that a show to throw me off? I'd fallen for it. It didn't make me mad; it disappointed me. If it were true, how did I allow such a sophomoric head fake to work?

A feeling came over me. Was it uneasiness? A form of anger? Then I realized it was embarrassment. I shook it off. This wasn't over by a long shot. I'd get to the truth.

Desmond was sitting at a desk, talking on the phone. I marched toward him. He was writing as he spoke. I knocked a knuckle on his desk, and he dropped his pen.

"Just wanted to say hello. I'll see you soon."

I hopped in my car, anxious to confront Ann about Desmond.

53

—————

I left Ann another voice mail. The drive by her house was a waste of time, and now she wasn't answering her phone. I wondered where she was as I made my way home.

Sitting at the light on Orange Blossom and Livingston, a white sports car turning onto Livingston caught my eye. Wedge-shaped, it accelerated like a slingshot and grew smaller as I followed it in my rearview mirror.

Tires squealing, I took off when the light turned green, hooking a U-turn. Traffic always moved swiftly on Livingston Road, but I was pushing it, going twenty miles over the limit.

The taillight of the Lamborghini flashed; he was making a turn onto Vanderbilt Beach Road. I cut around a Lexus and followed. I couldn't get close enough to read the plate number.

Its turn signal lit up again and it turned into the parking lot for the Alamo. It made no sense. It appeared he was going to the gun range. I swerved around an SUV and turned into the same lot.

My heart raced when I saw the Lamborghini pull into a

handicapped parking spot. I had to hand it to him; this guy had balls. I blocked the vehicle in and got out as the car's gull wing doors opened.

I marched over, stopping in my tracks when a prosthetic leg emerged. The driver was a woman in her thirties. I smiled and scurried back to my car. This day was shaping up to be a long one.

As soon as I got home, I went to grab some fruit for lunch. I opened the fridge, and a Tupperware full of pasta and turkey meatballs whispered to me. I paused before taking it and a fork to the den.

Stuffing a forkful of penne in my mouth, I clicked on the email Derrick had forwarded. Wyndemere might have been difficult to deal with, but the clip was professional. It was titled March 2nd, Entrance Activity, Hours 5:00 p.m. to 11:59 p.m.

I hit play. The quality was also good, though they could use additional lighting to sharpen the images. Using triple speed, I kept one eye on the screen and another on the meatball I was enjoying.

As the time stamp hit 5:55, I slowed the footage to normal. A line of cars formed at 6:07. I stabbed a piece of pasta covered in sauce. My mouth hung open. It wasn't the food. Talbot's white Genesis had stopped at the gatehouse.

Dropping the fork, I leaned in as his window rolled down. It was Talbot. He said something and a minute later was handed a slip of paper. Talbot tossed it on the dashboard and drove into Wyndemere.

I backed up the tape and froze it when Talbot was talking to the guard. The plate number matched. What had happened to the pass Talbot received?

Since it wasn't recovered from the car, there were only two possibilities: either he tossed it or whoever killed him did. I was convinced it was an attempt to erase proof Talbot had been to Wyndemere.

Now that we knew Talbot went to see Dawn Hill the day he went missing, the focus was putting together what happened after he cruised through the gate. Pushing the leftovers aside, I squared the laptop and hit play.

The later it got, the less traffic in and out of the community. I hit double time at 10:30 p.m. At 10:51, a van, driving a bit too fast, approached the exit. The driver had his hand on the side of his face. I paused the video, trying to determine if he was purposefully shielding his identity.

It was impossible to tell if the driver was just tired, but that didn't stop the speculation that Talbot was bound in the back of the van. I went back to the video. We needed to see if Talbot left in his own car, what time, and if he was alone.

The film just crossed 11 p.m. when my phone rang. It was Ann Talbot. "Hello, Frank?"

"Yeah, it's me. I've been trying to reach you."

"I know. That's why I'm calling."

"Where were you?"

She hesitated. "Where was I?"

"Yeah, that's right."

"I'm not sure I like your tone."

"I came by your house."

"I'm sorry I wasn't home, but I was at the spa."

"You went to the spa?"

"Yes, a friend of mine from church said I needed cheering up and treated me to a facial at the Ritz."

I took my foot out of my mouth and said, "I hope you enjoyed it. Why didn't you tell me you hired Tony Desmond to run your husband's firm?"

"I didn't know I had to ask you."

"You don't, but you should have told me."

"I don't know why you're so upset over it."

"You're having an affair with him."

"I'm no longer involved romantically with him."

"Oh, come on now. You expect me to believe that?"

"You can believe what you like."

"Don't you see how this looks? Your lover takes over the business. What's he going to do next? Move in with you?"

Click. "Hello? Ann?" She'd hung up me.

I punched her number in. "Now, hold on a minute. I got a right to know what's going on here."

"There's nothing going on."

"Don't you understand how this looks?"

"I don't care how it looks. It's simple. I needed someone with the licenses to keep the business going. And there was no time to waste; clients were looking elsewhere. Tony was available, and I asked him. That's all it was. I actually felt the way it came together was the best thing to happen since John disappeared. It was like God was helping me get through it."

"Okay. I hope you understand why I questioned it."

"I guess in your profession you're always looking for the bad in people."

I wanted to tell her it wasn't necessary to look for it, it showed up on its own. "Maybe. Anyway, sorry to bother you. I'll be in touch."

"I'm starting to lose faith."

"Hang in there. We're close to solving this."

I didn't know what to make of her. Was this part of her act? Was it really possible for her to feel no shame at bringing the man who slept in her husband's bed to his office and not be concerned with the optics?

After rubbing my eyes, I hit play and studied the black-and-white footage as it rolled. Where was Talbot? He'd exceeded the time frame allowed for his sexual games.

54

"Derrick, Talbot went to see Hill on the second. He drove into Wyndemere just after six p.m."

"What time did he leave?"

"That's the thing. He didn't, at least until just before midnight. I need you to see if we can get the next twelve hours."

"I'm on it."

"Good, but I can't wait on it. I got to go see Hill."

"You sure you don't want to wait?"

"I need to get a better sense of where this is leading. After you dropped me off, the guy from Talbot's office called me about some mail Talbot received, so I stopped by." Then I heard myself ask, "You'll never guess who was there." Was he rubbing off on me?

"I don't know, who?"

"Tony Desmond."

"The guy Ann was having an affair with?"

"Yep. He's working there."

"I don't like it. You talk to her?"

"Yeah, she claims they needed someone, and Desmond was out of work. She didn't see why I questioned it."

"She's a smart woman. Can she be that naïve?"

"If she's playing us, I'm going to go nuts."

"Desmond is an architect, not an engineer."

"I know, but she said he had the licenses to keep the business going."

"That don't sound right. Let me dig into that some. I'll let you know what I find."

"Sounds good. Talk to you later."

"Oh, hang on. I got a list of the owners in the Mercato building from the property tax records. I'm going to start ruling out whoever I can."

Derrick had not only turned into a good detective but a productive one as well. So much of what we did involved following hundreds of leads and processing untold amounts of information. Efficiency was as important to an investigator as the sense of smell to a dog.

I SLIPPED into the last parking spot in the lot of Hill's design firm. Announcing myself to one of the reception girls, I noticed Hill with three women discussing a mock bedroom setup.

"I'm sorry, sir, but Dawn is working with a client."

"Tell her it's an emergency, a personal one."

She exchanged glances with her coworker and walked over to Hill. She whispered in her ear, and Hill looked my way and frowned. Hill said something to one of the women and marched over.

"Can't you see I'm working?"

"Unless you want to do this here, I suggest we go somewhere private."

I wanted to see her office, but she took me to the same room where I'd met her previously. This time all the fabric books were lined up on shelves. It told me she was neat and demanded the same from the people she hired.

She closed the door behind her. "Make it quick. This is an important client."

"You lied to me. You said John Talbot or Silverman, as you know him, wasn't at your place on March second."

"It wasn't a lie. I just confused the dates, that's all."

It was good I didn't need to tell her about the video. "Come on now, you're trying to tell me you don't remember the night he went missing?"

"I don't keep tabs on him. All we had was a casual relationship."

"Having kinky sex is casual?"

"I'm not even going to dignify that with a response."

"What time did he leave?"

"I'm not sure. I fell asleep, and when I woke up, he was gone."

"And what time was that?"

"I don't know but in the middle of the night."

"Who else was there that night?"

"Nobody. Just the two of us."

"You're the last person to see him alive—"

"You think he's dead?"

"Nothing else makes sense."

"Maybe he took off. He didn't have the best relationship with his wife."

"What did he say about her?"

"Not much, just that he wasn't happy and that she didn't understand him."

I had to agree with Ann. Based on what we'd learned about what turned him on, I didn't get it either. "He say he felt threatened by her?"

"Not directly, but you know when something is there."

"No, tell me."

"He just kind of would say things."

"What kinds of things?"

"I don't remember exactly, but he was very unhappy. I felt bad for him."

She wasn't giving me anything to work with. It was probably a diversion, but normally they gave you something to run down. "Being you were the last to see him, I'm going to need a better time line to work with."

"I told you I fell asleep. I wish I could help you but . . ."

She was either truthful or knew about the gate video. "I understand, but could you narrow it down, say before midnight or later?"

"I woke up in the middle of the night, like two or three in the morning to go to the bathroom."

"You look at the clock when you get up, right?"

"Yeah."

"So why don't you know the time you got up?"

"It was a month ago, the nights kind of run together."

That was true, but not when something major put a stake in a date. "If you're not being truthful, I'll find out. There's no shortage of doorbell and other types of cameras."

"What does that have to do with getting up in the middle of the night?"

My phone vibrated; it was Derrick. "A light goes on, a door opens, a car leaves, it catches everything these days."

Hill stood. "I don't have any more time for this. I have to get back to my clients."

Her body language wasn't as confident as her statement.

I started my car and put the air on before calling back Derrick. "What's up?"

"You're not going to believe it."

"Believe what?"

"Desmond doesn't have the licenses. Talbot's firm is renting them from a retired engineer by the name of Charles Wei. I checked with the county business office."

This case was a bouillabaisse of lies. "Why would Ann say that, then?"

"She jumped the gun with her lover, or maybe Desmond has something over her."

"I don't know, why take a job if you're blackmailing her?"

"True. I'll dig around some more. How did you make out with Hill?"

"She said she mixed up the dates and fell asleep, so she doesn't know when Talbot left."

"Yeah, right."

"We need the entrance surveillance."

"We should have it later."

"Good. And if it's Ann, we can assume Desmond helped her. If it's the Lamborghini driver, he's got enough goons to help him, but if it turns out to be Hill, she had to have help. But who?"

55

THE SUN WAS SHINING AS I SAT IN THE PARKING LOT. According to Blade, Tony Desmond left the office at five on the nose. Now that I was running my own little business, it pissed me off that the guy in charge of John Talbot's business was a clock-watcher.

The sky darkened minutes before five. An almost black cloud had obscured the sun, but there were blue skies to the west. Though I was here for over a decade, I still couldn't believe the variance in weather from neighborhood to neighborhood.

As a couple of fat drops splattered onto the windshield, I saw Desmond bolt out the door. I jumped out as the rain began coming down. What was it about this case? Was somebody's guardian angel pulling levers?

"Mr. Desmond! Hold on a minute."

He looked at me and ducked into his Audi SUV. I knocked on the window, and Desmond hiked a thumb to the passenger side. I scurried and hopped in, hit by the smell of leather.

"Thanks, the sky just opened up."

"Welcome to the tropics. What do you want?"

"I'm curious how you ended up working here."

"They needed someone, and I was available."

"They using your license?"

"No. Engineers and architects are two separate professions."

"Ann Talbot said you had the license she needed to keep the firm operating."

"Really? She may have misunderstood. There is a lot of overlap, and I know how to run a project, but we had to rent a license."

"I know."

"If you know, why are you wasting my time?"

"Trying to understand why Ann said what she did."

"You have to ask her."

"Are the two of you back together?"

"What do you mean?"

"Romantically, sexually?"

"No. This is purely a business thing."

The rain was getting heavier, and I was running out of legitimate questions. "I find that hard to believe."

"Why?"

"She's a helluva good-looking lady."

"I've moved on."

And it was time for me too. I pulled my jacket over my head and splashed my way to the car.

I started the car and turned the air-conditioning vents away from me when Derrick called.

"What are you doing?"

"Drying out. I got soaked talking to Desmond."

"It's raining over there?"

"Oh, is it ever. What's up?"

"Mendoza came through. I'm on my way to get the video."

I picked the front of my wet shirt off my chest. "Super. Meet me at the house."

"Give me half an hour. And by the way, I started checking into Hill. I figured if she had a brother or steady boyfriend, they'd be someone she might have called to help her move the body, if it was her, but she doesn't have any."

"Last night I was thinking about the large withdrawal Talbot made. Maybe he said something to Hill, and she set him up."

"But it looks like she's got a good business. I can't see it for fourteen thousand."

"We don't know anything about her business. Maybe she's in trouble; maybe there's been other withdrawals."

"It's possible. We'll have to sniff around some."

"What about the list of people who own at Mercato?"

"I narrowed it down some. But there are two that kind of stood out. They were the only two titled just to one person. Both of them male. One has an Israeli name, and the other is Hispanic but close to the spelling of the owner of the Mercedes."

It wasn't exactly scientific, but it was something, and I'd nailed plenty of crooks with less than that. I raced home, anxious to change my clothes.

Dry and swallowing the last of a chicken burger, I answered the door and let Derrick in. He held up the thumb drive. "Got it."

I took the drive and headed for the den. "Let's hope it helps."

"We'll see. And I ran the two Mercato names. There were no hits on the Spanish guy, but this Israeli, Benedid Golan, has two interesting convictions."

"For what?"

"Take a guess."

"Money laundering."

"Nope."

"You gonna tell me or what?"

"Prostitution for high rollers. He ran a couple of operations in my old town, DC."

"How much sex can one case take?"

"As you like to say, there aren't many coincidences; they're clues."

It was close, but what I liked to say was that what others called coincidences, I called evidence. "I can't see a connection. Do you?"

"I got a couple of ideas but need to think them through."

I popped in the drive, and Derrick moved his chair to the corner of the desk. The time stamp moved from midnight March 2 to early a.m. on the third. There wasn't much activity. I toggled from normal speed when a car entered the picture and fast-forwarded when it was quiet.

Just after 1 a.m., a white car came onto the screen. Derrick leaned in, giving me a good whiff of his cologne. "That might be him."

I slowed the tape. "It's a Genesis."

"Can't see who's driving."

I froze the frame as it passed the gatehouse. Zooming in on the plate, I said, "It's Talbot's car. The question is if it's him driving."

"He's been there seven hours. Either he fell asleep, or he's some kind of porno star."

"Or he's dead."

"Rewind it and zoom in on the driver."

My finger was hovering over the play button. "All right, here we go."

"He's got his hand up, blocking his face."

I hit pause. "It could be Talbot."

"Hold on, what's that on his arm?"

"It looks like a tattoo on his wrist. I don't think Talbot is the type of guy to get one."

"I don't know, it seems like everybody has a tattoo these days."

As someone who loved to walk the beach, he didn't have to tell me. "I wish we could ask the lab to see what they could do with this."

"Linda has a friend whose husband is a digital something or other. He said he massages all kinds of video. Let me take it to him."

"Get moving. I'm going to check with Ann about the tattoo. We need to know if it's Talbot or not."

Derrick took the drive, and I drove to Talbot's house. As soon as I turned onto her block, I saw it.

56

SITTING IN ANN'S DRIVEWAY WAS AN AUDI SUV. DESMOND was there. I was betting it wasn't a business meeting as I rang the bell. I was about to knock when I finally heard footsteps.

Desmond opened the door. His shirttail was out. I couldn't resist. "What are you doing here?"

"We had a couple of things to discuss, about the business."

"Sure. There must be a million things to talk about. Where's Mrs. Talbot?"

"She's in the bathroom. Come in, you can wait in the kitchen. Let me tell her you're here."

He disappeared down a hallway and emerged a minute later.

"She'll be out in a second. I got to get going."

"I'm sure you do."

"I'm having dinner with one of our clients."

"Let me guess, it's a woman."

Desmond shook his head and walked out.

Ann had on a red jumpsuit with cuffed legs. I wondered how Mary Ann would look in something like that.

"Hi, Frank. What brings you around?"

"You said you and Desmond were not having an affair."

"That's right."

"Then what was he doing here?"

"Talking over business."

"Come on, Ann. You can be straight with me. It's the only way we'll find out what happened to John."

"I'm telling the truth."

"You said Desmond had the licenses you needed to keep the business going."

"That's what I thought originally. I just figured an architect and engineer were almost the same thing."

She was too smart to believe that. "You're doing it again."

"I'm not lying, Frank. Trust me, it was embarrassing to find out I was way off base."

"Are you going to replace Desmond with someone who has the proper licenses?"

"I don't think so, certainly not right away. I'd feel terrible about it."

"And you're not bothered by how this looks on the outside?"

"I learned a long time ago that the minute you stop worrying about what people think is the minute you start becoming yourself."

I liked that but was afraid of who she might be. "Did your husband have any tattoos?"

"John? A tattoo? He'd never get one. Why?"

"We might have a line on who drove his vehicle."

Her face darkened. "Someone was driving his car?"

"We're looking at the possibility. I've got to get on my way."

As she showed me to the door, I said, "By the way, I like the way you decorated this place. When did you redecorate?"

"About a year and a half ago."

"Came out nice. Who'd you use?"

"Uh, uh, I can't believe I can't remember. I'm drawing a total blank."

That was tough to swallow. Working with a decorator meant you were hitched at the hip for a good six months.

Driving home, I made a call. "Gesso."

"Hey, Sarge. It's Luca, how are you?"

"Good, Frank. How's it going with you and the family?"

"Everybody is good, thank God. And yours?"

"Same here, all good. But I know you didn't call to talk about the family. What's up?"

"I'm closing in on the Talbot case. The guy that went missing a month ago. I could use a little help."

I didn't like the silence.

"Look, we know Talbot was in Wyndemere right before he disappeared. And now we have video of someone else driving his car out of there."

"Okay."

"Can we get some help with the traffic camera footage, maybe follow this guy and get some intel on him? He could be the guy who killed Talbot."

"He could be a car thief."

"No way. If so, what happened to Talbot?"

"I'm sorry, Frank, but we got rules about outside sharing, you know that."

"I know, but I was just looking for some—informal help."

"You want to bring in what you have, and we can sit down with the sheriff?"

"Not ready to do that."

"Call me when you are. Sorry, Frank."

It pissed me off. Though I got it, I had worked alongside these guys for years. It wasn't like I was asking someone to drop charges. I was working a potential homicide case. All I wanted to do was avoid putting a bow on the gift I was going to give the sheriff.

I hung up, called Derrick, and told him we were on our own. He said, "Geez, you'd think with all the legwork we did, they'd pitch in a little."

"They got rules, you know."

"That's bullshit. I can reach out—"

"Don't go around Gesso. Trust me, he'll never forget it if we do."

"He can hold a grudge."

I thought about playing the guessing game he liked so much, but said, "Ann said her husband didn't have any tattoos."

"We got to hunt down whoever was driving his car."

"I'm going to run through everybody coming in, say from seven on."

"You don't need to do that. Anybody without a transponder has to stop at the gate. They may even have to show ID. I'm pretty sure they keep some kind of a record about who they're visiting."

How had I forgotten something so fundamental to most communities down here? The only explanation was chemo brain. "Yeah, I was thinking of that, but most places don't need to present any ID."

"I know, as long as they call or text the gate, they'll get waved right in. Let's get Mendoza to call them and get a time and name for anybody going to see Hill."

"Thanks, I'll check the tape and grab a plate number."

"What do you want to do about the Israeli? I'd go see him, but Linda will kill me if I miss my doctor's appointment."

"Happy wife, happy life. Text me what you got, I'll run over to see him."

––––––––

CHANCES WERE slim that the Israeli would agree to talk to me. But I knew the secret to success was tied to increasing the surface of luck, and that meant you had to create opportunities for it to shine.

I breezed past another art gallery on Mercato's main drag. The planned village was busy, but how many high-end stores could survive in a place crawling with tourists? I made a left and hit the call box. No one answered. I tried again before leaving.

Toojay's diner had a decent pastrami sandwich. It was something Mary Ann had forbidden me to eat. I looked both ways and headed over to satisfy my craving.

57

I ANSWERED DERRICK'S CALL. "FRANK, JUST HEARD FROM Mendoza. The gate at Wyndemere said a John Smith came through at ten forty on March second."

"Anybody else?"

"That's all they got."

"Unless Hill was doing a doubleheader, it's got to be our guy. I'll check the tape and let you know."

Fast-forwarding the footage, I realized it was the first easy thing to come along in the case. I hit play as the time stamp crossed 10:30 p.m. Nine minutes later, a blue Ford Focus rolled up to the guardhouse.

I stopped the tape and jotted down the plate number. I studied the footage. Wearing a baseball cap, the driver was leaning away from the window. I hit play.

The guard stuck his head out the slider briefly and retreated. Ten seconds later, he held out a slip of paper as the gate lifted.

The driver reached out. I hit pause. I zoomed in. He had a tattoo. I shook my fist and hit play. The Focus was swallowed by the darkness.

I plugged the plate into the DMV portal. The 2008 Ford Focus was registered to a Lee Nash. His address was listed as 10890 Isle of Pines Drive in Fort Myers.

It was time to see what this guy looked like. Hitting the license tab, I pulled up his photo and vitals. With downcast hazel eyes, Nash's face was pockmarked. He had a thin nose and sandy hair parted in the middle.

Thirty-six years old, Nash was six feet and a hundred and eighty pounds. He might struggle without help, but he had the heft to move a dead Talbot around.

There was no mention of any motor vehicle violations or even a parking ticket. I plugged his name and social into the crime database. Nothing.

I called Derrick. "The guy's name is Lee Nash. He's thirty-six from Fort Myers."

"All right, we're getting close."

"One thing bothering me is he's got no record. Not even a ticket. He doesn't fit as the killer."

"Maybe Hill killed Talbot and called Nash to get rid of the body."

"I've been thinking the same thing, but still, getting involved with a corpse?"

"Maybe Hill didn't tell him what was going on."

"Could be, but I don't know."

"Let's go see him and find out."

"I want to bat around a time line first. We know Talbot got there just after six, they do whatever it is the two of them are into, and they're finished by eight, eight thirty."

"Could be later. Maybe he brought something over to eat or she made him dinner. Then a little foreplay, blah blah blah. Don't forget, Talbot told his wife he'd be home around ten."

Ten? I remembered it as nine. Chemo-brain again? "Okay.

So, somehow, either intentional or by accident, Talbot ends up dead."

"If it was accidental, why not call nine-one-one?"

"She panics. Afraid what it'll look like. It'd ruin her reputation."

"Hill doesn't know what to do but needs to get rid of the body and calls her friend Nash."

"We don't know they're friends. Maybe Nash was sent by someone else."

"Either way, Nash gets there just before eleven."

"But doesn't leave until one. Why?"

"Good question. It couldn't take more than twenty minutes to move him into the trunk of a car."

"Unless they needed time to clean up. Maybe there was a lot of blood. It has to be something like that."

"Let's go see him."

<hr>

WE EXITED Route 75 and took 80 east. Passing the Manatee Park, I said, "We're heading to Fort Myers Shores."

"Plenty of water to dump a body out here."

"Yeah, that concerns me."

"If we don't have a body, it's going to be tough to get a conviction."

It wasn't impossible but miles more difficult as prosecutors would have to convince a jury that a death took place. Any defense attorney worth his weight would plant ideas that Talbot had decided to leave his cheating wife. The fact he had at least one bank account his wife didn't know about and had withdrawn large amounts of cash would add to the argument.

"Sooner or later it pops up. Our job is to make sure it's sooner."

We made a turn, passed the Davis Boat Ramp, and Nash's street was the first one of a series featuring canals in their backyards. The neighborhood of well-maintained homes was steps off the Caloosahatchee River, which fed into the Gulf of Mexico.

Derrick said, "Pretty neat spot. What's this guy do?"

"All I got was a couple of corporate positions in administration. Last one at Echo."

"What's that?"

"They manufacture outdoor equipment for landscapers. They're headquartered in Fort Myers."

"Chainsaws?"

"Yeah, but let's not go there."

"Yet."

Nash's one-story home had a Key West look with a metal roof. It was smaller than the other homes. I snuck a look between the homes, and his dock was empty, making me worry we'd wasted the trip.

Derrick rang the bell, and I stood on my toes, trying to see more than the foyer ceiling.

"I'll be right there."

"He's home."

We stepped aside as the door swung open. Nash had on a long-sleeved T-shirt and black shorts. Like his DMV photo, he didn't look directly at us, saying, "Hello, what can I do for you?"

Derrick said, "We'd like to talk to you about Dawn Hill."

As he blinked, I could see fear seeping out of his pores. "Uh, who?"

"Your friend Dawn Hill, the decorator."

"Oh, yes. Actually, we're not that close of friends."

I said, "Close enough to visit her after ten at night."

Nash ran a hand through his hair, and I caught a glimpse of a tattoo on his wrist.

58

"Uh, I wasn't trying to mislead you. We're relatively new friends is all I was trying to express. Is that okay?" I nodded and he said, "Why don't you gentlemen come in."

No woman was living here. The place was spartan, and there wasn't a throw or pillow in what passed for the family room.

"This is a nice spot to be. Been here long?"

"About ten years. When I came down from Chicago, I saw this place and that was it."

"You have a boat?"

"Nah, I never got around to it."

That lengthened the odds Talbot was at the bottom of the Gulf of Mexico. "Don't feel bad, neither of us are boaters."

"Can I get you something? Some water, a soda. Whatever, if I have it, it's yours."

"A bottle of water would be nice."

"Regular, or would you prefer sparkling?"

"Regular."

Nash ducked into the kitchen, and I took a look around.

Three awards for employee of the year at Echo were the only things hanging on the wall.

He handed us bottles of Poland Springs. I said, "You seem to have found a home at Echo."

"Yes, I'm lucky to be there. My superior is demanding, but I prefer that over being directionless."

"What do you do there?"

"I'm the administrative assistant to the chief operating officer."

"How did you meet Ms. Hill?"

"You know, I don't remember."

"But you said you met her recently."

"Let me clarify, I really don't want you to misunderstand. When I was looking to update my house, she was recommended to me as a decorator. I visited her studio but never followed through after that."

"And how did you become reacquainted?"

"Through Facebook. You know the algorithm is good at suggesting people you may know."

Derrick cut in, "What were you doing at her house on the night of March second?"

Nash looked like he swallowed a golf ball. "I'm not sure of the date, but I go there from time to time."

"Do you have or have you had a sexual relationship with Ms. Hill?"

"Excuse me, but that's a private matter."

I said, "Are you into bondage and that sort of thing?"

He squirmed and looked at his hands. I followed with, "I'm just asking, not judging. People do all sorts of things to get their rocks off, I'm told."

"I-I really want to be helpful, but I've got to be going."

Derrick said, "Do you know John Talbot?"

"Hm. No, the name doesn't ring a bell."

I handed him a photo of Talbot's car leaving Wyndemere. "That's you, driving Talbot's car."

"Oh, that's whose car it was. You see, Dawn said a friend of hers had left his car at her house. She asked me to bring it to him."

"Where did you leave it?"

"Oh, geez. You can't expect me to remember the address. It was a month ago."

"Was it in Naples? Bonita? Up here?"

"Somewhere around the Bonita-Estero border."

"So you were just helping a friend?"

"Yes, I'm a very loyal person and enjoy helping others."

"How did you get home after dropping the car off?"

"I used Lyft. I prefer them over Uber."

"You drove all the way to Naples, got the Genesis, and took a Lyft home?"

"Yes, it really isn't that far of a drive."

"What about your car?"

"Uhm, Dawn brought it to me the next day."

"Why didn't she bring her friend's car?"

"I didn't ask her, but I can see how that would have made sense. But, oh yeah, now I remember, she was extremely tired that night."

"Did you murder John Talbot?"

His eyes bulged. "Of course not. I couldn't do anything like that."

I believed he didn't kill him, but his answer confirmed his involvement. "What did you do with Talbot's body?"

Nash stood. "I don't know what you're talking about, and I'd like you to leave."

"One more question."

"No, I'm sorry. Please leave, now."

We hopped into the Escape. Derrick said, "What did you think?"

I handed my water bottle to Derrick. "Bag this and get the DNA. It'll match one of the unknowns found in Talbot's car. Either way, he's involved. The question is, how deep is he in?"

"He doesn't seem like a killer."

"I tend to agree, but you never know. He's a bit off, in my mind."

"Okay, let's say he's infatuated with Hill and goes to see her. When he gets there, he sees Talbot and loses it."

"It's a theory, but we'd have to confirm there was a relationship. I think there was, but we need proof."

"That Facebook crap was bullshit. He probably found her the same way Talbot did."

"Maybe they were doing some twisted threesome thing that led to a kind of passion killing."

"I've seen some BDSM people do some crazy shit on the internet."

"We got to stick with what we know. At this point, Nash either got rid of Talbot's car or the body and the car."

"It'll be interesting to see what Hill has to say."

"I'd bet it all that Nash is on the phone with her right now."

"No doubt. This is going to be fun."

I didn't want to offend Derrick, but I felt Hill would shut down, maybe even lawyer up, if both of us showed up. "Maybe, but chances are, once she sees the both of us, she'll go quiet."

"I remember my old CO; he said to never double-team someone you wanted to squeeze info out of."

"It does complicate things. Everybody gets defensive when they're outnumbered."

"Drop me off. I'll have the bottle analyzed."

"Are you sure?"

"Absolutely. If Hill gets a lawyer, we're screwed."

"We'd have to turn it over to the sheriff, and I'm not ready yet."

59

———

As I swung onto Hill's block, I saw a truck parked in front of her house. Three men were on the roof, tossing tiles into a dumpster on the driveway.

I parked across the street, making sure the laborers saw me crossing the lawn. When she opened the door, Hill had a look of surprise on her face.

"Oh, I thought you were the roofers."

"Glad to see you finally got the approval to go ahead."

"Me too. The green was hideous. Look, I really don't have time. I have a Zoom call scheduled in a few minutes."

"This won't take long." I wasn't lying; Hill would probably ask me to leave when I cornered her.

Following her in, I scanned the place. It was too bad I couldn't take a couple of pictures to show Mary Ann. "You should put this place in a magazine."

She smiled. "Once it's all done, I'll add it to my portfolio. People love the before-and-after shots."

You could hear the roofers walking on the roof. "I saw someone who wanted to use you to redecorate."

"Who was that?"

"Lee Nash."

She didn't flinch. "He didn't have the budget to go ahead with the project. But we became good friends, so it was a win-win anyway."

I'd bet Nash would now say they were buddies as well. "Good enough to call in the middle of the night for a favor?"

"I didn't call him."

"Really? So why'd he come here?"

"Well, it's none of your business, but I'll tell you only to get you off my back."

"Go ahead."

"Well, Lee and I had a little thing going. Same as Silverman, or Talbot, as you call him."

"So Nash liked getting bound up and abused?"

Hill frowned. "Abuse? That's a complete distortion of our relationship."

"Let's back up a second. Are you saying that Nash just happened to show up here looking to have sex with you?"

"Yes."

I didn't want to get off track. "Okay, he comes over, unannounced, you say."

"Yes, like I said, we were good friends."

I was tired of her bullshit. "Good enough to help get rid of a body?"

"What did you say?"

"When he arrived, what happened?"

"I don't know. I was sleeping."

"So Talbot answers the door, lets a stranger into your house, and gives him his car?"

"Lee isn't a stranger. He and John knew each other."

"Not according to Nash. He said he had no idea who Talbot was."

"That's because he knew him as John Silverman."

I couldn't remember using the alias when talking with Nash.

"Talbot aka Silverman went to your house just after six p.m. His car, driven by Lee Nash, was seen leaving around one a.m. He was alone. What happened to Talbot?"

"I told you I fell asleep, and when I woke up, he was gone."

"Without his car?"

"He said something about having an appointment to bring his car in early the next day. Maybe, since he wasn't feeling good, he asked Lee to drop it off."

"And Nash, just dropped everything, inconveniencing himself, to help Talbot?"

"Lee is a nice guy. John and him are very similar in wanting to help people."

"What happened to John?"

"I have no idea. I wish I knew; he was a dear friend."

"Come on now. You're trying to tell me he disappeared while you were supposedly sleeping?"

"Yes. Look, I have no time. My Zoom call starts in two minutes, and I have to organize my presentation."

Leaving, I told myself I had to be patient. Nash and Hill had settled on the same story, but anytime you had a secret between two people, it was only a matter of time before it came out. The only way it wouldn't was if one of them were to die.

I wanted to drive straight back to Nash, but tonight we were going out to dinner as a family. Driving home, I thought over the chances of something happening to either Hill or Nash. If it was Hill who did Talbot in and Nash who dumped the body, Nash could be in danger.

We settled into an outdoor table at AZN in Mercato. It was a prime spot for people watching, and the food was good the first time we'd come. I excused myself under the guise of going to the restroom and composed a text:

Hey, Doc, what kind of wine goes with Asian food?

Riesling.

How about a red?

Try a merlot or malbec.

Thanks. You're a lifesaver.

I grabbed the menu and scanned it, picking out an Argentine malbec.

"What are you having, Dad?"

"I'm thinking the salmon. It was good last time even though they overcooked it."

"Mom says if it's not swimming, you say it's dry."

"Well, Mom is a comedian, but I still love her." I pecked her cheek as the waiter came with our wine. He popped the cork, and I did a shortened version of Bilotti's ritual before flashing a thumbs-up.

I clinked glasses with Mary Ann and said, "Here's to the two prettiest women in town."

"This seems kind of heavy."

I took a shot. "With Asian food, you need something to compete with the spices they use."

"I think a white would go better. Something crisp, like that sauvignon blanc we had Friday night."

What had I created? "If you want, I'll get you a glass. More for me that way."

"Nah, it's okay."

I put my nose into the glass and inhaled. When I lifted my head, I saw it—a white Lamborghini pulled up behind a Bentley at the valet station. I put the glass down and focused on the sports car.

It took an old-timer five minutes to lower the Bentley's convertible and get out. The purr of the Italian sports car reverberated as it crawled to the podium.

Its doors scissored open, and the mystery man unfolded himself. He took the ticket and headed to the escalator.

I stood. "I'll be right back."

60

"WHERE ARE YOU GOING, FRANK?"

I turned around. "Order me the salmon, medium rare. I'll be back in a minute."

Eyes on the alleyway, I weaved through the tables. Mystery man was at the top of the escalator. Watching him walk toward the Silverspot Cinema, I hit the stairs two at a time.

Reaching the landing, mystery man, in the midst of other moviegoers, disappeared into the theater's foyer. I jogged to the ticket taker. "What movie did the big guy, blue shirt, go to?"

"I don't know, sir. I just take the tickets. You'll have to move aside, there are people behind you."

I looked at the list of movies playing. There were four possibilities. My phone rang, it was Mary Ann. "I'm on my way."

I hustled down the stairs. The Lamborghini was parked in the "look at my car" spot. A guy in shorts was taking pictures of it. Really? Of another person's car? I took my camera out and snapped the plate, making sure it was legible.

MARY ANN WAS on me about the case intruding on family time. She was right, but it wasn't easy resisting the urge to investigate who owned the Lamborghini. We had gone to bed, and between the license plate and another idea I had, I couldn't sleep.

Popping a pod into the coffeemaker, I sent a text, hoping my request for an appointment would be granted.

I grabbed my laptop as the coffee began to flow. My phone pinged; my ask had been granted but earlier than I wanted. I had to get moving. I put a dash of milk in the mug, opened the DMV portal, and plugged the sports car's plate in.

Considering what came up, I made a call.

"Derrick, I saw the Lamborghini last night at Mercato and grabbed the plate number."

"Great. Whose is it?"

"It's registered to a company named Deep Water Ventures, Inc. They're out of Miami."

"Figures."

"Do me a favor and track down who's behind it."

"Sure. Text the details."

"Thanks, I got an appointment. Talk later."

I sent the details to him and hopped in the Escape. Once again, I had avoided mentioning who I was going to see. Despite my firm belief in the value of seeing one, telling someone, even my partner, I was going to visit a head doctor wasn't easy.

She opened the door and that fresh-baked-cookie smell hit me. "Hello, Frank, good to see you."

"Likewise, Doc."

"Come in."

Bruno had her uniform on, a dark blue pantsuit. "Say, Doc, what do you use for that baking smell? A diffuser?"

She smiled. "A diffuser? No. Baking is therapy for me."

"What, do you bake every day? Every time I've been here, the smell makes my stomach growl."

"Not every day, but five, six times a week."

"Wow. What do you do with all of it?"

"I drop off trays at nursing homes. It brightens their day a bit."

"That's nice. I'm sure they appreciate it."

"I hope so, but it's good for me as well."

"The giver gets more than the receiver."

She was a good person, and while I sat there wondering why she wasn't married, she said, "That's very true. Sit, tell me what you wanted to discuss."

Settling into a gray club chair, I was glad it wasn't a personal issue that I needed help with. "I'm working on that case I mentioned to you. It may involve some BDSM, but I have nothing hard on that."

"What do you think I can help with?"

"We talked about submissive people the last time. And the missing man, by all accounts, is submissive. I'm interested in what motivates them."

"There are varying degrees. What makes you believe your missing man has a submissive personality?"

"Well, he's not the one I have questions about, but trust me, I spoke with two women, neither of them his wife, and he enjoys being dominated."

"I see. You said he's not the person you're interested in."

"Right. Here's two scenarios of what I think may have happened. One is where Talbot, the missing man, is with a woman friend, playing their role games. Something happens to Talbot, either intentional or by accident, and he dies."

"Oh my God."

"I know, it's crazy. The woman panics and calls a friend for help with the body."

She shook her head. "Sounds like a movie."

"I wish it was. The other situation has Talbot with his lady friend. The woman, for whatever reason, wants to murder him. She asks this friend for help in killing Talbot."

"Two very different levels of involvement."

"I know."

"And you want help profiling this friend?"

"Not exactly. I'm pretty sure he's submissive like Talbot. He goes to the same woman, and when we've talked to him, he was tripping over himself trying to be nice."

"That is a characteristic."

"What would it take for someone to help kill or hide a body?"

"My experience is limited when it comes to criminality."

"I understand, but I'd appreciate any insight you have."

"Assuming this is a dominant-submissive relationship, the first point is whether it is limited to sexual interaction or if it rules the entire relationship. In your two hypothetical scenarios, it would have to guide the entire bond between them."

"If it does, what exactly does that mean?"

"That the submissive person enjoys being controlled by their partner and wants to please them in every way possible."

"So someone could force them to do something?"

"No. The submissive one isn't forced to do anything they don't want to. A slave they're not, but their desire is to fulfill the wants and needs of their dominant."

"So they'd follow a command out of wanting to please their partner."

"Yes. They would put the needs of their partner above everything else."

"Even killing someone if asked by their dominant?"

"I've never heard of that and believe it would involve a psychosis of some kind."

61

Bruno said she'd never heard of it, and I believed her. The problem was what she'd said before that—that a submissive person would put the wants and needs of their partner above everything else.

The zillion-dollar question was whether that included murder or covering one up. It felt like some kind of mind control, but I knew it wasn't. I got the thing about keeping their partner happy, but could it involve another person in a crime?

Someone would rebel when they realized they were being manipulated, the key point being if they realized it. During my career, I'd run into a handful of cases where a completely innocent person was drawn into a crime under the guise of helping someone.

In every case, it was close relatives: a brother, father, wife, or husband. Could a friend, a recent one at that, be pushed into committing a crime? It sounded like something in a novel. I called Derrick.

"How'd your appointment go?"

"Good. You find anything on the Lamborghini?"

"I don't get why anyone would use companies for cars. Maybe it's the liability or something."

"Could be, or an attempt to avoid taxes. What's the story?"

"Deep Water Ventures is owned by a New York corporation called Growth Enterprises, and they're controlled by Fair Weather Corporation, also in Manhattan."

"New York? It can't be to save taxes."

"Amen. Anyway, according to New York State, Fair Weather is owned by four people, twenty-five percent each."

Sometimes you had to pull teeth with Derrick. "And they are?"

"Looks like a husband and wife or maybe sister-brother duo of Briana and Joseph Libowitz, and a Barry Levy, and Gregory Vucvich."

"Any of them reside in Florida? Or got records?"

"Yep, Levy and Vucvich are out of Miami, but neither of them looks like our guy."

"They have records?"

"Oh, do they. Vucvich served a term for attempted murder, and Levy has a string of drug-related arrests, all for distribution."

"What is our guy doing driving a car owned by them? Why would they let him use a two-hundred-thousand-dollar car?"

"Good questions."

"Find out what this Deep Water outfit does."

"I'm on it. Talk later."

"Hold on, when did the lab say the DNA analysis would be done?"

"Didn't say, but I told Arc Point it was urgent."

"We gotta push them."

"It doesn't matter, we have him driving the car on video. I got to run. Linda just got back from Publix."

I hung up and went into the kitchen thinking Derrick was wrong. It mattered. The location of DNA could help build a story as to what happened and dispute excuses. Bottom line was, the more proof we had, the more solid our case became.

Popping a pod into the coffee machine, Mary Ann came in. She was brushing her hair.

"You had a good swim?"

"The usual. We got to tell the pool guy, it looks like there's some algae by the stairs."

"The water's too warm."

"Maybe, but it feels good."

"Oh, we got a thousand-dollar bonus for solving that jewelry scam. Maybe we can use it toward the salt filter."

"Wow. That was nice of them."

"It sure was."

"What's going on with the other case?"

"We're struggling over a couple of scenarios on what happened to Talbot."

"What are you thinking?"

"Well, Hill and Talbot were together at her house doing whatever it was they did together. Did she kill him before calling her friend Nash? If she did, it was because she needed someone to help her move the body."

"She couldn't handle the body herself?"

"No. He outweighed her by a good sixty pounds. She'd need help to get him down the stairs and, I'm figuring, into Talbot's car."

"Where was Talbot's car?"

"According to the neighbors, he parked on the street. But with Talbot dead, Hill probably moved his car into her garage, where they loaded the body in, and Nash got rid of it."

"Either way, all three of their DNA would be on the garage stairway, the garage, and the trunk."

"If they used Talbot's car. There's a chance that Nash didn't know Talbot was dead, and Hill just needed help getting rid of his car."

"I don't know, why involve another party?"

"She was scared and panicked."

"She have a record?"

"No."

"It's possible she freaked out. What's the other scenario?"

"Hill gets Nash to kill Talbot."

"Why would he do that?"

"Nash is another one of those submissive types. He did it to please Hill."

"How romantic. Would you do that for little ole me?"

"It sounds crazy, but Dr. Bruno said it's possible."

"It seems far-fetched, but after five years in homicide, anything is possible."

"I'm leaning toward Nash transporting and hiding the body."

"If all he did was move it, it probably wouldn't qualify as a desecration crime."

"The car was found stripped, without the corpse. He had to have gotten rid of it."

"Probably. You might want to see about checking the trunk of Hill's car for Talbot's DNA."

"You forget I'm not working for the sheriff anymore?"

"It might be time to bring it to them."

I exhaled. "I need to give it a little more time. We're also following an interesting lead on a guy that had a run-in with

Talbot, and he's connected with a bunch of thugs, one with an attempted murder conviction."

"Now, that sounds promising. What was the argument about?"

"Talbot damaged the guy's Lamborghini in a fender bender."

"You remember that guy from Miami that beat that old woman up at Waterside?"

I sure did. If it wasn't for a good Samaritan, she might have been killed. Bringing up the incident triggered a memory from the assault.

62

Derrick was calling. I picked up. "Hey, what's going on?"

"Just heard from the lab. Nash's DNA matched one of the unidentified samples collected from Talbot's car. It was in the interior but also the trunk."

"Bingo."

"Yeah, but you want to know what's really interesting?"

No, forget it. "Uh, yeah?"

"Hill's DNA wasn't found in the trunk."

"What? How can that be?"

"Maybe Nash put Talbot in by himself."

I smiled. "Or he put his luggage in and was going to the airport. The reality is Nash doesn't seem strong enough to do it himself."

"I wish we could bring him in and grill his ass."

"You got that right. I hate to admit it, but private investigators don't have the tools to solve a homicide."

"I know. It's frustrating. All we can do is tee it up for the sheriff."

"And you know how much I like doing that for Chester."

He laughed. "You think he's going to leave?"

"He's got a little too much ambition not to take the Orlando position."

"I wonder who'd replace him."

"He's been grooming Dempsey for two years."

"He's a good guy."

"Let's hope he stays that way if he gets it."

"After he finishes Chester's term, he'd have to run and get elected."

"We may have to spend whatever currency we have with Chester sooner rather than later."

"You want to go to him now?"

"We need eyes on our mystery man, twenty-four seven. There's no way we can do it ourselves."

"I know three or four guys who'd jump at the chance to moonlight."

"See how much they'd want, and I'll run it by Ann. I'm gonna take a run at Nash."

Driving to Fort Myers, I called Chester. "Frank, it's great to hear from you. How are you and the family?"

"All good, sir. How about you?"

"Busy, tying up loose ends. I hope you called to say you're ready to come back."

"I'm still thinking things over."

"Take your time, but not too much. I wouldn't want my successor to fill the position."

"I understand, sir."

"Good. Now, what can I do for you?"

"I've been working a missing-person case that I believe may be a homicide."

"You have to bring it in."

"I'm not ready yet. We're close, but it's still unclear whether there is a conspiracy or not."

"What can I do to help?"

"Two things, if you could. There's a shady group run by a couple of felons. They're out of Miami, and rather than keep eyes on them, I could use help with some of the interagencies."

"Such as?"

"I'd like to see what Miami-Dade has on them. Also, we have a strong suspicion this gang is involved in drugs. We don't want any more of that here, so anything the DEA has could be crucial to shutting them down."

"This sounds dangerous. I don't want you taking any unnecessary risks."

"I wouldn't put Derrick or me in danger. We're not engaging them."

"Okay. I want you to be extra careful."

"We will."

"You said there were two items. What's the other?"

"I'd like to speak to the prosecutor's office and see what kind of leeway there is in enticing someone to talk."

"You're looking to cut a deal with someone?"

"No, just to see what an offer might get us in terms of presenting a case your office could close quickly."

"If you're that close, why not bring it in, and we'll get this across the finish line together?"

"I need another couple of days, max. Do you think you can help?"

"Send over the names you want me to run interagency interference. I'll handle it."

"Thank you. Though I'm not even sure I'd dangle a deal, can you speak to the prosecutor?"

"I'll advise them you might call."

"Thank you, Sheriff."

"I trust you see the benefits of working within the department."

I did, but I also hated begging. "Yes, sir."

—————

SOMEONE WAS BACKING a boat between two pilings at the house next to Nash's. Two boys, fishing rods in hand, waited to disembark. I wasn't into fishing, but being out on the water with your kids had to rate as a great day.

Making my way between the homes, I waved to the children. Nash was hosing off his modest lanai and sprayed his leg when he saw me.

"Sorry to scare you. I saw you were out back."

"Uh, no problem. You took me by surprise."

I lowered my voice. "We need to talk."

"About what?"

"You and Dawn Hill."

"I told you everything."

"I think it would be best if we did this inside."

Nash nodded and shut the water off. He opened a slider. "After you."

The faint smell of bleach was in the air. It was Nash's cleaning day.

"Can I get you something?"

"No, thanks."

"Please, sit."

I sat, and Nash started cracking his knuckles. "Tell me again how you came to drive John Talbot's car."

"But I did—"

"I'd appreciate hearing it again. It will clear up a few things."

"Of course. Well, it was simple. Dawn called me and

asked me to come over. When I got there, John answered the door. He said she was sleeping."

"And you didn't leave or try to wake her?"

"No. Dawn needed her rest. She had been working hard, too hard, if you ask me, and I decided not to disturb her."

"And Talbot asked you to take his car?"

"Yeah, he said he wasn't feeling well and needed a favor."

"And how were you going to get your car?"

"Dawn would drive it over."

"How did you know she would? She was sleeping?"

"I just figured, you know."

"Okay. So Talbot wasn't feeling good, and you helped him out."

"Yes, that's all it was."

"And what time did you get there?"

"A little before eleven."

"What were you doing for more than two hours?"

"Uh, nothing, talking. Time kind of slipped by for the two of us."

"But he was sick."

"Yes, but not right away."

"When?"

"I don't know, maybe after an hour, around midnight."

"Why didn't you leave then?"

"I was concerned whether he was going to be all right or not."

"He asked you to take his car?"

"Yes."

"What did you do?"

"What do you mean?"

"He gave you the keys?"

"Yes. I took them, got in the car, and drove off."

"You got in the driver's seat?"

"Yes. You didn't open any other doors?"

"No."

"How about the hood or trunk?"

He shook his head. "I didn't open either."

"How do you explain your DNA being found in the trunk?"

63

Fear flashed across his face. "My DNA? That's impossible."

"I'm afraid not. Two separate samples were collected."

"How could that be?"

"You tell me."

"I swear, I don't know."

"I do. You not only opened the trunk, you put something in it."

"What could I possibly put in there?"

"The body of John Talbot."

"I didn't do it."

"What? Kill him, or hide his body?"

"I'd like to call a lawyer."

Nash didn't realize he didn't have to talk to me. But it could be he was either ready to confess or was looking for a mouthpiece to hide behind.

"Did Dawn Hill ask you to kill Talbot?"

He shook his head. "No, no. Please, I really need an attorney."

"Why? If you didn't do anything wrong?"

He stood. "Please, I'd like you to go."

"If you agree to help us, I'll speak with the prosecutor's office, and as long as you didn't murder Talbot, a deal can be made."

Nash walked to the door and opened it. I followed behind. "There's not going to be much time. If Hill talks first, you're not going to get any consideration."

I handed him my card and walked to the car, certain Nash was making a call. The question was whether it was to a lawyer or to Hill.

Forty minutes later, I swung into the parking lot of Hill's design firm. Walking to the door, my phone rang. It was Chester.

"Hello, sir."

"Frank, looks like you're onto something. The DEA is working a case on that gang. It was started by Miami-Dade, but McMurray is leading it now."

"Is the scope of the investigation beyond drugs, like a homicide?"

"You know how tight-lipped the feds are. They want whatever you have on them."

"I need a little more time. I don't want the homicide I'm working to get buried."

"Not going to happen. From what McMurray said, they're close to bringing them down and want to debrief you immediately. What time can you get to their Fort Myers office?"

"Uhm, I'm in the middle of something—"

"McMurray is expecting you this afternoon. I'm surprised he hasn't called you already."

The DEA agent was a good guy. Though he was a company guy, he'd shared info with me over the years. I'd have to take a shot to save my case with him. "I'll reach out and firm it up."

"Good. Let me know how it goes."

As we closed the conversation, another call came in. I figured it was McMurray and let it go to voice mail. I needed time to think things over.

My mind raced. I tried to figure out the best way to handle the intrusion. Why had I asked the sheriff to reach out to DEA in the first place? I should have known it would either go nowhere or end up exactly where I found myself.

Was I hoping for a confirmation these guys were killers? If they were high-level drug dealers, they had to be. As frustration clouded my thoughts, I deployed Bruno's advice and got out of the car.

It was time to change things up, move on to something different, and that was Hill.

Taking a deep breath, I swung open the design firm's door. I asked for Hill and was told she wasn't there. I took a walk around to be sure and left. Now what?

Pulling my phone out to call Derrick, I saw the voice mail flag. I listened to the long message. Twice. It wasn't totally unexpected, but it looked like the end was within reach.

64

I was seated next to Lee Nash in the rear of an unmarked car. It had been a while since we turned off Alico Road. The last building we'd seen was nothing more than a pile of cinder blocks.

We continued east for ten more minutes when Nash said, "Please make a right."

As soon as we turned onto the dirt roadway, I knew we were in the neighborhood. The path ran through the middle of an abandoned sand quarry.

We bounced along for half a mile and Nash said, "Please slow down. If you can turn off, right after those boulders, we'll be close."

I had to ask, "How did you know this place existed?"

"A friend of mine worked for Vulcan Quarries. I couldn't believe there was sand so far inland, and he had me out here before they closed it."

"I remember being surprised myself."

After objections by environmentalists over dredging and pumping sand from the bottom of the Gulf, counties had been forced to truck sand in from Immokalee to replenish the beaches.

It didn't make sense because the steady caravan of dump trucks and the heavy machinery to spread it over miles of beaches spewed dirty exhaust in the air.

"Please stop."

The officer driving hit the brakes, and the other vehicles in our group stopped behind us. Nash looked at me, and I raised a finger.

"Let's wait for the dust to die down."

There was a rap on my window. It was Sergeant Gesso. "All right, let's get going."

"I hope you understand I had no choice. I knew it was wrong, but I couldn't say no to Dawn."

"Of course. Let's do this, so we can get it behind you."

He nodded. "Okay. It's right over there."

Nash headed toward a small pile of rocks. Gesso said, "All right, everybody, fan out, and keep your eyes open."

Nash slowed down. "I'm really sorry to drag everyone out here."

"It's all right. Where is the site?"

He pointed to a small depression. "There."

"How deep is it?"

"Four or five feet. I wanted to be sure he . . . he would be okay."

"Sarge, it's over there. It's about four feet or so below the surface, but be careful."

Holding shovels, two officers in protective gear walked over. When they started digging, Nash said, "I'm sorry, but I can't watch this."

I asked an officer to bring Nash to the car and keep an eye on him. It was difficult to imagine Nash driving here in the middle of the night to dump a body. I believed it likely Hill had been on the phone with him to keep him on track.

After forty minutes of careful probing, an officer said, "I think we hit it, Sarge."

The officers exchanged their shovels for hand spades and donned face masks. Two minutes later, the outline of a body wrapped in plastic took shape. I put my sleeve to my nose and moved closer.

Decomposition was visible through the cloudy plastic. I knelt down. "Sarge, it's Talbot. It's time for you to bring Hill in."

It was the sucky part of the job. Though time had made any other outcome unlikely, it was like losing an elderly parent; you knew the end was coming, but it still wasn't easy.

In the movies, the person knew as soon as they opened the door. I got it if you showed up in uniform, but I didn't expect it with Ann. I'd been here a dozen times, many of them unannounced. Rehearsing my lines, I hit the bell.

Ann opened the door, leaning back when she saw me. There was a reason I didn't play poker.

"May I come in?"

She nodded and stepped aside. A bossa nova was playing, and the sliders were wide open. I swept the room for a remote but came up empty. It was the perfect example of not knowing what another person was going through.

She still hadn't said a word. "Ann, why don't you have a seat?"

Lowering herself onto the couch, she said, "I know why you're here. You found John, didn't you?"

"I'm sorry, we did."

She looked at her hands. "Where?"

"In an old sand quarry in Fort Myers."

She dabbed a tear away with a forefinger. "Did he suffer?"

"We don't think."

"How did he die?"

"We're not sure yet. There'll be an autopsy, and we'll learn more."

She nodded but said nothing. I had to get out of here before the crying started.

"Someone should be here with you. Can I call anyone for you?"

She swallowed and took her phone out. "I'll call Sally, she lives next door."

"That's good." I stood. "I'm sorry for your loss, Ann. I really am."

As far as the case was concerned, my job was over. But I needed to know what had happened. Did some twisted sex result in Talbot's death, or had an argument triggered it?

I HAD CALLED THE SHERIFF, politely airing my concerns that the lack of homicide experience in the department might hinder Hill's interrogation. Though Chester didn't come out and say it, he quickly agreed to have me talk to Detective Mulberry. I laid out the facts and theories to him.

A no-nonsense man, Mulberry was a twenty-year veteran, but most of it was spent in robbery before moving to the major crimes unit. He took notes, asked the right questions, and appreciated my advice. But most importantly, he supported me watching the interrogation via video feed.

Passing on coffee, I took a bottle of water with me into

the viewing room. I was jittery as it was. The screen came to life, and there she was, Dawn Hill, staring right into the camera. Her lawyer, Sonia Gott, was jotting down notes on a yellow legal pad.

When Mulberry came into the room, Hill stiffened. Gott patted her hand and said hello to the detective.

Mulberry recited the formalities and said, "Ms. Hill, this is your chance to tell us what happened to John Talbot, also known as John Silverman."

65

HILL LOOKED AT HER LAWYER, WHO NODDED. "I DIDN'T DO anything. He just died."

"Then why didn't you call nine-one-one?"

"I don't know. I was scared."

"Was he, you, or both of you using drugs?"

"No, I never used."

"And Mr. Talbot?"

"I don't know for sure, but he didn't take anything at my house."

"Had he ever engaged in drug use?"

"Not that I'm aware of."

"An autopsy is being performed as we speak. It'll detect the presence of illicit drugs. Do you want to amend your statement?"

"He didn't do anything that I saw at my house."

"What were you doing when, as you say, he just died?"

"Having sex."

Hearing her say it that way made it sound transactional, which, I guess, is what it was. I wanted Mulberry to dig into her bedroom preferences, and he didn't disappoint.

"I understand you and Mr. Talbot practice dominant and submissive behaviors using bondage and other untraditional measures."

"It's more common than you think, Detective. We do role-playing but nothing more."

"And yet Mr. Talbot is dead."

Gott said, "My client has already stated that she is unaware of what caused Mr. Talbot's death."

"I heard her, Counselor. Problem is, I don't believe it. Now, I want to hear about you and Talbot having sex."

Gott said, "That's a private matter."

"Not when someone ends up dead. Now, take me through it." Mulberry was growing on me.

"John enjoyed being bossed around."

"I understand he liked to have a dog collar around his neck."

"Not really. I think once or twice we did that. He was just into pleasing me."

"He was your slave?"

"That's not what it's like."

"You have to punish him?"

"It's not what you think. It's more teasing him, sexually speaking."

"How often did you hit him?"

"Never. You're not listening to me."

"Was Talbot tied up when he died?"

"No."

"Were you?"

"No."

"So you were in the middle of having sex when he died?"

"Yes."

"Was he penetrating you at the time?"

"Yeah."

"From the front, back, side?"

"Doggie style."

"And he just dropped dead right in the middle of it?"

She nodded. "Yes."

"What happened?"

"Well, he just kind of fell back. I didn't know what was going on because, you know, he wasn't finished."

"What did you do then?"

"I kind of looked behind me and called his name. But he looked weird, and I checked his pulse."

"On his neck?"

"Uh, no, his wrist, but there was nothing."

"And what time was this?"

"I think around eight thirty."

"Why didn't you call for help?"

"I was scared."

"Why? You said you didn't do anything."

She shrugged. "I was afraid of how it would look. I figured something like this would be in the papers, and I have a business dealing with the public."

"You expect me to believe that Talbot was dead for two hours before you called Lee Nash to help you hide the body?"

"It wasn't two hours. Maybe an hour and a half, but I didn't know what to do. I was going to call nine-one-one and even had the phone in my hand a couple of times."

I wondered if the techies could tell if she had partially dialed 911 when Mulberry said, "But you didn't. Instead, you started a conspiracy to hide the body."

"It wasn't a conspiracy—"

Putting a hand on her client's forearm, Gott said, "We'll stipulate that Ms. Hill asked Mr. Nash to properly bury the body. She was traumatized by the death and unable to think clearly."

Mulberry kept pressing Hill, but she stuck to her story. When he ended the interview, Gott asked that Hill be released, but Mulberry said she was going to be detained on suspicion of murder.

As the lawyer objected, I left, wondering what, if any, crime they could hang on Hill without new evidence. With the autopsy the key place to find proof, as soon as I got into the parking lot I tapped out a text: *Hey Doc, let me know when you're done with Talbot.*

Pulling onto Goodlette Frank, my phone pinged a text. It was Bilotti: *I'm finished. Just started writing the report.*

I hooked a U-turn and at the next light texted back: *Need five minutes. Meet me in the parking lot.*

As soon as I got onto Airport-Pulling, my phone rang. It was Derrick. "Frank, they're letting Nash go."

"It seems a little early to do that."

"Hill didn't implicate him."

"I know, but if she did, she'd be screwing herself by admitting she orchestrated it."

"I don't think they're gonna charge Nash with anything more than a first-degree misdemeanor. It seems crazy; the guy put a body in a trunk and buried him."

"There was no desecration. If he had put him in the Gulf, he'd be facing a second-degree felony charge. Now, he'll get off with a thousand-dollar fine for not reporting the death, unless there is some way we can prove he was in cahoots with Hill."

"Do you think he was involved?"

"I don't know what to think. Under normal circumstances, I'd say hell yeah. But Dr. Bruno said a submissive person probably wouldn't commit a murder, but the desire to please their dominant partner was strong enough to do something crazy, and this certainly qualifies."

"You talked to Dr. Bruno about it?"

"Uh, yeah, I ran into her at Publix and figured I'd bounce it off her."

"You didn't say anything."

"It was nothing much more than what I grabbed off the internet. Look, I'm just about to pull into Bilotti's parking lot. I'll call you after I'm done."

I was still a good ten minutes away from the medical examiner's building but didn't want to get hung up on Dr. Bruno. It was immature, but I wasn't as comfortable as I should have been talking about my therapist.

66

———————

BILOTTI PUT ON SUNGLASSES AS HE EXITED. HE SCANNED THE lot. I waved and pointed to a bench in the shade of an oak tree.

We shook hands. He said, "Nice day."

"It is. I don't know how you stay cooped up in that icebox all day, Doc."

"When I'm engrossed in the work, I lose track of time and place. You're interested in the Talbot findings?"

"Definitely. How'd he die?"

"Cardiac arrest."

"Are you sure? No drugs or anything?"

"Nothing evident. The toxicity panels will take a couple of days to come back, but his heart gave out."

"It doesn't make sense. Why would Hill panic like she did?"

"They could have been engaged in autoerotic asphyxiation."

"You said that before. That's where they choke themselves to heighten an orgasm, right?"

"Yes."

"There any signs of strangulation?"

"No, but his heart evidenced damage of the kind we see from deprivation of oxygen. Its weakened state made it vulnerable."

"This guy liked to be collared, and you're saying there was nothing like that?"

"If strangulation triggered cardiac arrest, there would have been markings and petechiae."

"So you're saying his heart had been weakened from being choked in the past, and it just happened to give out when he was screwing Hill?"

"That doesn't mean they weren't using a plastic bag to cut off the flow of oxygen—"

"That's got to be it! He died with a bag over his head, and that's what made Hill panic."

"That's plausible."

"What can you give me to support it?"

"I hate to disappoint you, Frank, but the autopsy is inconclusive in that regard."

"How can that be?"

"Without physical evidence, such as a bag or a ligature of some kind, we just don't know."

"But you said his heart was damaged from a lack of oxygen."

"Yes, but the cause of that damage is unknown. A previous suffocation, strangulation, or near drowning could have caused it."

"Damn it."

"Sorry, Frank."

"It's not your fault, Doc. I appreciate the info. I've got to get moving."

A wave of heat hit me when I opened the car door. I'd

forgotten to crack the windows. I started the car and called Derrick.

"Hey, Bilotti said Talbot had a heart attack."

"Every man's dream, huh? Buying the farm while you're getting some."

It wasn't my ideal way of checking out for a fifty-year-old. "His heart was damaged from a lack of oxygen and gave out."

"What from?"

"I'm thinking it's from putting a bag over his head to get his rocks off."

"That's why Hill freaked out."

"Bingo. The problem is proving it."

"She can't say she didn't know."

"I don't know. In her statement she said they were doing it doggie style."

"You think she made that up to cover?"

"It would have been smart of her."

"She hid the evidence."

"I don't know what she could be charged with. Maybe reckless endangerment? Getting rid of the bag would be withholding or destroying incriminating evidence, but if it can't be proved she put the bag on Talbot or failed to remove it, there's no crime."

"How the hell they going to prove that?"

"Unless she confesses, I don't see it happening."

"Well, at least we did what we could to solve it on our end."

"I guess so."

"And Nash is off the hook."

"Yeah, looks like everybody is going to walk. I'll talk to you later."

As I drove home, the unresolved nature of the case

gnawed at me. A man died before his time. Was it his own doing, or had someone played a role and wasn't going to be held accountable?

I called Mulberry. "Hey, Frank. What's up?"

"I heard the cause of death on Talbot was a heart attack."

"Yep, his ticker gave out." He snorted. "Guess she was too much for him."

"Maybe, but something is bothering me."

"I'm all ears."

I told him about the autoerotic angle.

"Really? People do that?"

"I know it's crazy. I'm thinking it might be worthwhile pressing Hill on it. She could come clean."

"She's due to be released this afternoon. I'll pull her in and lean on her, see what she says."

"Great."

"I'll let you know."

I was glad Mulberry was willing to play ball rather than move on to another case. There were still a lot of good people out there.

Pulling up my driveway, the phone rang. "Mr. Luca?"

"Yes, who's this?"

"Pete Stapleton. You're a private investigator, right?"

"Yes. What can I do for you?"

"I run a fabrication company on Old Forty-One. I'm pretty sure one of my employees, or there could be two of them involved, are stealing from me."

A new case was just what I needed to dull the Talbot mess. "What do you think they're taking?"

"Precious metals. Not like gold or anything, but we do a lot of plating with zinc, and the inventory levels ain't matching the units we ship out."

"I see."

"Think you can figure out what's going on?"

"Be happy to take a crack at it. Text me your contact details, and I'll send over an engagement package."

I walked in the house. Mary Ann was reading on the lanai.

"Hey."

"You're home early."

"Yeah, got tired of getting beat up."

"What happened?"

I filled her in on the Talbot case.

"It's frustrating not knowing what happened. I'm sorry."

I didn't want to tell her Mulberry was taking another run at Hill. "I know, but on the good side, it looks like I just picked up another client, and the DEA is about to do major damage to that drug ring."

"See? Things balance out."

"I'm going to take a dip in the pool."

I changed and grabbed a towel. Stepping through the slider, my phone rang. It was Mulberry.

67

I HAD TO ADMIT IT, I WOULDN'T HAVE BEEN ABLE TO CRACK Hill either. Mulberry took another run at her, but she stuck to her account of events. Yet trying to find a way to accept it was another story.

I kept telling myself, it was better to solve a case without knowing what happened than it was to know what happened and not being able to prove it.

I needed a dose of B therapy. It was always easier to call Bilotti over Bruno, plus I had something to ask him.

"Hello, Frank. How are you doing?"

"Pretty good. But the Talbot case is still grating on me."

"You have to learn to let cases go, or they'll drive you to drink."

"That's not a bad thing."

"True, but remember life is too short to drink bad wine."

"Amen. Say, one thing I'm not understanding is about the heart attack. You said it was because of the lack of oxygen."

"Correct."

"What exactly happens?"

"The deprivation of oxygen causes an alteration of the

chemistry of the blood. That distortion triggers a change in the heart's rhythm, and in this case, led to cardiac arrest."

"I see. But doesn't a lack of oxygen damage the brain?"

"Definitely, but the length of time it's deprived plays a large role."

"So a short time damages the heart but not the brain?"

"No. They both suffer as a result. But people, especially those with histories and DNA predispositions, have different outcomes."

"It's so complicated."

"It is. Say, I've got to get going."

The interstate was backed up, and I got off the Bonita Springs Road exit. I swung onto Livingston Road. When I saw the sign for Vasari, I made a left into the community.

I took something out of the glove box. Stuffing it in my pocket, I walked to Bradshaw's coach home. Traffic had forced me this way, so I had to seize the opportunity and take a shot.

A woman with a Jamaican accent answered the door.

"Hi, I'm Frank Luca. I'm a friend of Brittany's. Is she available?"

"Yes, but she doesn't talk too much."

"Just wanted to say a quick hello."

"Come in. The missus is in there. I got to finish the laundry."

Bradshaw was in a wheelchair parked in front of a TV. "Hey, Brittany. How are you?"

She smiled and struggled to eke out a hello.

"How you feeling?"

She rocked her head.

"Tell me what happened to you."

"I . . . I . . . I . . . don't . . . know."

"Did someone hurt you?"

She shook her head.

"Are you sure?"

She nodded.

I pulled out the plastic bag and held it in front of her. Her eyes went wild and she moaned. I jammed the bag in my pocket, called for the aide, and left.

TALBOT'S FUNERAL was two days ago. I couldn't wait any longer. I didn't know what to expect when I rang the bell. I figured the house would be filled with depressing flower arrangements.

When Ann answered the door, I was surprised, but it had nothing to do with the lack of floral pieces. She was wearing a black pantsuit.

"Hi, Frank. Come in."

"How are you doing?"

"Okay, I guess. The funeral was difficult . . ."

"Sorry. I don't want to upset you. I can come back."

"No, it's okay. What's on your mind?"

I was going to lead with the Bradshaw revelation, but telling her about another woman her husband had a sexual relationship with made little sense.

"I never asked the question directly, and I think it's important to get to the truth."

"Okay."

"You said you and your husband never engaged in any BDSM type, uh, sexual relations."

"That's right."

"Did he ever ask you to use a plastic bag or another method of restricting oxygen while engaging in sex?"

Her face crumpled, and she cast her eyes down.

"Forget it. It's okay."

She tried to smile.

"Are you going to be all right?"

She nodded.

"I've got to get going."

I sat in my car thinking about Ann and what she had to deal with. Shifting into drive, my phone rang, it was Mary Ann. She reminded me to pick up milk. It was good she called; I had forgotten.

The Publix parking lot in Park Shore bordered on an ice-skating rink. Not wanting to get dinged, I parked in the rear of the lot by Amore, where I saw a mother and daughter laughing as they loaded groceries into an SUV.

It was Mrs. Coyle and Carla. I debated going over to them but didn't want to upset the vibe by bringing up bad memories. I cut through a row of parked cars to avoid them.

Seeing mother and daughter reunited squashed the depression out of me. I almost skipped into the grocery store.

WE CLIMBED INTO BED. I was exhausted. Mary Ann said, "What do you have going on tomorrow?"

"I have a meeting on the new case."

"It'll be good for you to start something new."

"Yeah. Oh, I forgot to tell you, I saw the Coyle mother and her daughter at Publix. It looks like they've ironed out their issues."

"That's wonderful."

"I couldn't think of a better way to end the day."

Mary Ann slung her leg over mine. "Are you sure about that?"

Little Luca rose like Lazarus. I rolled over and pressed

into her. I didn't think the day could get any better, but man, was I wrong, in a good way.

The next book in this series is, Buried At The Lake. Find it in eBook & Paperback.

I hope you enjoyed reading this book as much as I enjoyed writing it. If you did, I'd appreciate it if you would write a quick review on Amazon or your favorite book site. Reviews are an author's best friend and even a quick line or two is helpful. Thanks, Dan

OTHER BOOKS BY DAN

Complicit Witness

Push Back

Ambition Cliff

You can keep abreast of my writing and have access to books that are free of discounting by joining my newsletter. It normally is out once a month and also contains notes on self- esteem, motivational pieces and wine articles.

It's free. See bottom of my website: www.danpetrosini.com

ABOUT THE AUTHOR

Dan is a USA Today and Amazon best-selling author who wrote his first story at the age of ten and enjoys telling a story or joke.

Dan gets his story ideas by exploring the question; What if?

In almost every situation he finds himself in, Dan explores what if this or that happened? What if this person died or did something unusual or illegal?

Dan's non-stop mind spin provides him with plenty of material to weave into interesting stories.

A fan of books and films that have twists and are difficult to predict, Dan crafts his stories to prevent readers from guessing correctly. He writes every day, forcing the words out when necessary and has written over twenty-five novels to date.

It's not a matter of wanting to write, Dan simply has to.

Dan passionately believes people can realize their dreams if they focus and act, and he encourages just that.

His favorite saying is – "The price of discipline is always less than the cost of regret"

Dan reminds people to get the negativity out of their lives. He believes it is contagious and advises people to steer clear of negative people. He knows having a true, positive mind set makes it feel like life is rigged in your favor. When he gets off base, he tells himself, 'You can't have a good day with a bad attitude.'

Married with two daughters and a needy Maltese, Dan lives in Southwest Florida. A New York native, Dan has taught at local colleges, writes novels, and plays tenor saxophone in several jazz bands. He also drinks way too much wine and never, ever takes himself too seriously.

He puts out a twice-a-month newsletter featuring articles, his writing and special deals and steals.

Sign up at www.danpetrosini.com